Home is where the heart fits . . .

Summer Murray is ready to shake things up. She doesn't want to work in risk management. She doesn't want to live in Hartford, Connecticut. So she plans a grand adventure: she's going to throw out all the stuff she doesn't want and travel the country in her very own tiny house shaped like a train caboose. Just Summer, her chihuahua-dachshund Shortie, and 220 square feet of freedom.

Then her take-no-prisoners grandmother calls to demand Summer head home to the Pacific Northwest to save the family bakery. Summer has her reasons for not wanting to return home, but she'll just park her caboose, fix things, and then be on her way. But when she gets to Cat's Paw, Washington, she's shocked by her grandmother's strange behavior and reunited with a few people she'd hoped to avoid. If Summer is going to make a fresh start, she'll have to face the past she's been running from all along . . .

Visit us at www.kensingtonbooks.com

D1263902

Books by Celia Bonaduce

Tiny House Novels
Tiny House on the Hill

Fat Chance, Texas Series
Welcome to Fat Chance, Texas
Slim Pickins' in Fat Chance, Texas
Livin' Large in Fat Chance, Texas

Venice Beach Romances
The Merchant of Venice Beach
A Comedy of Erinn
Much Ado About Mother

Tiny House on the Hill

Celia Bonaduce

LYRICAL PRESS
Kensington Publishing Corp.
www.kensingtonbooks.com

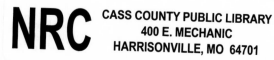

Lyrical Press books are published by
Kensington Publishing Corp. 119 West 40th Street New York, NY 10018

All Kensington titles, imprints, and distributed lines are available at special quantity discounts for bulk purchases for sales promotion, premiums, fundraising, and educational or institutional use.

To the extent that the image or images on the cover of this book depict a person or persons, such person or persons are merely models, and are not intended to portray any character or characters featured in the book.

Special book excerpts or customized printings can also be created to fit specific needs. For details, write or phone the office of the Kensington Special Sales Manager:
Kensington Publishing Corp.
119 West 40th Street
New York, NY 10018
Attn. Special Sales Department. Phone: 1-800-221-2647.

Kensington and the K logo Reg. U.S. Pat. & TM Off.
LYRICAL PRESS Reg. U.S. Pat. & TM Off.
Lyrical Press and the L logo are trademarks of Kensington Publishing Corp.

First Electronic Edition: August 2017
eISBN-13: 978-1-5161-0235-8
eISBN-10: 1-5161-0235-5

First Print Edition: August 2017
ISBN-13: 978-1-5161-0236-5
ISBN-10: 1-5161-0236-3

Printed in the United States of America

To Team Tiny:
Big Thanks

Chapter 1

Summer Murray stared at the three large boxes marked KEEP, GIVEAWAY, and TRASH.

This is useless, she thought, frowning at the overflowing KEEP box. *I'm supposed to be getting rid of stuff.*

Summer was moving. She *had* to downsize. Overwhelmed with the prospect, she'd read article after online article on the subject. All the experts seemed to agree the "three-box" method would make it easier to get organized. But getting organized and downsizing appeared to be two distinctly different beasts.

She hugged a black wool coat to her chest, and took in a deep breath. The coat was an unfortunate impulse buy—a waistcoat worthy of the U.S. Calvary, circa 1865. She slipped her arms into the sleeves. The coat was from China, a country that really did not understand the concept of American breasts. At least, it didn't understand the concept of Summer's breasts.

The coat had three strikes against it: It didn't fit, she had not worn it in a year (she'd not worn it *ever*), and it had been out of style for almost 150 years. Summer, at 28, was still barely young enough to go the costume route should she so choose, but costumes really weren't her thing.

I will give this away, Summer willed herself, shrugging out of the too-tight coat. *I. Will. Give. This. Away.*

She stuffed the coat into the GIVEAWAY box. She looked down at it. The coat's coal-black buttons stared back at her as forlorn as a baby seal adrift on an ice flow.

Fine!

Summer rescued the coat and dumped it into the KEEP box. After all, she lived on the East Coast, where it was certainly cold enough to need a wool coat, even with global warming. Perhaps she could take it to a tailor and get the bustline let out. She wondered if there could possibly be eight inches of extra fabric in those seams.

Summer had first moved in to her riverfront two-bedroom, two-bath apartment four years ago, after graduating with her master's and landing a job with a big insurance company in Hartford, Connecticut. She had originally set up the smaller bedroom as a home office. But after three months at her job downtown in a cubicle, the last thing she wanted to do was spend any more time in an office—home or otherwise. Especially one with overhead lighting. She'd read an article online about turning an unused room into a closet, and hired a handsome carpenter named Hans to build her a dream storage space. Summer tried to engage him in conversation, but Hans only seemed interested in his job and sports—neither of which Summer understood. By the time he'd finished working for her, Summer had bookcases along one wall for shoes, purses, scarves, hats, and various other accessories; double-hung poles for shorter pieces along another and a strong support for longer items along the third wall. She took pictures of his handiwork and showed them to her colleagues at work.

All her friends said it was the most spectacular closet they'd ever seen. They also took a great interest in Hans. Except for Aiden on *Sex and the City*, none of them had ever heard of such a skilled handyman. And even in the insurance capital of the world, eligible men in their late twenties and early thirties seemed to be in shorter and shorter supply.

Egged on by her friends, Summer toyed with the idea of inviting Hans for dinner. She didn't really have much luck with the opposite sex. A few dates and her passion always cooled. She was the Goldilocks of the dating world, always looking for the one who was "just right." She suspected she and Hans had nothing in common, but standing in her beautiful closet, she thought perhaps she should throw caution to the wind and just take a chance. As she reached for her phone, she happened to look up at the beautiful chandelier and realized—even as gorgeous as it was—it was still overhead lighting. You can disguise something, but it's still what it is.

She never made the call.

* * * *

Summer hadn't thought about Hans in months. She wouldn't miss him when she left Hartford, but she sure would miss this closet. She held a pair of black leather espadrilles in her hands. Last spring, she'd twisted her ankle in them. Surely she could part with them! She strode purposefully toward the GIVEAWAY box but stopped just inches short of tossing them in. Was it the shoes' fault she fell? Hadn't she learned her lesson and would be more careful next time? They were just so damned cute!

She stared at the paltry GIVEAWAY box. There was a T-shirt from a marathon she'd run five years ago, a pair of pajamas, and one pair of jeans that were too big. She'd bought them online and thought about taking them to a tailor but then decided it was a comfort knowing there was a pair of jeans not just in the universe, but in her actual closet, that swam on her.

In the KEEP pile were the jeans that were too small. Summer usually bought jeans when she'd been dieting. They usually fit for about a week before she'd gain her seven pounds back. But she made it a rule to never get rid of a pair of pants until she could fit into them again. The too-small jeans had been around so long they were out of style. But she worried if she gave in to chucking them, she'd never have incentive to lose the weight. She knew it was preposterous, but who was she to thumb her nose at this unfounded fear? Even superstition had some foundation in reality.

She stared at the jeans, then the espadrilles, then back to the jeans. Something had to give.

A knock at the door saved her from a decision.

"Hello?" came a familiar voice from the hallway.

It was her neighbor Mary-Lynn Laite. Mary-Lynn insisted that everyone call her Lynnie.

"Lynnie just sounds friendlier, you know?" Lynnie explained when Summer first moved in.

There was no denying it, Lynnie was fanatically friendly. Summer hadn't been in the building a week before Lynnie offered to keep a spare key in case of emergencies. "Emergencies" seemed to translate into "any time I want to get into your apartment."

"Hi, Lynnie," Summer called. "I'm in the closet."

If there was one person to whom she didn't need to explain the layout of her apartment, it was Lynnie.

Somewhere along the road of Lynnie's fifty-five years, she'd decided she was meant to be in the center of things. Lynnie knew everything about everybody in the building, and was happy to spread gossip among the tenants. After Summer had made her big decision to leave not only her job but the town of Hartford, Lynnie (and therefore everyone in the building) seemed to know about it before she'd even turned in her notice at work.

"How are you doing, sweet pea?" Lynnie said through her permanently sorrowful I'm-on-your-side expression.

"Plugging along, I guess," Summer shrugged, espadrilles in hand.

"Want to take a break?" Lynnie asked, holding up a plate of cookies. "Chocolate chip *and* oatmeal raisin. Gluten-free, of course! Pick your poison..."

When Lynnie got her diagnosis and learned that wheat would have to be banished from her world, you would have thought her life was over. She'd thrown herself on Summer's couch, begging for help.

"I've got something called celiac disease," Lynnie said.

"So...that's no flour, right?"

"It's worse than that," Lynnie said. "Did you hear me? It's a *disease*. Not just flour, but soy sauce, beer—all kinds of stuff. How am I supposed to live without bread?"

"There's gluten-free bread," Summer said. "I've seen it in the freezer at the market."

"How can *you*, of all people, think frozen bread is worth eating?" Lynnie whimpered. "It tastes like sawdust."

Summer wished she'd never mentioned that her grandparents owned a bakery.

"There has to be a decent gluten-free bread out there," Summer said.

"I think you should experiment with some of those gluten-free flours and see what you can come up with," Lynnie said.

"Why should I experiment?" Summer asked. "I can eat wheat!"

"Bread is in your blood!" Lynnie said heatedly. "You come from a long line of bakers."

No matter how many times Summer told her that only her grandparents on her father's side of the family were bakers, Lynnie insisted on the long-line-of-bakers lineage for her.

Lynnie finally wore Summer down. Summer brought an automatic bread maker. Just the thought of her grandmother finding out that she had one terrified her. Still, in time, Summer crafted a sweet-enough, moist-enough, sort-of-flat-but-edible bread. She handed the bread maker and recipe to Lynnie and moved on. Lynnie had taken it from there, and now was turning out gluten-free treats on a weekly basis. Give a lady a loaf a gluten-free bread and she'll eat for a day. Give her a bread maker...

Summer studied the cookies.

"Which one is better?" Summer asked, realizing how much she was going to miss these treats.

"I think the oatmeal raisin," Lynnie said. "Try one."

"Sure," Summer said, munching on the cookie.

She wasn't sure if she'd just gotten used to the heaviness in Lynnie's gluten-free offerings, but this one wasn't bad.

She gave Lynnie a thumbs up as she tossed the espadrilles in the GIVEAWAY box. Lynnie looked shocked.

"You've going to give away those darling shoes?" Lynnie asked. "If you are, I'll take them."

Lynnie had laid claim to just about everything in Summer's apartment—whether Summer was taking it or not.

"I haven't decided," Summer said, putting the shoes on a shelf and leading Lynnie and the cookie to the kitchen.

"I saw a big red truck in your parking space," Lynnie said. "You seeing somebody new?"

"No," Summer replied, hating herself for answering but knowing there was no point keeping anything from Lynnie. "It's mine."

"Wha...?" Lynnie froze mid-bite.

"I'm going to need it." Summer shrugged, pleased that she'd caught her neighbor by surprise for once.

"Why'd you buy a big old truck?"

"To tow the house," Summer replied.

"I was hoping to hear you'd come to your senses," Lynnie sighed and put her half-eaten cookie down.

"That's very...supportive of you," Summer said, hoping to end the conversation. Lynnie's lack of faith sometimes shook her to the core.

"I just don't want you to regret anything." Lynnie said, her "I'm on your side" expression going into overdrive. "I mean, you got a degree in risk management for a reason, right?"

"I guess so," Summer said, wondering if it really had ever been her goal to get a job in insurance. "But when I was choosing a major in college, risk management sounded a lot more exciting than it was. In the real world, it turns out to be too much management, and too little risk."

"Making felt purses to sell at craft fairs and dragging a tiny house behind a big truck?" Lynnie asked. "That's risk without the management, if you ask me."

I didn't ask you.

"I'm stuck in a job I don't want. Living a life I don't want. I just need to simplify things," Summer said. "And you're only young once, right?"

"Can't argue with that!" Lynnie sighed, looking around the half-packed apartment. "But I don't know how you're going to get all this stuff into 300 square feet."

"220 square feet," Summer said patiently. She'd explained all this before.

"Those tiny houses are just a fad, you know," Lynnie said. "If you want to live like a vagabond, the RV people have already figured everything out."

≀"Except how to make it feel like home," Summer said.

"I'm sure you could make an RV feel like home," Lynnie said. "You just don't want to put your mind to it because an RV is not trendy."

"Why are you defending RVs?"

"Why are you attacking them?"

"Just because I don't want to live in one doesn't mean I'm attacking them," Summer said, wondering why she was even having this conversation. "I just love the whole idea of living the life I choose, without crazy overhead, in a cute house."

"But 220 square feet!" Lynnie shuddered.

"It has two lofts."

"How is Shortie supposed to climb a ladder? Or does he only get to live on one floor?" Lynnie asked, a tinge of outrage in her voice for Summer's half Dachshund half Chihuahua companion.

"There are stairs to the bedroom loft," Summer said. "I've seen smaller dogs than Shortie climb stairs."

"Where?"

"On that TV show about tiny houses," Summer tried not to sound defensive. "He'll figure it out."

At the sound of his name, Shortie waddled into the room. Both women stared at him. He had the huge ears and eyes of a Chihuahua, and the body and two-inch inseam of a Dachshund. He did not look like a dog who was going to navigate a tricky staircase.

Summer looked defiantly at Lynnie, but Lynnie had already lost interest in the dog.

"I guess you won't be taking those two chairs by the fireplace," Lynnie said, switching gears.

"I guess I won't," Summer said, waiting for what always came next.

"I can take them off your hands if you'd like." Lynnie said. "I mean, anything that will help you *simplify* your life."

"Sure. Thanks."

"I'm going to miss you," Lynnie said as she got up and dusted crumbs off her jeans. "I mean, you and me have been a regular Mary Richards and Rhoda Morgenstern."

Summer nodded. If it weren't for TV Land and Hulu, she wouldn't understand half of Lynnie's references. Lynnie saw herself to the door, mercifully leaving the cookies behind. Summer grabbed one, scooped Shortie off the floor and plopped them both down on one of the now-claimed chairs.

"Are we crazy?" Summer asked Shortie, giving him a pinch of an oatmeal-raisin cookie.

Visits with Lynnie always left Summer questioning her decisions. Was she happy? Was she doing what she really wanted to do in life? Exactly what *did* she want to do in life?

It was while she was asking herself the hard questions one day while folding laundry that she held up a sweater that she recognized by the pattern was hers, but by the size of it, it belonged to the toddler down the hall. She realized she'd washed and dried her favorite cashmere sweater on hot.

She raced to the computer and looked up how to un-shrink a cashmere sweater. Even the Internet, with its trove of false promises, gave her no hope. But a DIY video showed her how to turn it into a funky purse. She hauled out her hand-me-down sewing machine and followed the video's instructions. The purse came out a little lumpy, but she had to admit, it was pretty cute. Everyone at work wanted one. A tiny seed was planted that this might be something to explore.

It wasn't until she was at a viewing party for a colleague who had participated in a home renovation TV show that her new life plan materialized. Previews for the program *Traveling in a Tiny House* had everyone discussing the pros and cons of living this new vagabond existence. That night, Summer went home and started following several tiny travelers on Instagram. Within a week, she'd flown to Cobb, Kentucky, where the Internet said she'd find the perfect home. She met with Bale Barrett, who used to sell real estate and was now making small homes on wheels at *Bale's Tiny Dreams*. Bale was a startlingly large man to be selling tiny houses. His shoulders took up the entire width of the front door—a fact Summer pretended not to notice. She also pretended not to notice his green eyes, long legs, sun-flecked hair, or his calloused workman's hands. She was a sucker for a man whose hands felt like they knew how to earn a living. She sure wasn't going to meet anyone like that in the lunchroom at work. But there was more to Bale than his looks. He was a man following his dream! Inspired, she picked out a tiny house shaped like a caboose—if she was going to make a statement, she was going to make a *statement*. Summer wrote Bale a check and promised she'd be back to pick up her house on wheels in a month. She was ready to put her plan into action.

"If you change your mind," Bale said, covering her hand with both of his. "You call me. This is a big decision and I want you to be happy."

As she sat in the airport for her flight home, giddy with possibilities, she worried the Bale-ness of the situation might have gone to her head. She took a deep breath and fired up her computer. Typing in "Buyer's Remorse" with her manicured nails, she read article after article. According to the Internet, she had two choices: continuing with the purchase or renouncing the purchase. She looked at the situation as an impartial observer: assessing the risks, the rewards, and the financial burden. All her professional instinct said to cancel the check. But she remembered the sandpapery texture of Bale's big hands and flew back to Hartford to detonate her life.

Back in the kitchen, Shortie gave her a slobbery kiss, which startled her out of her reverie. Summer first saw Shortie on Facebook—a friend of a friend of a friend needed to find him a forever home. She drove the sixty miles to Danbury to take a look at him. It was love at first sight for both.

Summer's cellphone vibrated on the counter. She looked at the screen: It was her Grandmother Murray, known to everyone, family and townspeople alike, as Queenie. Summer had been avoiding her grandmother's call for almost a week. Summer had sent Queenie an e-mail, letting her know that she was quitting her job and exploring other options. What she left out were the truck, the tiny house, and the idea of earning a living selling purses made from old felted sweaters. Shortie looked at her as if to say: "You can't put it off any longer." Summer took a deep breath and answered the phone.

"Hi Queenie," Summer said, bracing for the worst.

"Clarisse, you need to come home," Queenie said.

Summer winced. Only her grandmother still called her by her given name.

Even at seventy, Queenie had a stately authoritative voice. Anyone else who said, "You need to come home" might sound petulant, like a five-year-old refusing to share. But from Queenie, it sounded like a command.

"I'm sort of busy right now..." Summer started.

"You've been busy since you left for college," Queenie said. "It's been ten years. I'm beginning to take it personally."

"You've seen me...around," Summer said lamely.

She knew her grandmother didn't mean family holidays with her parents. It was obvious to the entire family that Summer had avoided the town of Cat's Paw her entire adult life.

"Anyway, I need to see you," Queenie said. "So whatever bee is in your bonnet, let him loose. The bakery is falling apart. Get yourself and your fancy college degree up here and straighten things out."

Her grandmother rang off abruptly. Summer stared at the phone.

Simplifying her life just got very complicated.

Chapter 2

Summer stared at the phone. She commanded herself to call her grandmother back and let her know as gently as possible that she was not planning on coming back to the Murray family bakery under any circumstances. When her grandfather died after Summer's graduation from college, she'd been backpacking in Eastern Europe and hadn't been able to get back for the funeral. Summer loved her grandfather Zach Murray dearly. He'd named his bakery Dough Z Dough—the most fantastic name Summer, as a kid, had ever heard. As an adult, she wondered how Grandpa ever managed to convince Queenie to accept the Z.

She would have made an exception to her boycott for his memorial, but if she were being honest, she was happy for the excuse not to return to Cat's Paw. She mourned her grandfather and wept at the thought of never seeing him again. He'd died unexpectedly of a heart attack, leaving a family and a town devastated.

Summer thought about the last time they'd seen each other. The two had been out walking only a few days before Summer was to return to San Francisco for her senior year of high school. She'd lost her footing in a tangle of soft ground. She grabbed for her grandfather's strong arm, as one of her legs slipped into the earth and seemed to be dangling in space. Grandpa Zach righted her.

"Ouch," Summer cried, seeing blood trickling from her leg.

"Careful," Grandpa Zach said, studying the wound and the landscape. "You stepped in a patch of wild salmonberries. Lots of thorns."

Grandpa Zach gently removed a few thorns, then took out a handkerchief and cleaned Summer's scratched legs. "Looks like you'll live," he said. "I think we should find out why you almost disappeared into the earth."

Summer loved that her grandfather turned everything into an adventure. She felt a little timid at the prospect, but, while she was too old to think they'd discovered a secret passage to the middle of the earth—there was *something* going on!

They looked at each other for a few seconds. Gingerly moving some of the salmonberry branches aside, they started digging. They cleared enough branches to stare down into an old circular brick hole about ten feet deep. Summer got down on her knees and peered inside.

"What is this?" Summer asked, sitting back on her heels.

"An old well," Grandpa Zach said.

"It doesn't have any water in it," Summer said.

"Must have dried up. Wasn't any use to anybody anymore. That's probably why somebody covered it up."

"How long do you think it's been here?"

Grandpa Zach said he had no idea, but it must have been there before he'd bought the property.

"This is super dangerous," Summer said. "We should fill it in."

He vowed to fill it in. He'd wait until next spring to tackle the project, he said.

"But somebody could get hurt," Summer insisted.

"The salmonberries have done a pretty good job keeping people away from here," Grandpa Zach said. "I'm sure we'll be safe until next year."

It hadn't occurred to Summer at the time, but Grandpa Zach must have known it was a job that was going to be too much for him. Summer wondered how long her grandfather knew he had a weakened heart. Her eyes stung with the knowledge that she could never ask him.

There were all the childhood memories that made the summer so special year after year. But there was something else. She knew her grandfather was instrumental in ending her romance with Keefe Devlin. She always thought she'd have time to confront him and ask for an explanation. Now she would never get the chance.

Grandpa Zach was gone, but Queenie still loomed large. Summer rehearsed the conversation and realized the gentle approach would never work with Queenie.

Summer would need to be firm!

She practiced her firm approach, knitting her eyebrows fiercely. She stabbed at the keypad on her phone.

"Hello, Queenie?" Summer said in a voice two registers higher than she'd anticipated.

"Are you calling to let me know when you're arriving?" Queenie asked.

"No...." Summer could feel her resolution fading, but she tried again. "Not exactly."

"Well, you call me back when you have a date," Queenie said. "I expect you'll need to give work two weeks' notice."

"I have something I need to say, Queenie," Summer said, summoning her resolve.

There was dead silence from Connecticut, up to the satellite that connected their calls and down to Washington.

"Yes?" Queenie finally asked. "If you have something to say, say it. These cell phone minutes aren't cheap."

"I'll see you in about two weeks," Summer said. She let out a sigh of resignation. Nobody could out-fierce Queenie.

She looked at Shortie after she hung up the phone.

"I didn't actually lie to my grandmother. I didn't say 'I've already quit work,' I said, 'I'd see you in two weeks,'" Summer said to the dog. "I know you're judging me. But you don't know her! I need those two weeks to wrap my head around this."

Fierceness might just take some practice. She marched into the closet, reached into the KEEP box, took out the too-small black wool coat, and heaved it into GIVEAWAY. Shortie snorted.

Summer continued packing through the night. She thought back to happier times at her grandparent's lavish Victorian on the outskirts of town. When she was a kid, the house had been her haven. Both her parents were teachers, and from the time Summer was a newborn, they would drive her to Washington as soon as school let out in San Francisco and pick her up again in late August. Summer looked forward to the trip to Cat's Paw as far back as she could remember. Family lore had it that her first two-syllable word was Summer, which she said as her father packed one last bag into the car and it was evident that they were on their way to her grandparents'. Summer became her nickname from then on.

She surveyed her closet. After hours of decision-making, the GIVEAWAY box was still half empty. Summer shook her head—she deemed it half-full. Heading to Washington was going to require a change of attitude.

From now on, more positive thinking.

Summer curled up on the sofa with her MacBook Air and fired up her favorite search engine. She hesitated. What exactly did she want to research? Estrangement? Forced reconciliation? She clicked on a link or two, but all the articles were about families...and family wasn't exactly her problem. She wasn't sure how to define the difficulty facing her, let alone seek an answer on how to fix it.

She stared at the screen. Running away from Cat's Paw was easier than looking at the situation head on. Her parents, still living and teaching in San Francisco, were easy to avoid—either her mother or her father always had some type of research or other project that filled their time once Summer headed off to college. A few days at Christmas and a once or twice a year visit with them was always easy to manage. It wasn't hard to find a legitimate excuse when one of her parents suggested they meet up at Queenie and Grandpa Murray's place. Once Summer was in college, she could always summon a research project of her own.

The day Summer drove away to college, she promised herself there was no going back to Cat's Paw until her heart had healed. Or until Keefe Devlin no longer worked for her grandparents. It had been ten years. Much had changed over the years—her grandfather died, Queenie was getting older, the bakery seemed to be in some sort of peril, but two important facts stayed the same: Keefe Devlin was still in Cat's Paw, and Summer had been true to her resolution that she would never go back.

Until today.

She typed in "reconciliation" on Google and clicked on a link: ARE YOU READY TO RECONCILE? 5 QUESTIONS TO HELP YOU DECIDE.

She typed in her answers:

1, *Can I handle the possibility of being rejected a second time?* (No. But I'll never give him the opportunity.)

2. *Have we both experienced significant emotional growth since going our separate ways?* (I can't imagine he is capable of emotional growth.)

3. *Can I trust myself to set and maintain clear, respectful boundaries?* (I think ten years' worth of boundaries is a pretty good start.)

She paused at the next question:

4. *Do I feel the need to confront the person from whom I'm estranged? Do I?*

She decided to skip the question.

5. *Am I still angry?*

This one was easy. She pointed the mouse to the top of the screen, changed it to thirty points, and then typed in the word YES.

She submitted her answers and waited for the analysis. It came back in less than a minute.

"You are not emotionally ready to resolve your issues. You have work to do in your emotional arena before engaging in a reconciliation. For more information, please send $59...."

"You lost me at emotional arena," she said as she closed the computer. She was always willing to believe that online advice was gospel—as long as it was free.

Chapter 3

Queenie expected Summer to be in Washington in two weeks and Summer was going to make the most of that time. As she made her final preparations to leave her old life in Connecticut, she tried to convince herself that her rising excitement was due to picking up her tiny house and starting a whole new adventure—even if the adventure wasn't exactly what she'd planned. But that was the whole point of adventure, wasn't it? She could make purses in Washington as easily as any of the other forty-nine states. There must be craft fairs in Washington. Keefe Devlin be damned. He was nothing more than a relic from her past. She felt her emotional arena was filling up just fine.

There was another reason the thought of jumping in her new truck and heading toward Kentucky gave her goose bumps: Bale Barrett was waiting in the Bluegrass State with her custom-made house. If Keefe was yesterday's news, maybe Bale would be tomorrow's headlines.

Summer dubbed her truck "Big Red." The day she was leaving Hartford, she and Lynnie loaded the truck bed with everything Summer needed to set up her new household in the caboose—or at least, everything that would fit in the caboose. She had a small box of dinnerware. As much as it pained her, she only kept two plates, two bowls, two cups, four glasses (two large and two small), and two sets of utensils. She'd tried to only pack service for one but decided she didn't need to completely give up on the idea that there might someday be someone else eating in the little dining area.

All the research she'd read pointed out that when you lived tiny, you actually "lived in the world and less in your house." Her first instinct was to get rid of everything else, but her discipline deserted her. The truck bed contained a few well-thought-out appliances—and her two Bernina sewing machines. Summer saw the sewing machines as the key to her craft-fair future, so they got pride of place in the truck.

Summer tried to tune out Lynnie's chatter as panic rose with every trip she took down the apartment stairs. But hard as she tried, snippets of Lynnie's conversation worked their way into her brain.

"Hey, Lynnie," Summer said, interrupting the steady flow of Lynnie's patter, "Would you stay with Big Red while I go get Shortie?"

"Well, of course, I will," Lynnie said, a look of solidarity replacing the maternal haranguing.

Summer bolted up the stairs. She wanted to be alone in the apartment for her goodbye. Lynnie had volunteered to call a local charity to come get the three huge GIVEAWAY boxes and all the furniture, so it didn't have that final, empty appearance that always tugged at Summer's heart during past moves. With all the furniture still in place, it was as if the apartment didn't understand it was being left behind. She scooped Shortie into her arms and stared out at the river.

Hard as she tried, Lynnie's words still rang in her ears: *Just because you saw this on television doesn't make it a good idea...I don't see how you expect to live with just a truck full of stuff...You can always change your mind....*

Summer had quit her job. She'd spent all her money. Her grandmother had summoned her. While mind-changing was no longer on the table, it was hard to ignore Lynnie's other points. As she surveyed the truck bed from the window, she did wonder how she was supposed to set up housekeeping with so few *things*. And as far as making a life-altering decision based on a few televisions shows...well...it might not have been her smartest move. But she'd made decisions based on less. Case in point: the reason she was in Hartford with a career in insurance was because a school counselor told her she had good problem-solving skills. It occurred to her years later that the one who was good at problem solving was the counselor—one student had a problem with her life's direction and the counselor pulled a career out of a hat. Problem solved for the counselor.

Summer didn't really feel she was very good at her job, anyway. She was too emotional. Even if one didn't particularly like one's job, one still wanted to be good at it. When she liked a particular businessman or woman, she found it hard to put the kibosh on his or her plans. She would often argue that a business could be classified as risk but just as easily be classified as opportunity. Her bosses were losing patience with her. That fateful day when Summer pulled her favorite sweater out of the dryer, found it miniaturized and decided to turn it into a purse—now *that* was problem solving.

"I'll be much better at making purses," she muttered to Shortie.

Shortie, staring out the window, was losing patience. He started to squirm. "Okay, okay," Summer said. "We're out of here."

While Lynnie stood impatiently on the sidewalk waiting for her dramatic farewell, Summer strapped Shortie into his car seat, a boxy affair that took up an extraordinary amount of room in the back seat of the cab. A new vehicle for Summer meant new restraints for Shortie.

"I know you're going to hate this," Summer said, feeling guilty that Shortie was no longer going to be riding shotgun or poking his head out the window. All her research pointed to a doggy booster anchored to the middle of the backseat and a harness pulled snugly across his broad chest. The dog looked at her with alarmed what-the-hell? eyes as she snapped the harness into place. "Sorry dude, but this is for your own good. The videos all say you'll get used to it."

But Shortie's eyes said otherwise.

Summer turned her attention to Lynnie. She was surprised to see tears misting in her neighbor's eyes. Summer tried to remember Lynnie's every little annoying quirk, but one-by-one they deserted her and she found herself in the older woman's embrace.

"I'm going to really miss you," Lynnie said in a jagged voice.

"I'm going to really miss you, too," Summer said—and, to her surprise, meant it.

Summer inhaled sharply as she caught a glimpse over Lynnie's shoulder of the apartment complex and the river beyond.

Maybe I could still change my mind! Most of my stuff is still in the apartment, after all.

But Summer was resolved to look forward, tough as that was.

"Thanks for taking care of everything," Summer said, disengaging herself from Lynnie's embrace. "Not having to deal with the furniture and the rest of the stuff has been really great."

"Oh, now," Lynnie said. "What are friends for? And remember, you can always come back."

"I know," Summer squeaked.

"I mean it," Lynnie continued. "You go get this crazy idea out of your head and come right back here. There's security, a solid paycheck and probably a nice man waiting right here."

Summer remembered why she wanted out. She gave Lynnie a quick peck on the cheek and jumped in the truck. In a moment, Hartford, Connecticut, was nothing but an image receding into her past—or at least into her rearview mirror. She thought about Lynnie's parting words and felt better about her choice. She didn't want security, she didn't even necessarily care about a solid paycheck.

But she had to admit, that "nice man" part sounded pretty damn good.

Getting to Cat's Paw, Washington, by way of Cobb, Kentucky was far from a straight shot. As much as Queenie was bad-vibing Summer to get to the bakery as quickly as possible, Summer was determined to stick to her plan—or as much of her plan as possible now that she was going to help her grandmother on the other side of the country.

She knew Queenie would never approve of the tiny house philosophy, let alone a real tiny house, so Summer just didn't mention she'd be bringing one with her. And it wasn't just the tiny house. She's mapped out a route of thrift shops along the way where she planned on stocking up on cashmere and wool sweaters. Of course, stocking up had a whole new meaning when a person was going to live in 220 square feet. Maybe she'd just buy the most appealing sweater in each store. She caught a glimpse of herself in the rearview mirror and frowned. She knew that was never going to happen. If she found five sweaters that appealed to her, she was going to buy them. It occurred to her that there was a huge barn up at Queenie's house and maybe she could keep her new stash of bulky sweater in there? She shot a look at Shortie in the back of the cab. He refused to meet her eye, indignant that he was strapped into a booster seat.

"You're no help," Summer said.

Summer sighed. All the research she'd done insisted that he would get used to it. She hoped so, since this was his future.

"At least you know what your future holds," Summer said.

It was only four hours to Philadelphia from Hartford, but Summer pinned it in Google Maps as her first stop. As soon as she'd made up her mind to make her sweater-purses, she started taking an interest in the wardrobes of all the ladies, and some of the men, at work. She found herself following a plus-sized woman named Breeze, who always wore gorgeous clothes (including knockout cashmere and wool sweaters that would shrink beautifully), making notes and sketches and, if she could get away with it, taking photos. Breeze finally confronted Summer in the hallway, asking if she needed to call Security. Summer stammered out her reason for following her. Luckily, Breeze took the stalking as a supreme compliment. She told Summer that the secret to her entire wardrobe was a thrift store in Philadelphia called *Bodacious and Curvaceous* that catered to curvy ladies.

"You should definitely go. You won't have to limit yourself to puny purses from small, medium, and large sweaters," Breeze said proudly.

"Honey, you'll be able to create messenger bags with some of the loot you'll find there."

Summer checked out *Bodacious and Curvaceous* online and determined it would make a great first stop on her road to bohemian purse-maker. But now that she was on the road, she wondered if she would have been better off finding a thrift shop closer to Hartford. While traffic flowed smoothly down I-95, Summer was perfectly confident behind the wheel. But when Google Maps' mechanical voice began to navigate her toward the intimidating George Washington Bridge, her hands broke out in a sweat.

Summer had driven all kinds of tractors and snowplows when she was a teenager at Flat Top Farm, her grandparents' property, but nothing had prepared her for this. She tried not to look over the rail where she could see so much *water* from the cab. Shortie was causing a disturbance in the backseat; he must have known he was missing something. Summer's right butt cheek suddenly started to vibrate as she realized she was drifting into the lane to her right. She remembered when she bought the truck the salesman mentioned this feature: The seat would pulse when the car detected a crash threat. Summer's palms were buttered with a new layer of perspiration. Had she been about to crash, and on the George Washington Bridge? She checked her odometer; she was a little more than one hundred miles from Connecticut. She'd barely gotten underway! Was this a bad omen?

She gripped the steering wheel with both hands and didn't breathe again until she was off the bridge. Once she felt secure, she checked the side and rearview mirrors and glided cautiously to the left. The seat signaled her negligence and her left butt cheek jiggled.

"Oh, come on," Summer said indignantly to the seat. "That wasn't even a *swerve*! No way was that a crash threat!"

She arrived in Philadelphia with only an hour until *Bodacious and Curvaceous* closed.

Plenty of time to scoop up some treasure.

Summer crept along Spruce Street looking for a parking space. One butt cheek then the other vibrated with outrage. Summer watched the clock: forty-five minutes till the shop closed. She gave up, pulled in a valet lot, and then realized that valet parking was probably not going to be something she should be spending money on. But between the interactive seat and the fact that no space seemed large enough for Big Red, her nerves were shot.

She dug through her purse (a midsized red slouch bag made from a J. Crew Christmas cashmere) for Shortie's Therapy Dog jacket. When planning her trip, Summer mentioned to Lynnie that she had concerns about traveling with Shortie. She could find hotels all along the route that would take him, but what was she going to do with him at stores? Lynnie then suggested getting a therapy dog vest online.

"But he isn't a therapy dog," Summer said, looking dubiously at Shortie.

"That's not the point," Lynnie said.

"I think that *is* the point."

"Well, if you want to play strictly by the rules," Lynnie said. "Then you go ahead and knock yourself out. I know you'd never leave Shortie in a car by himself...so how do you expect to buy a cup of coffee or do all that sweater shopping?"

Lynnie had left it at that. That night, just for curiosity's sake, Summer googled "therapy dogwear," and came up with myriad choices in all sizes, styles, and patterns. Some even came with official looking badges. Summer wasn't one to break rules, but struggled with her decision. Was a bogus vest better than tying Shortie to some outdoor furniture while she did her shopping? Just the thought of his little eyes following her into a store made her tear up.

Summer bought a cute blue and silver coat with two paw prints on either side and a smiling canine on the rump. She attempted a faux-therapy-dog outing, initially exhilarated by her outlawing. But when attempting to enter a store, Summer saw a man with a real therapy dog and couldn't bring herself to pass herself off as someone who needed emotional support.

At her exit interview at work, Summer brought up the Shortie problem as one of her main concerns for the trip. If there is one thing people in insurance can do, it's get the ball moving. In no time at all, Shorty was licensed as a bona fide emotional support dog. It did cross Summer's mind that her friends in high places might have actually thought she was in desperate need of a support dog, but she preferred to think they were all just animal lovers.

Fishing the coat out of her bag, she released Shortie from his chair, cinched the coat around his middle and snapped on a leash. Shortie looked startled and confused, like he'd been released from one prison just to be rowed downstream to another.

Summer put him on the ground and appraised the look. The real therapy dog coat was dull, so while she had the legal paperwork, she still had him wearing his original cute outfit from the Internet. It wasn't out-and-out breaking the law, but still she felt like a renegade. The coat was made for a slightly longer dog, so the fabric jutted out over his head. When Lynnie first saw him in it, she thought he looked like an armadillo. Summer couldn't really argue and vowed to make him a jacket out of a man's argyle sweater when she had her business up and running.

Summer was proud of herself. Besides the fact that she had gotten over the challenge of her first bridge, she was three hours closer to the tiny house and her future—not to mention three hours closer to Bale—and was on her way to her first sweater purchase!

I've got this! she thought.

Shortie seemed anxious to stretch his little legs, and pulled at his leash. But before Summer had taken no more than ten steps, her cell phone rang. She halted and dug in her purse again. She could hear it, and she could see it flashing with lights that would have made a disco proud, but she couldn't put her hands on it inside the slouchy purse. *I'm going to have to figure out how to put a few pockets in these purses*, she thought.

She noticed that the purse seemed to be stretching, and not in an attractive way. Maybe there was more to this sewing than met the eye. She finally managed to fish the phone out of her purse. She whipped back her hair to answer it as Shortie strained at his leash in order to christen the tires of a tantalizingly close Mercedes Benz.

"Hello?" Summer said, giving Shortie a little more leash.

"It is I," Queenie said.

Summer chided herself on not checking the number before she answered. She'd have to be more diligent. The best way to keep Queenie in the dark about her plans was to just not talk to her. Avoidance had served her pretty well up until now and she saw no reason to mess with success.

"Hey, Queenie," Summer said, inching closer to the Mercedes. There was no reason for both she and the dog to be miserable. "What's up?"

"Just checking in on you," Queenie said. "Making sure you haven't changed your mind about coming up here."

"Why would I do that?"

"I don't know," Queenie said. "I told Keefe you were coming and he said he'd be surprised if you showed, so I'm just..."

"Keefe?"

"Yeah," Queenie said. "Keefe Devlin. You remember Keefe Devlin, don't you?"

"Of course I remember Keefe Devlin!" Summer said, trying to keep her voice even. "What's it to him if I show or not?"

"He's just trying to make plans," Queenie said. "He's still the manager of the shop, you know."

"I've got to go, Queenie," Summer said. "You can tell Keefe I'll be there sooner than I thought. Whether he likes it or not."

"No need to act like a fishwife," Queenie said. "Keefe is just doing his job. I'm sure he doesn't care if you show one way or the other."

"I believe you," Summer said as she hung up, tears stinging her eyes. She was jerked out of her melancholy by a harsh male voice.

"Hey!"

Summer looked around. The angry voice belonged to a red-faced man in a green T-shirt and baseball cap. He strode over to her.

"Your dog peed on my tire," the man said accusingly, pointing at Shortie.

Summer looked down at Shortie, standing triumphantly by a spreading puddle.

"I see that," Summer said.

She wondered if she should apologize, but decided against it. After all, *she* hadn't peed on his tire. Why were men always causing trouble?

The man glared at her, then at Shortie, then jumped over the puddle. He opened the door, got in and drove away, screeching out of the parking lot.

Summer looked down at Shortie again. The man had not upset Shortie, who was all set to move on with his day. Summer gave the leash a little tug and they headed toward the store.

"You're a very wise man, little guy," Summer said. "Never sweat the small stuff, right?"

She strode briskly to the store. A sign on the door read: "We're closed! Thank you for your business and have a bodacious and curvaceous life!"

Summer sat on the front stoop and put her head in her arms. Nothing was going according to plan. Her phone buzzed. This time she looked at it. It was Bale in Kentucky.

Chapter 4

"Hello? Hello? Hello?" she practiced three different approaches to the word before answering.

"Hello?" she finally said into the phone, settling on the sort of smoky secretarial I'm-having-sex-on-my-desk number she'd never gotten to use at work.

"This is Bale," he said. "Bale Barrett—with the tiny house."

Various sentences popped into Summer's head: *Yes, I have you on Caller ID* (too pathetic?)...*I only know one Bale* (too haughty?)...*Is something wrong?* (too risk-management?)....

She settled on: "Hi, Bale."

"I'm finishing up the house," Bale said. "I was just double-checking to make sure you still want to use the horse trough as a bathtub."

Summer had seen a tiny house online with a galvanized steel watering trough converted into a bathtub. It embodied all the romance of the tiny house adventure she envisioned. When Bale barely blinked at the complexity of the concept, she was thrilled. But now, the thought of arriving at Queenie's with a bright red tiny house shaped like a caboose with a bathtub made from a horse trough gave her severe doubts.

Galvanized was taking on a whole new meaning.

"Are you having second thoughts?" she asked.

"I think that's my question," Bale said with a deep rumbling laugh.

"Oh!" Summer tried to recover some ground. "No, I'm not having second thoughts. Unless you have another idea."

"I'm been thinking about you," Bale said. "And I do have another option."

You're thinking about me?

"I'm listening," she said.

She thought she sounded the epitome of sophistication.

"I just did a shower installation using half a whiskey barrel," he said. "I have the other half of the barrel and thought that if you wanted a shower instead of a tub, you might like it."

Summer wandered Spruce Street aimlessly, curvaceous sweaters forgotten. Lost in conversation while Shortie sniffed at every new tree, there was something sexy about discussing her bathing options with a handsome man in Kentucky.

Summer pictured herself climbing into the half whiskey barrel and realized the vision of lounging in a horse trough with bubbles up to her shoulders was a much better image than her climbing clumsily over the side of a half barrel.

"I think I'll stick with the tub," she said.

"You got it," Bale said. "See you in two days, then?"

"Looks like it," Summer replied. "I'm in Philadelphia right now and tomorrow I should be in West Virginia."

"Beautiful country out there," Bale said. "Are you going to Dolly Sods?"

"Are you kidding?" Summer replied. "Why drive through West Virginia if you aren't going to Dolly Sods?"

"That's my girl!" he said. "Well, wish I were going with you, but I have a bathtub to build. See ya."

"See *ya*," Summer answered clumsily. As Queenie's granddaughter, poor diction did not come easy.

She knew she shouldn't read anything into his offhand remark, "I wish I were going with you," but her resolve deserted her. She felt a little giddy with the anticipation of seeing him and the fact (well, the supposition) that he sounded as if he couldn't wait to see her.

Summer checked the battery on her phone. She was down to twenty-three percent. She always filled up her car at a quarter-tank and always recharged her battery at twenty-five percent. But she was a new, more reckless version of herself. She decided to throw caution to the wind.

"Come on, Shortie," she said, pulling him and his therapy jacket into a coffee shop.

The shop was nearly deserted. She headed toward a small booth in the back, walking straight-backed, as if training Shortie how to act in a public place. The doctor who gave Summer Shortie's license cautioned her that the dog needed to be well-behaved in all public places. Shortie was clearly not a method actor. His tail wagged and he made eye contact with every patron, whether they were smiling at him or not. She promised him if he would just not cause a scene, there would be bacon in his immediate future. Whenever he went off script, Summer, knowing dogs had exceptional hearing, would just whisper "bacon" under her breath. It seemed to work every time.

She managed to tuck them both into the tiny back booth, just as the waitress appeared. She wore a name badge that read: My Name is Mindy. She had jet-black hair pulled tightly into a ponytail, bright red lipstick, and she was chewing gum.

"I'm Mindy," the girl said robotically. "Do you have any questions?"

"Yes," Summer said, looking up at her. "What are Dolly Sods?"

"Beats me," Mindy said, nodding toward Summer's cell phone. "What does Wikipedia say?"

Summer used her remaining cell phone battery to discover The Dolly Sods Wilderness, known to outdoorsy types as Dolly Sods, is a wilderness area in the Allegheny Mountains located in eastern West Virginia. The unusual name came from an eighteenth-century family in the area named Dahles, tacked on to the local term for an open mountaintop meadow called a "sods." Over time, the area's name was shortened to Dolly Sods.

"I guess the thrift stores of West Virginia will have to wait," Summer said to Shortie, who was much more interested in licking the bacon grease from Summer's fingers. "Looks like we're going hiking tomorrow."

Google Maps directed Summer into West Virginia the following morning.

The rocky plateau at the very top of Dans Mountain in The Dolly Sods Wilderness left Summer literally breathless. The almost 5,000-foot elevation gain was slow going, but spurred on by Bale's endorsement and Shortie's exuberance, she'd made it to the top after losing her way several times. This wilderness was aptly named; the paths were marked only with footprints. She guarded her cell phone as she forged streams, carrying Shortie through rushing water that could easily have carried him away.

Summer perched on a breathtaking overlook. Shortie stretched out beside her. He was obviously enjoying Mother Nature. She'd never taken him hiking before, in part because she thought his little legs would be an impediment, but, she had to admit, mostly because she didn't hike. She thought back to hikes she'd taken with her grandfather in Washington every summer. From her bedroom at her grandparent's property, she could see Mount Rainier when the mountain was "out"—the few days a years when the fog didn't obscure it. She smiled at the memory as she looked down at Shortie. Maybe they'd take up hiking when they got home. She caught herself off guard. It had been years since she'd thought of Washington as home. Although the topography in the Allegheny Mountains was very different from the Cascade Mountain Range in the Pacific Northwest, the feeling of being part of a bigger picture was the same. When her dreams of a life with Keefe unraveled the summer she'd turned eighteen, she headed to college determined to show him she'd be fine without him. She wondered if she had proven anything except that she could be stubborn enough to stay away.

Summer had gone over their brief but shattering story a million times, each time hoping some new piece of information would reveal itself. What had gone wrong with Keefe? Since she was six years younger than Keefe, he acted like more of a big brother even while she was tending a crush that spread across her soul. She remembered watching him after work at the bakery. He'd whip off his apron, hop on his motorcycle and roar across town to pick up Evie, a local girl with the longest legs Summer had ever seen. Summer prayed that when she grew up, she'd have legs like Evie's—legs that cause everyone to stop dead in their tracks to watch her climb onto the back of a motorcycle.

The summer Summer turned seventeen, everything changed, almost. She never got the long legs.

As bittersweet as the memory was, Summer couldn't help but relive their first kiss. She had radar when it came to Keefe, always knowing where he was—either at the house (he lived over her grandparents' garage), at the bakery, or in town with or without Evie. She'd heard that Keefe and Evie had broken up while she was home in San Francisco, but it didn't seem to make much difference in her own relationship with him. She'd somehow lost track of him one brilliantly sunny day. She wandered down by the lake on her grandparents' property and suddenly there he was, fishing. They saw each other at the same time. He waved and, with her heart pounding, she managed to get herself to the creaking little dock without stumbling on her shaking legs. She was surprised to see him fishing from the dock. Keefe was known throughout Cat's Paw as the best fly fisherman in the area.

"Hey, little girl," Keefe said as she sat down beside him. "You caught me slumming."

"I'm not so little," Summer said, trying not to sound disappointed. She hated it when he called her that.

"No, I guess you aren't," Keefe said. "I keep forgetting you're all grown up."

Summer steamed. Every year, as soon as she'd get to her grandparents, she'd run to find Keefe, to show off how grown up she'd become. And every year, he'd seem surprised that she was there. Ruffling her hair, he'd say: "Hey, little girl, you back for the summer?"

Clearly, he had not been counting the days until he saw her again.

"You know, Clarisse," he said, watching the water for any sign of shadow below the surface. "I've been..."

"Don't call me that," Summer said. "Only my grandmother calls me Clarisse."

"Sorry," Keefe said. "No 'little girl,' no 'Clarisse.' Any other new rules?"

Summer tried to smooth out her scowl. Practicing enticing expressions she saw online, she thought she'd perfected a come-hither look, only to catch a glimpse of herself in the mirror. She looked like an unpleasant child.

"Just call me Summer," she said.

"I think I can wrap my old brain around that," he said.

"You're not old!" Summer said.

He was always bringing up their age difference.

"I'm twenty-three," he said. "Old enough to know better."

"Well, I'm old enough to know better, too."

"I guess you are."

She couldn't explain it, but she saw an interest in his eyes that she'd never seen before. She couldn't explain it, but it was there. Her breath caught.

He sees me.

Without warning, he leaned in, smoothed back her hair and kissed her. She had fantasized about this moment her entire life, but now that it was happening, she couldn't lose herself in the moment.

He's kissing me!

Stop thinking.

But he's kissing me!

Whatever was passing between them jerked to a stop as Keefe's fishing line demanded his attention.

"You caught something," Summer said, as they both leapt to their feet.

In seconds, Keefe had reeled in a small trout. She watched him handle the fish carefully. He took the hook gently from the fish's mouth. Lying on his stomach, Keefe gently lowered it back into the water, moving the tail back and forth and side to side. The trout swam away. Keefe got back to his feet and dusted off his jeans.

"I guess that little guy was too small," Summer said, wanting to sound knowledgeable. She knew that not everybody lived up to the catch-and-release rules of Washington State, but Keefe did.

"Yep," Keefe said, squinting into the water and not looking at her. "That fish has some more living to do before it's ready to be reeled in for good."

He walked away. Summer stayed on the dock.

That was it? That *couldn't* be it.

Keefe kept his distance the rest of the summer. When she came back the following year—when she was eighteen—Keefe seemed to think that maybe it was time to reel her in.

Summer stopped reliving the past. She could construct every moment they'd spent together. She knew the moment he started to slip away, but no amount of rehashing was ever going to change that.

She took a deep breath and relaxed into the mountains. She hated to admit it, but now that she'd come to terms with going back to Washington, she longed for the rugged beauty of the place. She hadn't realized until now, exactly how much she'd put behind her.

She wondered if she was making excuses for herself, now that she was heading back to Cat's Paw.

Or maybe it really *was* time?

Chapter 5

It had been years since Summer had done any serious hiking. Her thigh and calf muscles were reliving every moment of yesterday's march in Dolly Sods. She'd had a restless night as her feet cramped and her legs twitched, but in the morning she'd driven across the border into Kentucky and she perked up. Her GPS told her she was only two hours from Cobb, her tiny house, her new life, and Bale. She'd orchestrated her trip to pull into Bale's parking lot at exactly six o'clock that evening, which was closing time. She'd pictured conveniently arriving in time for dinner—if he were so inclined. She'd even researched dog-friendly restaurants in the area, so Shortie wouldn't be a hindrance.

But now her legs were screaming at her. She couldn't get up or down without grabbing onto a steady surface and pulling herself up or gently lowering herself down. There was no way to achieve any of this without grimaces and groaning of the most unflattering kind. She was torn: Call Bale and say she would be there by closing time or limp into a hotel. Call him and say she'd see him tomorrow and pray her legs felt better by morning.

Summer decided to call and make excuses for this evening. The last thing she wanted to do was limp into her new adventure. She touched the button on her phone that would let her chat hands-free. When the phone at the other end of the line started ringing, she gripped the steering wheel with both hands. She was shaking from head to foot.

"Hello, Summer," Bale said.

He's entered my name into his phone! She thought, giving Shortie a thumbs up.

"Hey, Bale," she said. She looked in the rearview mirror. Shortie, who had been dozing for the last hour, raised his head at the unnatural tone of his human's voice. "Listen, I was thinking…since it's so late, maybe I'll swing by in the morning. It's been a long couple of days, you know, with all that hiking. My dog is beat."

Might as well spin this, she thought, avoiding Shortie's gaze.

"That's fine," said Bale, "I understand exactly how the old dog feels."

Summer started. Was Bale old? How old could he be? He was so handsome. But he was distinguished, which means he wasn't *young*. She was twenty-eight. He was…maybe forty? Keefe flashed through her mind. He was now thirty-four. Maybe she had a thing for older men.

"Are you still there?" Bale asked.

"Yes, sorry," she said, snapping out of her reflective mood. She realized she was aimlessly driving up and down the same gravel road. "Weird phone connection for a second."

"No problem," Bale said. "I'll see you first thing…are you in a red pickup truck?"

"Yes," Summer said, surprised. "How did you know?"

"You keep driving past me," he said. "Look to your left."

Summer did as instructed. She could feel the blush immediately creeping up her cheeks as she saw Bale standing in the *Bale's Tiny Dreams* parking lot. He waved extravagantly. She finger waved back.

Now what?

She knew she had to pull in.

As nervous as she was about seeing him after all these months, her pounding heart was due in part to the fact that perched on the edge of the lot sat her brand new fire-engine red caboose!

It took her breath away.

Rolling to a stop in the parking lot, she forgot all about her legs and jumped out of the truck—which made her remember her legs. She gripped the door handle fiercely with her left hand to keep upright as Bale approached.

Handshake? Hug? Cheek kiss? Double cheek kiss?

While she was still making up her mind, Bale reached out for a hearty handshake, the option she had been most likely to reject.

"Looks like you made it after all," he said.

"I did!" she said with over-the-top enthusiasm.

Calm down.

"Let's take a look at your pup," Bale said, looking in the front window.

"He's in his car seat," Summer said. "In the back."

"Your dog is in a car seat?" Bale asked. "How does he stick his head out the window if he's in a car seat?"

"He doesn't," Summer said. "My research said this was the safest way to travel with a dog."

"Safest, maybe. But doesn't sound very fun," Bale said, peering in the back window at Shortie, who was getting restless as he intuited Bale's attention. "May I?"

At her nod, Bale opened the back door and unbuckled Shortie, who leapt into Bale's arms. Summer watched, furtively testing out her legs as Shortie put on an exaggerated show of gratitude for being released from bondage.

Bale put Shortie on the ground. The dog took it as his cue to start sniffing everything in sight.

"Let me get his leash," Summer said, but she wasn't sure she could move yet without yelping.

"He's fine," Bale said, spreading his arms to show that there was nowhere unsafe for Shortie to travel. "We're in the middle of nowhere. Let him read the newspaper."

"Pardon me?"

"That's what I call it when a dog goes sniffing around," Bale said with a grin. "He's getting all the news."

Shortie was acting as if he were starved for news. Zigzagging among the tiny houses, Summer's heart would stop every time he was out of her sight, then she'd breathe a sigh of relief when she'd spot his tail or his paws. She realized that she was going to have to adopt a more breezy attitude about life in general with the new life she was trying to cobble together, but she didn't really want to start with her dog. Finally, Shortie bounded back. Summer was in a quandary. She really didn't want Shortie roaming around, but she didn't want to offend Bale. Years ago, Summer had perfected the art of subtle control. With her legs still shrieking, she bent over and scooped Shortie up. Bale reached over and scratched Shortie's ears.

"He's a fine man," Bale said. "I can tell a good dog when I see one."

Etiquette crisis averted.

"As long as you're here," Bale said. "Want to check out the house?"

The thought of climbing the three stairs into the caboose sounded like torture, but the pull of her new life was hard to resist.

"Why not?" she said.

As they walked to the caboose, Summer checked out the competition: the other tiny houses on the lot. Though there were several styles, they were all on wheels and ready to head off to zoning laws unknown. Some of them were houses she'd toured on her first trip. There was a very modern silver-toned box with a teal door and a rooftop deck. She remembered that she'd been drawn to it, but at 350 square feet, it was too big for her to ever consider towing on her own. There was also a replica of a Victorian Manor perfect to every miniaturized detail. But it reminded her too much of

Queenie's house, so she crossed it off the list. She smiled at the thought of having purchased it and now driving it to Queenie's spread—an architectural mini-me on the front lawn. There were also a few new houses; there was a little number that reminded her of a Jules Verne's time machine with its steampunk sensibilities and a rustic log cabin. In one corner of the lot sat what looked like a canvas tent.

"What is that?" Summer asked, pointing.

"That's a yurt."

"A real yurt?" Summer asked. "I thought only nomads in Mongolia used them."

"They're getting popular with the tiny house crowd," Bale said. "A guy traded me this one for my smallest house. I'm going to study how to maximize yurt living."

"You think yurts might take over the tiny house trend?"

"Maybe not in Mongolia," he said. "But you never know."

"And what about the guy who traded it to you?" Summer asked, fascinated by the tiny house motivations of others.

"He said he'd stay in touch and let me know if it were possible to live comfortably in sixty-seven square feet."

"Sixty-seven square feet?" Summer's eyes widened. "Isn't that the size of a port-a-potty?"

"Twice the size, actually," Bale said. "But we don't really like to refer to port-a-potties in general. Bad for the image."

Summer looked at him to see if he was kidding. He winked at her. She flushed.

They had arrived in front of the caboose. She stared up at it.

Here it was! Literally, her dream come true. She hugged Shortie to her and kissed his head as she watched Bale climb up the stairs and unlock the glossy front door. He looked down at her and offered both his hands—his beautiful, workman's calloused hands, which had built this house just for her. She blinked back tears. So many possibilities could lead from this moment.

"Do you want me to take Shortie?" he asked.

"Sure!" she chirped, handing him the dog.

Grabbing the rail, she pulled herself up the three stairs and followed him into the caboose. The evening light was fast evaporating. It occurred to her that they were in *her* house and yet she had no idea where the light switch was. She could hear Shortie's little toenails on the floor as she watched Bale's shadow flick a switch that illuminated the space with a warm, inviting glow. The fact that he was so comfortable in her house made her slightly giddy. She sobered immediately when she realized how *big* he seemed.

"Is there something wrong?" he asked, reading distress on her face.

"Oh, no!" she said. "It's just a lot to take in."

"Check it out," he said, sitting in the built-in nook that was soon to be her new dining room.

Dining area, she reminded herself.

She loved the distressed wood Bale had used for the flooring and the built-ins. She'd asked for the couch and dining furniture to all be built-in, so she wouldn't have to set up the house every time she moved. She'd also required the dining table to be solid, since it would double as her sewing room. She snuck a peek at Bale now sitting at her table. She noted with satisfaction that *everything* looked sturdy.

When she'd ordered the caboose, she envisioned herself trekking across the country instead of being parked in her grandmother's yard, but the furnishings were beautiful and contained extra storage, so she still supported her original decision.

The kitchen was amazing. It had a real stove top, farm sink, built-in microwave, dishwasher, and cabinets stained a dusty grey. She ran her hands over the stainless steel countertops. It was perfect. She hadn't thought about it when she and Bale were going over design options, but she realized she could make a romantic dinner here, no problem.

She continued her tour. Behind the kitchen was a sliding barn door. Her heart started to pound. She smiled at Bale.

"Is this it?" she asked.

"That's it," he said proudly.

She slid the barn door smoothly to the side and gasped. In 220 square feet, Bale had managed to build a large walk-in closet. Shortie scooted in ahead of her and sniffed out every corner. Every inch was maximized.

"You can hang seventy-two dresses," Bale called from the dining area.

"That should do it," she called back, realizing her life working in a bakery would probably curtail her dress wearing.

She looked at a wall of extra-large white wire bins. Walking over to them, she pulled one open. It slid as smoothly as the barn door had. The workmanship on this place, she felt, was incredible.

"I know you said you were going to start making things out of sweaters," Bale said. He had moved into the closet doorway, his arms propped on both sides of the frame.

Sensing that this was his new territory, Shortie started barking furiously at Bale. Summer was horrified, but Bale just laughed.

"Glad to see he's protective," Bale said. "Now I won't have to worry about you out there."

Was he going to worry about me?

As Shortie quieted down, Summer thought now might be a good moment to throw her arms around Bale. She envisioned him pushing her up against the wire baskets and kissing her passionately. But they might bend the baskets…those tracks were tricky. She let the moment get away from her. Bale had moved out of the doorway.

"You have more house to see," he said.

Summer rubbed her eyes, clearing the daydream.

"Oh yes," she said. "The bathroom! I can't wait to see it."

Bale had talked her into a composting toilet. Summer had her reservations; she wasn't exactly sure they even worked, but she sure as hell wasn't going to start discussing plumbing with this man right now. She would go straight to the tub. Composting toilets might not be the stuff that dreams are made of, but tubs were *hot*.

The galvanized horse trough was set on a platform with a gorgeous oversized faucet. A rainforest showerhead hung from the ceiling and a circular curtain rod ring finished the tub. It was perfection.

"I love this," she said quietly.

She looked at Bale, who was nodding. He was a man who obviously took pride in his work.

"Check out the loft," he said.

Summer bit her bottom lip. The loft was always a concern. As much as she defended it to Lynnie, she wasn't sure Shortie was actually going to be able to navigate stairs. She saw Shortie wandering around the caboose and she had to stifle a laugh. He really was her partner in this adventure, deciding on favorable corners and surfaces. She put her foot on the first circular stair that led from the corner of the bathroom onto the loft. It was higher and steeper than she expected, although that left more room on either side than a traditional staircase. And every inch was valuable. There was also no handrail. This might be tricky navigation for Shortie *and* her. She pulled herself up and realized it was not just her legs that had muscle fatigue from the hike, her butt cheeks were screaming in indignation.

"You okay?" Bale said, sensing her distress.

"Yes," she said. "Just getting used to the pitch of the stairs."

She looked up to the loft. It was only seven large steps away. She could do it.

No, I can't!

It occurred to her that if she were honest with herself, this new life she envisioned encompassed more than just creating handbags. While the lofts in tiny houses didn't exactly shout *wild sex this way!* they did look romantic. Bale might be having those exact same thoughts. She braced her muscles and sprinted up the stairs.

She was an expert at getting into lofts without banging her head after inspecting so many of them. The process involved racing quickly up the stairs, bending your head without losing momentum as you reached the top step, launching yourself like Superman into the space, then elbowing your way, like a soldier on military maneuvers, to the center. She completed this exercise seamlessly, inhaled a few times to steady her breathing from the exertion and stuck her head into the space between the loft and the staircase.

"This is amazing," she called down.

Most of the tiny houses on wheels she'd looked at, both online and at *Bale's Tiny Dreams*, had pitched roofs. There really was only room to maneuver in the very center of the lofts. In the caboose, with its raised, flat roof, besides the addition of even more storage, she had plenty of room to move around. She felt herself naturally reverting to a walking style she'd learned on her walks around the wilderness outside of Cat's Paw when she was a kid. They called it "walking native," which meant propelling yourself forward in a partial squatting position. As you walked, you maintained a low stance. Her legs and butt would have none of it, but she knew she'd get her mojo back. After years of suppressing all memories of her summers in Washington, she was glad to see there was some positive experience still available to her – not just sadness and regret over a man who threw her over.

There's a handsome man at the bottom of the stairs, she thought. *Focus!*

"Ready for some company?" Bale called from downstairs.

Summer was startled out of her reverie.

"Um, sure!" she said, hoping she sounded jaded and sophisticated instead of eager and overly anxious.

She turned toward the steps to see Shortie's nose peeking over the top. He seemed to be floating until she realized Bale was handing him up to her.

"I don't think Shortie can navigate these yet," Bale said. "But if he can't figure it out, we'll figure it out."

Summer liked the sound of "we'll figure it out." She reached over and grabbed Shortie from the disembodied hands that offered her the dog. She wondered what it would take to make Shortie feel comfortable climbing the stairs. She looked down at Bale, who was smiling up at her.

She wondered what it would take to make Bale feel comfortable climbing the stairs, too.

Chapter 6

Just as she'd given up, Bale asked her if she would like to join him for dinner. He'd mentioned a restaurant called Crabby's. She was happy she'd done her research and already knew the place was dog friendly. She could skip the anxiety-ridden *what-about-my-dog?* conversation.

As soon as she got to her hotel room, Summer fired up her laptop. Looking for clues as to Bale's intentions, she scrutinized the restaurant's website. Crabby's was on the water, with a battered-looking patio built over the Kentucky River. She always thought of water-view restaurants as being on the romantic side, but there was no way to know if Bale felt the same way. She looked for signs of a dress code. The closest she found was a little disclaimer at the bottom of their menu which stated: no shorts, no flip-flops. Even with her limited wardrobe, she could pull that off. Shortie would wear his official therapy dog jacket.

Shortie watched her every move as she unpacked a clean floral skirt, a white lace top, toiletries and makeup. He tensed as she undressed and walked into the bathroom, then tried to wiggle under the bed when he heard the shower creak to life.

"Oh, no, you don't," Summer said, diving after him. "You need this more than I do."

Summer was sure he had the ability to read her mind, but two could play at that game.

With Shortie under her arm, Summer climbed over the side of the tub into the warm spray of the shower. She gave Shortie a good scrubbing and rinse, while he stared at her accusingly. She stepped lightly out of the tub, put him on the vanity, and rubbed him down with two towels. No matter how hard she tried to get him dry, when she put him on the floor, he shook himself and water droplets flew like bullets around the bathroom.

"Okay," she said, opening the bathroom door. "You can go, but stay off the..."

Shortie had already taken a flying leap and was on the bed rubbing his wet ears into the pillows. Summer studied the room. She wasn't a master of square footage calculation, but she thought it was probably bigger than the caboose, which was still at *Bale's Tiny Dreams*. Bale said he wanted to give her a few lessons on hitching and unhitching the caboose to Big Red. She felt a little guilty and positively retro letting Bale think she needed these instructions. While she was still getting the hang of driving something as powerful as her heavy-duty truck, her years hanging out with her grandfather had made her more than conversant with hitches and towing. But she warmed to any excuse that prolonged her time with Bale, not to mention prolong the time away from Cat's Paw, Washington, her grandmother and Keefe Devlin.

She'd probably been thinking more about Keefe Devlin in the last week than she had in the last ten years. That wasn't exactly true—keeping thoughts of him at bay for the first couple of years had been pretty rough, but she had been in college and managed to bury herself in her studies. Was it possible she had him to thank for her degree and job in Hartford? It occurred to her that if Keefe had not broken her heart, she might not have been such a good student.

She could feel her resolve against him loosen, but realized she resented her degree and her job, so he not only dumped her, but put her on the wrong path for most of a decade. But she would have the last laugh. Everything she'd learned about risk management would be applicable to running the bakery. She was going to run circles around him. Maybe even get him fired!

Of course, that would mean she'd be stuck running the bakery indefinitely, which would put the kibosh on her plans to roam the countryside as a purse-making gypsy.

Nerves gnawed at her as she stared into her uncertain future. She noticed the clock on her computer. She and Shortie had to meet Bale in less than a half hour. The thought did nothing to calm her.

With one final swipe of lip gloss, Summer unlocked Big Red, wrestled Shortie into his jacket and strapped him into his car seat—Bale's admonishments be damned. She climbed into the driver's seat and set the coordinates for Crabby's into Google Maps on her phone. She stared at the little car icon and the little walking man icon. It appeared Crabby's was a two-minute drive, but also a short ten-minute walk. She jumped out of the truck, released Shortie from the car seat, clicked on his leash, and headed down to the river. It was still light outside, but by the time dinner was over it would be dark. Bale would probably either walk her home or give her a lift. Of course, in this day and age, you couldn't count on that, but Bale had more than a hint of the Southern gentleman about him.

She wondered if Queenie would like Bale.

Shortie walked purposefully forward, oblivious to the many options that lay in his future.

Cobb was a cute place, with a tiny, pristine downtown. Victorian buildings with second-story bay windows and brightly colored gables gave the place a historic feel. Summer window-shopped as she made her way to the river. Most of the stores were just closing, but everyone seemed to be friendly, in that small-town way she remembered from Cat's Paw. Several of the proprietors interrupted their closing-up-shop rituals to pat Shortie, as Summer snuck peeks in their windows. As the new inhabitant of a tiny house, she knew she could no longer give into an impulse buy, but there was no harm in looking. At the end of the street, in the window of a thrift store already shuttered for the night, she spotted a mannequin sporting a purple cashmere sweater. The sweater had tiny pearl detailing around the edges and the color faded from a dark eggplant at the bottom to light periwinkle at the top. It was a beautiful garment. She had to have that sweater. She might even wear it a time or two before throwing it into a hot washing machine in preparation for its new life as a purse. Summer cupped her hands over the glass in the front door, hoping someone might still be inside, but there was no movement from the interior of the store.

I'll come back after my driving lesson tomorrow, she thought. She looked down at her phone. She was supposed meet Bale in five minutes. The sweater could wait!

Turning the corner, Summer saw Crabby's perched on the river's edge. The parking lot was full; Cobb, Kentucky, was more jumping than she'd imagined. She looked around for Bale.

Summer always thought you could tell a lot about a man by the type of vehicle he drove. She tried out a few on Bale. He clearly was too down-to-earth to be a sports car guy. Prius? Any man who thought you were stifling a dog by using a seat belt would never buy into a hybrid. SUV? Too citified. She could practically hear him snort in distain. Considering he built homes for a living, he probably had a truck. He might even have a truck just like hers. Although, probably not red. Bale didn't seem like the type to drive a flashy red truck. It was probably black or maybe the British racing green that was almost black, but more mysterious. You could only tell it was green in the bright sun. A color with depth. She decided that was definitely what he drove: a green British racing truck.

Summer was still scanning the parking lot when he flagged her down. He was standing in the doorway, already out of his car. There was no way to know what he drove at the moment, but Summer brightened at the possibility of her two minute ride back to the hotel in his British racing truck.

As soon as Shortie saw Bale, he started wagging; no dog could wag quite as enthusiastically. It started at his tail, but within seconds had encompassed his whole body. Wagging and walking were almost at odds with each other. Bale broke into a huge grin, which Summer hoped was for her, but suspected was for Shortie. That dog was irresistible.

"You found the place okay," Bale said.

Summer wasn't sure what to say. Was this a question: "You found the place okay?" Or a statement: "You found the place okay."

As she was contemplating an answer, Shortie attempted to launch himself into Bale's arms, a clumsy maneuver at best, now hindered by the therapy jacket. Shortie didn't seem to realize exactly how short his legs were. Jumping got him as far as Bale's knees. But Bale got the hint and scooped up the dog. Summer waited for Bale's attention to return to her as Shortie covered Bale with kisses—which she longed to do herself. At least Shortie wasn't constrained by convention.

"What's with the dress?" Bale said as he put the dog back on the ground.

"It's a skirt," Summer said, looking down at her attire in a panic. "Is there something wrong with it?"

"Not you," Bale laughed. "Shortie."

"It's his therapy jacket," she said as they both stared down at the panting dog.

He seems pretty well adjusted to me," Bale said. "I bet if you didn't keep him strapped to a car seat all the time, he wouldn't even need therapy."

"He doesn't need therapy," Summer said, coloring. "He *is* the therapy. Not that I need therapy. Although there is nothing wrong with needing therapy. I just…"

"I'm teasing you," Bale said. "Even here in good old Kentucky, we've heard of therapy dogs."

Summer wished they'd go into the restaurant and order some wine. This encounter was not going as planned.

"Shall we go in?" she suggested.

"Sure," Bale said, reaching down and releasing the Velcro around Shortie's midsection. He handed the jacket to Summer and rubbed Shortie's ears. "We're going to the patio, so you can go commando," he said to the dog. "Come on, boy! Walk like a man."

Bale stepped aside and let Summer and Shortie pass in front of him. Summer wondered if she should admonish Bale for taking such liberties with her dog, but when he guided her forward by placing his hand on the small of her back and gently propelling her forward, she decided against it. She'd wait for Bale to take liberties with her.

"Hi Bale," chirped the hostess. "Your usual table?"

"Thanks, Molly," Bale said.

"Is this your new dog?" Molly asked, stooping to pet Shortie.

"Can't say that he is," Bale said. "This is Shortie and this is my client, Summer Murray."

His *client?*

"Oh, did you buy a Tiny?" Molly asked over her shoulder as she led them to the patio.

"She bought the caboose," Bale said.

"Oh, I love that one!" pouted Molly, turning her duck lips on Summer. "I hate you."

I hate you, too.

Molly indicated a table right on the edge of the patio. The sky was turning shades of purple with the sunset and the river twinkled. Summer sat down, and after making sure there was no more adoration coming his way, Shortie scooted under the table. Bale sat opposite her and smiled. Molly was still with them.

"Can I get you started with a drink?" Molly asked. She looked at Bale. "The usual?"

Okay, I get it. You know him.

"Ladies first," Bale said, looking at Summer.

"I'll have a Prosecco," Summer said.

"What is that?" Molly asked, tilting her head.

"It's an Italian champagne," Bale said before Summer could respond.

"I don't think we have that," Molly said. "We have hard cider."

"Hard cider goes more with the ambiance," Bale said with a wink.

"Okay," Summer said. "I'll have a hard cider."

"We also have hard lemonade and hard punch," Molly offered. "If you're interested."

"I'll stick with the cider," Summer said, wondering how much farther her drink order could get from Prosecco.

"And I'll have the usual."

"I'll also bring a bowl of water for Shortie," Molly said. She beamed at him, and nodded sweetly at Summer. "I'll be right back with your drinks."

"Take your time," Bale called after her.

He's reading my mind.

Summer was distracted. Bale never looked confused, so she was aware she was holding her own in the small-talk department, but she was obsessed with knowing what Bale's "usual" was. Was he a hard drinking whiskey man? Maybe he was an abstainer? Wine drinker (he did know his Prosecco)? Beer?

Molly came back with Summer's cider, Shortie's water, and Bale's stout.

Summer couldn't help herself; she grinned like an idiot. She knew that stout was just a type of beer, but it had a touch of the mysterious about it. You could lose your keys in a glass of stout. Stout was *perfect*.

"Okay, Bale," Molly said. "Shawn will be your waiter today. See you around. Nice to meet you, Summer."

Molly returned to the front desk. Summer's eyes followed her. Maybe she wasn't flirting with Bale. Maybe she was just friendly by nature. Her heart lifted. She looked over at Bale who had disappeared momentarily under the table to give Shortie the bowl of water. He smiled at her when he sat up. Maybe *he* was just friendly by nature.

Her heart sank.

Chapter 7

"I don't know why I'm telling you all this," Summer sputtered.

She wasn't much of a drinker and after she'd had another hard cider, she'd told Bale all about her grandmother's phone call and her own derailed plans.

"Would it be easier if you weren't saddled with a tiny house?" Bale asked. "I can always take it back."

"Oh, no, that's not it at all," Summer said, reaching over and patting his hand. "The caboose is the only thing that makes the whole thing acceptable. I mean, I can still have at least a semblance of the life I want to live."

"Just on your grandmother's property," Bale said, signaling for the check.

"It sounds horrible, doesn't it?"

"I wouldn't say that," Bale said. "As a matter of fact, the whole point of having a house on wheels is you can literally roll with the punches. You can check out the situation with your grandmother and when the time is right, you can hit the road."

"I wish I didn't have to leave tomorrow," Summer said.

She waited, but Bale said nothing. Shawn, their waiter, arrived with the check. Bale and Summer both reached for it. Bale got there first. He put the leather check holder on the table and covered it with his hand.

"I've got this," he said.

"You really don't have to do that," Summer said.

Try as she might, a spark of hope that paying for dinner meant more than a thank-you-for-buying-one-of-my-houses. He put a credit card in the holder and handed it to Shawn.

"I'd love to see more of this area," she continued. "It really is beautiful here."

"We're not going anywhere," Bale said, signing the check and handing it back to the waiter. "Thanks, Shawn."

Summer tried to dissect Bale's conversation. Did he mean he'd like for her to come back?

"Dinner is over and all we've done is talk about me," Summer said, remembering having read an online article about how to keep the conversation going. "I don't know anything about *you*."

"Not much to tell," Bale said. "I was married once."

Summer held on to the word "was" as if it were a lifeline.

"Amicable divorce," he continued. "But we don't keep in touch."

Summer tried to hide her glee.

"I'm probably too invested in getting this tiny house thing off the ground to focus on any kind of personal life," he said. "As much as I'd like to."

Summer realized his eyes had taken on a more serious look. Her breath caught. Shawn appeared at Summer's shoulder, breaking the spell.

Damn you, Shawn!

"Anything else I can do for you guys?" Shawn asked.

"Nope," Bale said. "We're good to go."

Summer tugged gently on Shortie's leash and the little dog appeared from under the table. The three of them started to leave the restaurant, but half the people in it seemed to know Bale and stopped him to chat.

"We're going outside," Summer said. "Shortie has been cooped up long enough...if you know what I mean."

"Sure," Bale said. "I'll see you outside in a minute."

That was not the answer she'd been hoping for. She took Shortie up the block and smiled as he "read the newspaper," a phrase she'd never forget. She found herself standing in front of the thrift shop, staring at the purple sweater.

"I give up," Bale said, coming up behind her and startling her. "Do you want to wear that as a sweater or a bag?"

"Both," she said.

"You know something, Summer," Bale said. It was dark on the street and she couldn't make out his features. "You're going to be just fine."

"What do you mean?"

"You see the sweater as a sweater," he said. "And you see a life for it afterwards. Just like you—one life going to Washington, but a life afterwards."

There was more to this man than met the eye.

Summer took in a deep breath. If she were Bale, this would be a good time to lean in and kiss her.

But she was not Bale.

And he did not kiss her.

Summer tossed all night, waking every few hours to see Shortie's little back eyes glistening and staring at her in confusion. She awoke at dawn to find he'd jumped off the bed and was curled up in her open suitcase, sound asleep.

At least one of them got a good night's sleep.

Summer took a shower and pulled on her driving outfit—jeans, work boots, and a T-shirt. Since it was painfully obvious Bale was not interested in her, she'd initially decided against makeup and earrings. But a quick look in the mirror brought her up short. She dug through her purse, pulled out her makeup bag and grabbed the lip gloss and mascara.

"No sense looking like a bad sport," she said to Shortie, grabbing the silver hoop earrings she'd worn the night before. She held them up, then rejected them firmly. She found a tiny pair of silver studs and put them on instead. Bale might not notice, but earrings made her feel alluring. She stared at her reflection for a minute, then took the studs out, replacing them with the hoops. If earrings gave her confidence, she needed all the earrings she could get.

As Summer stowed her bag in the truck, Shortie, tail wagging furiously, put his paws on the running board and readied for a boost into the back seat of the truck cab. She knew she was being ridiculous, but she was smug that Shortie knew where he was supposed to ride and seemed happy about it.

Take that, Bale Barrett.

With Shortie safely strapped in, she drove to *Bale's Tiny Dreams* without consulting her GPS. She'd only spent a few hours in Cobb, but it was an easy town to navigate. Last night, she was hoping there would be a reason to extend her stay, but since that appeared to be an illusion, she was anxious to get going. She could probably get her house hitched to her truck, stop for the purple sweater and be on her way by midmorning.

She pulled into Bale's property. The red caboose had been pulled to the front of the lot. It looked as ready to hit the road as she was. She looked around for Bale, but the place appeared deserted.

She swung the truck around, so the ball was lined up with the coupler on the house. She got out of the truck and lowered the coupler to the hitch ball. She tightened the hand wheel on the coupler and studied it. It appeared nice and snug, just like her grandfather had taught her. She crossed the safety chains and locked the carabiners. She checked to see if there was enough slack to turn from side to side, then pulled the chains. Perfect! She connected the wiring harness from the trailer to the truck. Again, the slack was perfect for tight turns. She opened the driver door, started the truck, turned on the lights and set the right turn indicator going. She turned to go back and check the trailer lights.

Bale was behind the trailer. "Lights are good! " He called. "Right turn indicator is good!" He smiled. "You know your way around a trailer hitch!"

She couldn't help herself. She beamed.

"It's been awhile, but I guess you never forget," she said.

"Let me just take a quick look and you can be on your way," Bale said.

As Bale inspected the trailer connection, Summer studied Bale. As much as she hated to admit it, Bale seemed much more interested in the receiver hitch than he did in her. Even if he were interested in her, what would be the point? He was in Kentucky, riding the wave of the tiny house movement. She was on her way to Washington—and then to parts unknown.

She wondered if she should get out of the truck to say goodbye. Bale settled that question before she could worry about it. He came back to the window and knocked lightly on the door.

"Alright, you," he said casually. "Looks like you are good to go. Mind if I say goodbye to Shortie?"

"Be my guest," Summer said, trying not to sound disappointed with their farewell scene. Romeo and Juliet, they were not.

As much as they tried, her earrings were not helping.

Summer busied herself with her iPhone and resolutely did not look in the rearview mirror as Bale opened the back door and gave Shortie a quick pat.

"So, listen Summer," Bale said, leaning in the window again. "I don't know how long you're going to be in Cat's Paw, but there's a tiny house road show going on in Seattle later this month. I'll be heading up there. If you're still in the area, I'd love to see you."

"That sounds great," Summer said, trying to keep her voice modulated. She didn't want it to sound as great as she thought it actually was.

"Good," he said, smiling and backing away from the truck. "I'll be interested to see how the caboose is doing."

She tried to keep her happy face frozen in place as she waved and drove off.

As she drove to the thrift store, she tried not to cry.

The last thing you need right now is the emotional roller coaster of Bale Barrett, she thought.

By the time she got to the thrift store, she'd firmly pushed Bale to the back of her mind. If there was one thing she learned from her disastrous romance with Keefe Devlin, it was how to push a man from your thoughts.

She realized she couldn't park the truck with the tiny house on the street; there was no room. She circled the block slowly and parked in the very corner of a supermarket parking lot. She unstrapped Shortie and put on his leash. They marched quickly toward the shop. Summer looked at her phone: it was 10 a.m. Maybe the store wasn't even open. If it wasn't, she'd wait. She'd lost out on the gem trove that was in Philadelphia, she'd be damned if she'd give up this gem in Cobb!

She looked up from her phone just as they arrived at the store. She stared at the window. A woman was struggling to put a hideous green blouse on the mannequin that just hours ago wore the purple sweater of her dreams. Summer tried not to panic. Maybe they rotated the clothes ever day! She tapped on the window. The woman looked up.

"I'd like to buy the purple sweater that was here yesterday," she said.

"Sold it," the woman said, returning to her work.

Summer pulled smoothly on Shortie's leash and led him back to the truck. She felt dizzy. She wanted to clamber in the tiny house, climb into the loft, and hide. If the universe was trying to tell her something, it was not being subtle. But she couldn't hide. The best thing she could do for herself was get out of this town. She picked up Shortie and prepared to belt him in when she saw a brown bag tucked into the far corner of the car seat.

She put Shortie on the bench seat of the truck and pulled the package loose. She stared at it. *What was it and where did it come from?*

She opened the bag and her breath caught. It was the purple sweater. Bale must have put it in the car when he said goodbye to Shortie. She shook the bag.

A slip of paper fell onto the seat. She picked it up. It read: You'll never go wrong with imagination and a tiny house. See you around, Bale.

Had she read everything wrong? Was he interested? Summer wanted to go back to the tiny house lot. Such an elaborate gesture required an elaborate thank-you, didn't it? She quickly situated Shortie and jumped in the front of the cab. She started the engine, but quickly realized she could only go forward, not backward. It would be impossible to get back to Bale's without an awful lot of risky maneuvers. She looked in the rearview mirror. *Bale's Tiny Dreams* was only a few blocks. She could walk!

Summer put her head on the steering wheel. Heading to Washington had stirred up so many memories. She thought back to her romance with Keefe. She obviously had read *him* wrong. She wouldn't make that mistake again.

She put the truck in drive and headed west. It seemed to Summer that the universe certainly had its own sense of humor.

Chapter 8

Once on the road, Summer had no time to think about Bale. Driving Big Red with the tiny house behind her took all her concentration. She'd done her research and had found tiny-house-friendly RV parks across the country. She was surprised to find there were far more unfriendly parks, which wanted nothing to do with the Tinies.

When she was trying to plan her trip, she followed the advice of several tiny house bloggers, who suggested calling the various parks to ask questions, rather than just filling out a reservation sheet online. To the statement, "I'm going through your town soon and would like to reserve a space for my tiny house for one night," many of the managers of the parks would just hang up on her. One talkative gentleman said he liked the tiny houses he'd seen on television, but his private RV park didn't accept them.

"I don't take up any more room than an RV," Summer said.

"I know that," he said. "But this is an RV park and we only take RVs."

"Why is that?" Summer tried to sound pleasant.

"Because that's what we've always done. Besides, I don't think the mix would look good," he said, and hung up.

Summer Googled images of his RV park. *My caboose would be the finest-looking thing to ever grace his land*, she thought.

But the tiny house community was always helpful with advice and pep talks. They recommended she get a composting toilet and a generator, to make herself as RV-park compliant as possible. Once she found a few friendly parks, she'd be able to walk the walk and talk the talk, only her rig would be way cuter than any RV.

By the time she headed to Kentucky from Connecticut, she'd carefully mapped out her route. The trip to Washington was going to take six days. All her research suggested that four or five hours a day would be the most she'd be able to handle on her own. She'd become adept at Google Maps and plotted all her stops. It did cross her mind that the tiny house life was supposed to be offering her a new sense of freedom, but she'd never had to plan so carefully in her life.

Five hours from Cobb, Kentucky, got her within striking distance of St. Louis, Missouri. She pulled Big Red off Highway 64 and drove carefully down Old Lincoln Trail. She located the RV park she'd secured and pulled up to the front gate. Summer scanned the rows of assorted RVs. Some had awnings, some had pullouts, some were streamlined; she saw nothing that resembled any kind of tiny house or gypsy wagon, let alone a caboose.

A middle-aged woman appeared from an Airstream and walked toward her.

Summer was surprised to see concern knitting the woman's brow. In just one day, Summer had gotten used to being treated like a minor celebrity every time she pulled over to eat, get gas, or walk Shortie. It appeared all of America was happy to see a tiny house roll by, except this woman. She was wearing a shirt with TRIXIE embroidered over her left breast pocket, jeans, and dusty boots as leathery as her face. Summer hopped out of the truck, sensing there might be trouble ahead. Shortie stuck his nose in the air, misinterpreting the stop as a signal that freedom would soon be his. When it was clear he wasn't going anywhere, he begrudgingly settled back in his car seat.

"I saw on the books that a tiny house was coming in today," Trixie said, still looking at the caboose instead of Summer. "But I wasn't expecting a train!"

"It's not a real train," Summer said, fearing Trixie had something against that particular form of transportation.

"I can see that," Trixie said.

"Is there a problem?" Summer asked. "I have my paperwork on my phone."

"I don't have a problem," Trixie said, finally looking at Summer. "But you do. I don't see how you're going to get this thing in here."

Summer saw that Trixie had a point. She had no idea how she was going to navigate the narrow gravel pathways that threaded their way through the community of recreational vehicles.

"Where you coming from?" Trixie asked.

"Cobb, Kentucky."

"Don't know it."

"Outside of Lexington."

"Where you headed?"

"Cat's Paw, Washington."

"Don't know it."

"It's north of Seattle."

"So, I'm guessing this is your first day on a very long road trip."

"You certainly know your geography," Summer said lightly to the stonewalling manager. "It's going to be a very long trip. And today was really tough. I'm still getting the hang of driving this thing."

"I'll bet," Trixie said, turning on her heels. "We're closed."

Momentarily stunned, Summer watched as Trixie marched back toward the campground. Through the open car door, she heard Shortie give a let-me-out-of-here bark. Summer bleated after Trixie as she released Shortie's seatbelt and put him on the ground.

"Wait!" Summer called. "I have a reservation…"

"At my discretion," Trixie said.

She didn't turn around, but pointed to a sign which read

WE RESERVE THE RIGHT TO REFUSE SERVICE TO ANYONE—
AND THAT MEANS YOU.

"But I have nowhere else to go," Summer said.

She saw Trixie shrug her shoulders. Summer's plight seemed to have absolutely no effect on Trixie, but having said the words out loud, the reality of the situation hit Summer hard. She blinked back tears.

All the online research she had done about tiny house living counseled dipping your toe into the lifestyle, not jumping in with both feet. Summer was so enamored of the idea of freedom that, her risk-management training be damned, she went against that advice. Now, here she was, with everything she owned in the world, at the mercy of a heartless RV park manager.

"Well, hello, little fellow," Trixie said when she spotted Shortie. "Aren't you a cutie pie!"

A heartless RV park manager who loved dogs!

Summer calmed her features, if not her inner turmoil, and smiled brilliantly at Trixie, who was now down on one knee accepting kisses from Shortie.

"His name is Shortie," Summer said.

"Good name," Trixie said. "Can I pick him up?"

"Sure," Summer said. "He loves to be picked up."

She hoped Shortie wouldn't squeal with outrage. He hated being picked up unless it was his idea. Shortie seemed to sense this was a special circumstance, because he barely paused in his kissing as he was airborne into Trixie's arms. He was laying it on thick.

"He likes you," Summer said.

"I got a way with dogs," Trixie said.

"I can see that."

Summer waited. When Shortie had done all he could do to rectify the situation, he started squirming. Trixie put him back on the ground. Summer held her breath.

"Wal-Mart," Trixie said.

"Pardon me?"

"You can park this thing at Wal-Mart," Trixie said. "They have plenty of space."

Chapter 9

Summer located Wal-Mart and pulled in to the parking lot. It was getting late in the evening, so it was nearly empty. She sat facing the store's neon sign and pondered her options.

She decided she had none. She knew there would be a learning curve from the moment she signed the contract with Bale. The fact that absolutely everything that could possibly go wrong seemed to go wrong should not be coming as a surprise.

And yet, somehow it was.

Summer put her head on the steering wheel and let out a big fat gulping I'm-in-my-truck-and-nobody-can-hear-me-and-snot-is-filling-up-my-nose-so-I can't-breathe sob. Shortie whimpered in the back seat. Summer pulled herself together for the sake of her dog.

"Okay, Shortie," she said. "I'm alright. Time to woman up."

She crept across the perimeter of the parking lot, not ready to tangle with the few cars parked closer to the store. It was almost dark, but the store still seemed to be doing business. She glanced up at the blue and yellow sign: 24-Hour Center. She wondered if she should park under a bright light or snuggle up into a corner. She decided to check out all four massive parking areas that ringed the store before making a decision. It was sort of like shopping for a parking space.

She pulled Big Red and the caboose slowly around the corner and slammed on the brakes. She closed her eyes for a minute, afraid to believe what she was seeing. When she saw them, she let out a little whimper of surprise, and gratitude. In front of her was a small cluster of RVs parked discreetly—or as discreetly as you can park twelve giant RVs—around the edges of the parking lot. She inched toward them.

She pulled into a space that required no particular finesse. Before she shut off the truck, she made sure she could pull out in the morning without ever putting the truck in reverse.

This was heaven on asphalt. She was almost giddy with relief as she surveyed the triangle of parking lot loaded with new and old RVs.

My people!

An older man in jeans and a plaid shirt was checking the tires of the RV parked next to her as she shut off the truck. He waved to her as she let herself and Shortie out of Big Red. It felt good to stretch her legs. She hadn't realized how tense she'd been the last few hours.

"Howdy, neighbor," the man said. "That's some rig! First one I've seen up close!"

Summer beamed at him. She'd been so caught up in all the misadventures that she forgot that she was towing a very unusual trailer.

"Thanks. My name's Summer and this is Shortie."

"My name's Alf," he said, shaking Summer's hand and bending down to pet Shortie, who, as always, acted as if he were starved for affection. "So how do like living in a tiny house?"

"I don't know yet," Summer said, sneaking a peek at her home. "I just bought it."

"Welcome to life on the road," Alf said.

"Thank you," Summer said.

"That's a sweet little crummy you got there," Alf said.

"Excuse me?"

"Back in the day, they used to call a caboose a crummy," Alf said. "So, this is your first night as a blacktop boondocker, huh?"

Summer blinked at Alf. Was there an entire language she had to learn along with everything else she didn't know?

"I'm not sure what that is," Summer said. "But it's probably a safe bet to say that since this is my first night on the road, it's my first night as a …shortstop bootlegger."

"Blacktop boondocker," Alf said, squinting at her. "It means dry camping. You do know what dry camping is, don't you?"

Summer stared down at Shortie.

"It means you can't run your gennie," Alf added.

For the second time in less than an hour, Summer burst into tears. She buried her head in her hands.

"What did you say?" came a smoky female voice.

Summer looked up sharply, relieved to see that the comment was not directed at her, but at Alf.

"I didn't say anything," Alf said, visibly upset at having reduced Summer to tears. "I was just showing this little lady the ropes!"

"I'll take it from here," the woman said, letting a relieved Alf off the hook. She introduced herself as "Margie...not Marge, Margie."

"I'm sorry," Summer sniffed. "I'm just new to all this and I honestly couldn't understand a thing Alf said to me!"

"Oh, was he using that Depression Era–hobo lingo on you?" Margie said, shaking her head affectionately as Alf joined a few other men in the parking lot.

"Is that what it was?" Summer asked. "I mean, I wasn't around then..."

"Honey, *he* wasn't around then!" Margie said. "But when he retired from forty years in the insurance game, he's coming as close to living his dream as a 1930's train-hopping hobo as I'll let him. You know, the whole open-road thing, not knowing where you're going to land. Wal-Mart parking lots are about as good as it gets these days."

Summer thought this sounded like *her* original dream until Queenie called.

I don't have to stay in Washington. I can just stop in and calm Queenie down. How bad can things be with the Great Keefe in charge?

Thoughts of heading to Washington always led to thoughts of Keefe, so she put her destination out of her mind.

"I was in the insurance game, myself," Summer said, trying to match Margie's tone. "But I was only in it four years."

Margie looked at her, a slight tilt to her head, as if she were studying her.

"You quit after four years?" Margie said, looking at the tiny house and then back at Summer.

Summer braced herself for whatever Margie was going to say next. Maybe she could practice what she'd say to Queenie when Queenie got wind of her idea.

"You are a very brave young lady," Margie said.

Summer smiled. She sincerely doubted this was going to be Queenie's reaction.

"Thanks," Summer said, feeling lighter than she had all day.

She liked this version of herself. Brave, instead of insane. Getting back to business, she added, "But what exactly is dry camping?"

"Basically, it means you aren't using your generator," Margie said,

She explained that in many Wal-Mart parking lots, but not all, you were welcome to park overnight but not run your generator.

"Especially when the store is in a neighborhood," Margie said. "Keeps the noise down."

Margie cheerfully led Summer through the etiquette of dry camping at Wal-Mart.

"First, you find the store manager and ask if you can stay," Margie said, leading Summer by the elbow to the store.

Shortie, in his counterfeit therapy dog jacket, trotted at their heels.

"What if the manager says no?" Summer asked.

"Why would she say no?" Margie replied. "You got your purse?"

Noting that Summer had it, she continued:

"Because you also should buy a little something. Just to show your support. Have you had supper? They have amazing hot dogs here. You're not one of those vegans are you?"

Summer shook her head.

"And they have a great variety of dog treats!" Margie said.

"Oh no!" Summer said, stopping dead in her tracks. She hadn't planned on setting up her tiny house until she got to Queenie's, but she realized, without turning on the power, she'd wouldn't even be able to blow up her air mattress or turn on the lights.

Margie was sanguine when Summer explained her situation.

"This is Wal-Mart," Margie said proudly, as if she were an official Wal-Mart greeter. "We can get you a hand pump. And a flashlight, since you won't have any light."

"What about hooking up the plumbing?" Summer asked.

"Negative, Captain," Margie shook her head.

So I'm camping with a Depression Era–hobo and a Star Trek *First Officer.*

"This isn't a place to get comfortable," Margie said. "No cooking, no peeing, no showering."

"No showering?" Summer said with a hint of alarm. Clearly she could find places to eat and pee. But it was a long way to Washington with no shower.

"There are truck stops along all the major highways. You can get a shower there."

"How will I find them?"

"Oh," Margie said. "There's an app for that."

Finally, someone was speaking her language.

The manager was happy to let Summer and Shortie spend the night. True to Margie's word, Summer was able to purchase a hand-pump for the air mattress, treats for Shortie, two hot dogs for herself and a camping lantern. By the time she was lugging her shopping bags back to the caboose, she felt she'd taken a mighty step toward blacktop boondocking.

"You're the first tiny house I've seen in person," Margie said.

Summer nodded. The tiny house movement was sweeping the nation's imagination, if not its highways. She saw more television shows about tinies than she did actual homes. As she crossed the country, her house was the sensation of parking lots and truck stops. It seemed all her temporary neighbors were waiting to ask her questions.

If someone asked, "How can you live in something that small?" Summer would reply that it took discipline, but getting rid of anything extraneous was liberating. She didn't actually feel that way. She missed her belongings. But her online research all but guaranteed she'd feel that way soon.

There was also the question: "Why a tiny house instead of an RV?" usually asked by someone leaning up against their RV. At first, Summer took this to be hostility, but the RV crowd marched to its own drum. The inquiry usually came from a place of curiosity rather than condemnation.

"I like the idea of an RV," Summer would always say, as an homage to their mode of transportation and lifestyle. "But I just fell in love with the idea of taking a real home with me everywhere I went."

Summer was surprised to find how many people asked: "How do you have sex in that loft?" She always replied, "Very carefully." Although in truth, she still didn't have any idea.

"Thanks for everything, Margie," Summer said as she and Margie parted ways. "You've been a lifesaver."

"Ah, now," Margie shooed away the compliment. "We're all in this together."

Summer smiled. She liked the idea of being part of the nomadic tribe she'd stumbled upon.

"Who knows," Margie said, eyeing the caboose. "Maybe I'll get Alf to look at a tiny house one of these days. They're sure cute."

Summer hugged Margie and waved as the older woman disappeared into the evening mist. As she climbed onto her air mattress at night, and her eyes adjusted to the darkened loft, Shortie snuggled up at the bottom of the air mattress, Summer realized she was thinking more and more about how it was going to be to actually live in such a tight space. She was exhausted, but her mind wouldn't shut off. She was having too many thoughts, too quickly.

Summer fired up her iPad and turned to the page she'd stopped reading on her latest romance novel. The steamy scene did nothing to quiet her mind. She shut down the iPad and closed her eyes. Thoughts of making love in the loft drifted into her twilight sleep. Keefe wandered into her mind, but she replaced him with Bale immediately. She smiled. If anyone would know how to make love in a tiny house, it would be Bale.

There was no time to think about anything during the day. RVers and truckers tended to get up with first light. Against her will, she and Shortie were usually on the road by dawn.

Stopping at thrift stores proved to be challenging. Every morning she would "yelp" the local thrift stores, then set her GPS for anything that looked promising. Parking continued to be an issue. There were several stores she drove by, slowing down to look in the window, but knowing she'd never find a place to put the tiny house while she shopped.

Even with the hands-free option, Summer never went near her phone while she was driving. At every rest stop, she'd greedily grab her phone, dreading a call from Queenie. Hoping for a text from Bale. Neither came.

There were a few exceptions, and she made the most of them. In a tiny town in South Dakota, Summer found a gem of a vintage store with racks and racks of thick sweaters. Of course, a state in the Salt Belt—so named because they were traditionally so cold in winter large quantities of salt were applied to roads to control snow and ice—would have amazing sweaters!

By the time she was closing in on Seattle, twenty minutes south of Cat's Paw, Summer had spent six days on the road. If nothing else, she was now an expert in parking at Wal-Mart parking lots. She'd heard stories that RV parks and campgrounds weren't hospitable to tiny houses. But save for her initial jarring experience, she hadn't really found that to be the case. While she knew she had to find private campgrounds and RV parks, since federal and state regulations haven't caught up with the tiny trend, she just felt too inexperienced every time she arrived at a campground or RV park. Even after a few days driving under her belt, when it came time to stop, there always seemed to be an obstacle. She'd work up her nerve to approach her painstakingly chosen spot for the night, only to find either a non-navigable road for a novice, or a crowd of onlookers excited to check out her tiny house. So, Wal-Mart it was.

The trip went by in the blink of an eye. Summer had nothing to show for her travels but an armload of sweaters of questionable quality.

As Cat's Paw's Main Street came into view, Summer's heart skipped a beat. Her parents had told her the town had spruced itself up over the years, rising from the ashes of being a railway town, then a lumber town, but she hadn't seen it for herself. She knew Grandpa Zach and Queenie spent years trying to outrun the destruction of the historic buildings on Main Street. They finally won. Eight years ago, Cat's Paw was awarded placement not only on the State Historic Register but also on the National Historic Register. While Grandpa and Queenie did most of the heavy lifting, it looked as if the town took the honors seriously. Every business on Main Street seemed determined to preserve its historic charm.

She sat at the intersection of the two main streets, taking it all in. She stared at the bakery smack in the middle of the newly restored downtown. When she last saw it, the building was dull green painted over bricks... or maybe a dull grey painted over bricks. Summer couldn't remember which. She only remembered that it was dull. Now it, along with the other stores, had been sandblasted. The entire street was varying shades of dark red to light pink, with wood detailing in tasteful shades of maroon, green and beige. The store name, Dough Z Dough, remained the only cheesy note on the block.

She suddenly snapped out of her contemplation as Keefe suddenly appeared in the doorway of the bakery, wearing a long white apron over his jeans and light blue shirt. He looked as good as the town.

Damn it.

Her mouth went dry as she watched him. He was standing in the same spot as when he said goodbye ten years ago. She could still envision the day. The wind was insane that day. She stood in front of the bakery, holding her college acceptance letter. She had to hold onto it with both hands, to keep it from blowing away. While there must have been other people on the street, she only remembered him, standing there, reading over her letter.

"Wow!" he said. "Baylor University. Where is that?"

"It's in Texas," she said.

"Texas," he said.

"But this is just my acceptance letter," she said quickly. "I don't have to go!"

"Why wouldn't you go?" he asked, looking at his feet.

"I don't know," she said. "I thought maybe I could go to college around here."

"In Cat's Paw?" he looked up, surprised. "I don't think so."

Was he laughing at her?

"Not in Cat's Paw," she said. "But Seattle. Or even Portland. So I'd be....closer."

"Closer to me, you mean?"

Her face burned.

He doesn't want me to stay.

"Don't make any decisions based on me, Summer," he said, handing her the letter back. "We've had some good times, but this is your future. You need to get serious."

I thought we were serious.

Shortie startled her back into the present, barking as Keefe strode toward Big Red. His smile was as bright as ever.

It appeared you could go home again, even when you didn't want to.

Chapter 10

Luckily, the lure of the caboose brought more people than just Keefe to look over Big Red. Summer jumped out of the truck, released Shortie from his car seat and accepted the attention of the town. She pretended Keefe was not among them.

"Is that you, Summer?" Doreen, the woman who owned the hardware store asked. "It's been a million years since you've been here!"

"Ten years, actually," Summer said, accepting Doreen's kiss.

"Might as well be a million," Mr. Caleb, the owner of the *Cat's Paw Chronicle* said.

The impartial eye of the journalist was still not Mr. Caleb's strong suit.

"You have time for a story and a photo?" he asked. "My editor will kill me if I don't get one."

"Your editor?" Summer said. "I thought you were the editor."

"Not for the last three years," Mr. Caleb said. "Turned it over to Sherman."

"Sherman!" Summer tried to look pleased instead of startled. "Isn't that something."

Sherman Caleb was Mr. Caleb's son. Summer hadn't thought about him in years. With his blazing red hair, he was always painfully timid. He would come into the bakery and whisper his order. His face turning beet red in the process, almost matching his hair. Whenever Keefe called him "Shy Sherman," Queenie would frown and tell Keefe he was unkind, reminding him that not everyone was born with an outgoing personality like Keefe's.

"Thank Sweet Baby Jesus for small favors," Grandpa Zach would say.

Summer couldn't imagine Sherman being the editor of a paper, even one as small as the *Cat's Paw Chronicle*.

"So what do you say?" Mr. Caleb said. "Help keep me in good with the boss?"

Summer really had to get up to Queenie's place, but what could she say? Mr. Caleb snapped a close-up with his phone before she could even smile.

"This is certainly the grand entrance after all these years," said a woman about her own age.

The woman looked familiar. It took Summer a moment to place her after so many years.

"Evie?' Summer gasped.

"I wasn't sure you'd remember me," Evie said.

"Of course I remember you," Summer said. "I just had my mind on..."

"Parking?" Evie said, casting a glance at Big Red and the caboose.

"Something like that," Summer smiled.

She hoped the smile looked genuine instead of threatened. Keefe's ex-girlfriend was back in town? Eventually, Summer learned that Keefe and Evie broke up because Evie wanted to go to Cincinnati to work in her uncle's restaurant. Keefe said it was never a serious relationship and Summer believed him.

But in those days, Summer believed everything Keefe said.

"You're back," Evie said.

"I could say the same about you," Summer said. "And you look great."

There was no denying Evie looked better than ever. Her straight corn-silk hair was tied up in a ponytail. She had a slight tan and freckles dotted her nose. The legs still went on forever. The effortless effect was maddening.

"I've been back for five years," Evie said. "I came back for your grandfather's funeral. I thought I would have seen you there, but your grandmother said you were away."

"I was away," Summer said. "Very far away. Eastern Europe away."

Why was she being so defensive?

"Oh, I know," Evie said. "Anyway, it was a lovely funeral. It was a sad day for Cat's Paw, but wonderful to reconnect with...you know...all the great people here."

Who spoke like this? Was Evie running for office? Summer blinked. Did Evie mean she and Keefe reconnected? Was *he* the "great people?"

Summer wasn't sure if this was an entirely friendly observation.

"It's hard to sneak into town pulling a tiny house," Summer said. "Not that I was sneaking into town, of course."

"Of course. Those tiny houses are getting so popular!" Evie said in an I-wouldn't-be-caught-dead-in-one tone. "Did you know that there's going to be a tiny house convention in Seattle?"

"I did know," Summer said. "As a matter of fact, I have a good *friend*, actually the *friend* who built my house, who'll be there with several of his houses."

"That's cute," Evie said.

Wow, she's good.

Just thinking about seeing Bale again gave Summer a little boost.

"It's nice to be going back to the bakery," Summer said. "Working with Keefe. Just like old times."

Summer noticed Evie color slightly.

Score!

"Are you...staying?" Evie asked.

"For a while."

"I see," Evie said. "I have an ice cream parlor where the old drugstore used to be."

Summer was about to say, "I will," but realized Evie hadn't invited her to stop by.

"Every town needs ice cream," Summer said instead.

"And a bakery," Evie said. "Cake and ice cream; natural allies."

Allies?

Was this war?

"I'm glad I had a chance to say hello," Evie continued. "I'm sure we'll bump into each other again."

"Who is this you've brought with you?" asked a young woman whom Summer didn't think she knew. The woman was pointing to Shortie.

"This is Shortie," Summer said, holding the dog up for everyone to admire. People applauded.

"And what's *that* you've brought with you?" Mrs. Bell, the postmistress's voice rang out.

Summer could hear ripples of curiosity.

"It's a tiny house," Summer said, looking at the caboose as if for validation.

"Looks like part of a train," came another voice Summer didn't recognize.

She realized there were going to be a number of people she didn't know, which came as a shock to her. Ten years ago, anyone Summer didn't know was a visitor. Now *she* was the visitor.

"It's just the design," Summer said.

"Designed to get you out of town fast," Keefe's voice said.

She jumped as the crowd laughed. She spun on her heels as people surged toward the caboose. He was right behind her. As the townspeople climbed around the caboose, taking selfies and discussing how it worked,

Summer faced up to the fact that she was finally here and would have to deal with Keefe.

"Hi Keefe," she said. "You're looking well."

You're looking delicious.

"You too, little girl," Keefe said, leaning against the wheel well of her truck." Summer jumped at the sound of his voice. She remembered how much she used to hate it when he called her "little girl," but now the name wrapped around her like a favorite blanket.

"So what brings you back?" Keefe asked.

Was it possible he didn't know? She decided to play it cool.

"Just dropping by," Summer continued, trying on her nomadic-life-on-the-run persona she's wanted so much to become. "I'm just making the rounds."

"Of what?" Keefe said, looking around.

"The United States," Summer said loftily.

"I can see where you might want to start with Washington State," Keefe said. "You know, when you live in Connecticut."

Summer knew she sounded ridiculous. She just hopped in an oversized truck pulling a color-coordinated caboose three thousand miles to drop by? But she was stuck with her trajectory now.

"*Lived* in Connecticut," Summer said. "Past tense. Now I don't live anywhere."

She meant it to sound daring and fearless, but it just sounded sad.

"I'm just teasing you," Keefe said. "Whatever you want to do with your life is your business."

So basically nothing has changed.

"Good to hear," Summer said.

"And I'm really glad to see you," Keefe said, moving a step closer.

Summer could do nothing but stand her ground.

"How about a picture of the two of you?" Mr. Caleb asked. "You know, like the good old days?"

What good old days?

Keefe put his arm around her as Mr. Caleb, who had somehow retrieved an old digital camera from the nineties, approached. Time may march forward in Cat's Paw, but it marched slowly.

"Come on, smile," Mr. Caleb said testily.

Since Keefe was already grinning from ear to ear, he must be talking to me, Summer thought.

The challenges of coming home were mounting. It was hard enough to process dealing with Keefe and Queenie. She'd forgotten that every adult from her past was still going to boss her around as if she were a child.

"And turn that dog toward me," Mr. Caleb commanded.

She obeyed. Summer was grateful to have Shortie in her arms, so she didn't have to put her arm around Keefe. But the touch of his hand as it encircled her waist took her by surprise. It felt alien yet somehow perfect. She smiled for the camera and wondered if she and Keefe both stood just a moment longer together than was absolutely necessary.

"Okay, Summer," Mr. Caleb said. "Can I run a few questions by you?"

Keefe dropped his hand and bowed as if to say, "I'll leave you to it."

"Coward," Summer said with a hint of a smile.

She was shocked that it was so easy to fall back into playful banter.

Summer watched Keefe head back to the bakery, barely aware of the answers she was giving Mr. Caleb. She stuck with her mythology that she was planning on touring the states with her tiny house, reasoning that if Queenie hadn't mentioned to Keefe that she'd commanded Summer to return, she probably hadn't alerted the whole town. Before long, half the town seemed to be circling her for an impromptu question and answer session. Questions ranged from the personal, to the tiny house to Shortie. Finally, the crowd seemed satisfied and Summer was left standing with Shortie still cradled in her arms by her truck. She looked up the street and saw Keefe coming back out of the bakery, this time locking the door behind him. He had a motorcycle helmet in his hands. She tried to turn away before he saw her looking at him, but it was too late. He lifted the motorcycle helmet in greeting and walked toward her.

"That dog's paws ever touch the ground?"

Summer realized poor Shortie had been in her arms for nearly a half hour. She dropped him to the ground. Shortie ran immediately to Keefe, not playing hard-to-get in the least.

"You going up to the house?" Keefe asked.

"I drove into town because I thought Queenie would still be at the bakery," Summer said.

Keefe's smile faded.

"She hasn't been coming to the bakery much the last couple weeks," Keefe said. "But I can't get a straight answer as to why."

"When was the last time anybody got a straight answer from Queenie?"

"If you want to follow me," Keefe said, "I'll lead you up to the house."

"I know how to get to my own grandmother's house," Summer said.

"No you don't," Keefe said. "There's been a lot of changes since you were here...including a new route to Queenie's."

"I'm sure the GPS will get me there just fine," Summer said.

"The GPS is out of the loop," he said. "About four years ago, the creek behind the old mill flooded. It washed out the road up to Queenie's. They rerouted her whole mile-long driveway. You now enter up in front of the house instead of behind it. Looks good, but we lost the mill and the old schoolhouse."

Summer nodded somberly. In her mind's eye, she could clearly see the old mill and the schoolhouse, and could certainly see Keefe's apartment over the garage at the farm, but couldn't for the life of her visualize a new route to Queenie's. She had been gone a very long time.

"Okay," Summer said. "I'll follow you."

"That's my girl," he said.

I am so not your girl.

"I'm on the Fatboy," Keefe said, nodding toward a gleaming black motorcycle in front of the bakery.

"Nice bike," Summer said, giving him a thumbs up. All those days on the road, at truck stops and at Wal-Mart parking lots meant she knew her motorcycles as well as her RVs and fifth wheels.

By the time Shortie was strapped down in his car seat, Keefe's bike was in front of Big Red. They headed down Main Street, creating a mini-parade. Summer waved to the onlookers as they drove slowly out of town.

Summer's circuitous route to Cat's Paw from Connecticut had put more than 3,500 miles on Big Red. She'd seen the lush greens of the northeast, the tangle of trees that seemed to threaten to take over any un-mowed inch of land in the south and the endless plains of the Midwest. It was all beautiful, but, nothing beat the beauty of the Pacific Northwest. The drive to her grandmother's encompassed everything the terrain had to offer; towering trees, a creek racing beside the road, houses old and new, stately and homey. It was calming and exhilarating all at once. Summer concentrated on following Keefe. She had to admit – she'd never have found the old Victorian on her own.

Suddenly, they were in front of Queenie's home. Summer slammed on the brakes, as Keefe disappeared around the corner with a wave of his hand. She knew he was headed back to his apartment over the three car garage. Summer returned the wave but felt her pulse quicken. Was Keefe leaving her to face Queenie alone? She felt abandoned yet again as she stared up at the house. Unlike the cliché that insisted when you returned to your childhood haunts, everything looked smaller, she gaped at how huge the house actually was.

Nestled in large evergreens, the towering, gingerbread-style mansion was in fine form. The freshly painted exterior, including the wraparound porch, was a brilliant white. The roof shingles and shutters were a slate gray. With three chimneys, a tower, cupola and four gables, the Queen Anne had all the hallmarks of an ornate Victorian. But somehow, Queenie had wrestled it into looking refined.

Summer remembered as a child, she'd begged Queenie and Grandpa Zach to paint the house the bright pastels of the San Francisco Victorians she was familiar with. But Queenie would have none of that. Queenie always tried to give the mansion an unassuming look, but even in its muted tones, there was no hiding the exuberance of the design. It was like trying to rein in a wedding cake.

Summer recalled being driven up the coast from Northern California, through Oregon and into Washington. The year she turned sixteen, Summer started driving herself. The anticipation of summer in Cat's Paw didn't lessen with her jaded teenage years. Thoughts of two uninterrupted months with Keefe might have replaced images of berry picking with Grandpa Zach, but she was always excited at the prospect of time in Washington.

Staring at the front porch, she could envision Grandpa Zach coming out the door to greet her family as they all tumbled out of the car. He'd always picked her up and swung her around, even when she was too big.

By the time he'd put her back on the ground, Queenie would come out on the porch, wearing her white Dough Z Dough apron, wiping her flour dusted hands on her backside. Queenie wasn't big on smiling, but she always had a table laden with the most delectable baked goods. She pretended that she was just trying out some new recipes, but Summer's dad told her that was Queenie's way of saying, "I love you."

"Why doesn't she just say it?" Summer asked.

"That's one of the unsolvable mysteries of the world," her father said.

Summer thought it was impressive having an unsolvable mystery in your own family.

Summer blinked as Queenie came onto the porch, realizing with a pain so sudden and jarring it took her breath away, that the family tradition of Grandpa Zach appearing first was gone forever. As sure as she was that Grandpa Zach had something to do with the end of her romance with Keefe, it was easier to keep the flames of resentment going from three thousand miles. It just plain hurt, looking at the house and knowing he was never going to step onto that porch again.

But the rest was picture perfect. Queenie hadn't aged much in the last ten years. She still wore her hair in an impeccable French twist. Her clothes were perfectly pressed and her white Dough Z Dough apron wrapped smoothly around her trim waist. The apron wouldn't dare wrinkle.

Was it possible Queenie hadn't baked anything for Summer's arrival? The thought stung. Summer jumped out of the truck as Queenie approached.

"I see you got here, Clarisse," Queenie said.

"I did," Summer said. "It's wonderful to see you, Queenie."

"Mr. Caleb called," Queenie said, arching an eyebrow. "He said you were towing a train."

"It's my house," Summer said, steeling herself for the moment she'd been dreading.

"Mr. Caleb asked me what I thought about it," Queenie said.

"What did you say?"

"I said nothing, of course."

"Well, what *do* you think about it?"

"I don't understand it. Why do you need a dollhouse? I've got six thousand square feet right here."

"I just like the idea of my own space."

"Your own space?" Queenie repeated, looking back at the behemoth behind her, as if she were checking the house was still there. "I'm not using at least five thousand square feet of this. Help yourself."

"Thanks, Queenie, but I have my house and I intend to live in it."

"The nearest train yard is ten miles down the road."

"I thought I'd live in it here on the property."

"Do I hear a dog?" Queenie raised her eyebrows, somehow sidestepping Summer's declaration that she planned on living in the caboose.

"Yes," Summer said, relieved for the diversion, and getting Shortie out of the backseat. "This is Shortie."

Shortie shook his body from the tip of his nose to his tail, luxuriating in the stretch. He gave Queenie a quick appraisal, then started sniffing around the yard. Queenie spent more time considering him than she did the tiny house.

"I know you don't like dogs, but I couldn't very well leave him behind," Summer said, trying not to whine.

"I don't recall ever saying I don't like dogs," Queenie said.

"Every time Grandpa and I tried to bring one home, you said no." Summer could feel her voice reverting to that of a petulant teenager. "You're famous for not liking dogs!"

"Well, isn't that something!" Queenie said. "I'm nearly seventy years old, I've worked every day of my life. I've helped run a business, not to mention getting this town back on its feet, and I'm famous for not liking dogs. A life fully lived."

"Can we do this tomorrow?" Summer said, suddenly exhausted.

"Just keep an eye on him," Queenie said. "I'm not sure how Andre is going to feel about this."

Summer's eyebrows shot up. Andre? Did Queenie have a new...she could barely form the word in her brain...*boyfriend*?

"Who is Andre?" Summer squeaked.

"My Great Dane," Queenie said.

Summer gasped.

"You're not the only one full of surprises, I guess," Queenie said.

There went that eyebrow again.

"I guess!" Summer said, scooping Shortie up. Andre was certainly a wrinkle she hadn't anticipated. A big wrinkle.

"Let's go in. I made some peanut butter cookies," Queenie said, leading the way into the house. "Just trying them out for the bakery."

Summer grinned. She was happy some things never changed.

I love you, too, Queenie.

With a backward glance at the caboose, she grabbed her backpack and followed her grandmother into the house.

Chapter 11

Andre was stretched like a sphinx on the front porch. A majestic brindle, Andre appeared to have practiced the bored, regal expression of his matriarch. As Queenie and Summer climbed the porch stairs, Andre rose to his feet, calm and cool as Will Smith in an action movie.

At the sight of the other animal, Shortie started flopping in Summer's arms like a fish. He barked at Andre from his safe perch.

Have some dignity, dog!

Queenie introduced them without missing a step into the house.

"Andre," Queenie said, "This is Shortie...and my granddaughter, Clarisse."

"Summer," Summer said to the Great Dane as she followed her grandmother inside.

No use starting bad habits.

Summer stepped through the front double doors into the foyer. She knew she could count on Queenie to keep the house in Victorian splendor. The dark wooden staircase, with original trim, swept up the entire three floors of the house, gleaming with a century of wax. Small stained glass windows let in prisms of red, blue and gold light onto each landing. Summer reflexively dumped her backpack on the bottom step. She looked up at the rounded tower nook, which held an antique bench throughout Summer's life, and now embraced a small piano. Had Queenie taken up piano? Summer was about to comment on the instrument but held her tongue. Andre was enough of a surprise for one day.

The house showed its contempt for so-called open concept. The parlor, with its ornately tiled fireplace opened through pocket doors onto the living room. Summer never knew the difference between the parlor and the living room; they were about the same size and only company was invited to sit in either. Marching directly through the living room, they came to the dining room: a massive expanse with a table that could hold twenty people. Queenie had painted the walls and ceiling since Summer was here, but the three-tiered chandelier and the gleaming sideboards were still in place.

Summer could smell the cookies as they arrived in the kitchen. Summer was relieved to see the brick floor was still in place. The large kitchen in the Murray house was always getting a makeover with all the latest appliances, but the brick floor was a constant. Summer was surprised to see the kitchen was spotless. Usually, when Queenie was cooking, it was wall-to-wall and floor-to-ceiling flour. Now, a jar of peanut butter and a sole large spoon with the remains of a dollop of peanut butter sat on the enormous kitchen butcher-block island. Andre, who was following Summer through the house, suddenly bolted around her. He practically knocked her down, ditching his regal demeanor as soon as he spotted the spoon. Queenie held up the spoon.

"Sit," Queenie said.

Andre sat.

Shortie started to whimper as Queenie let Andre lick the spoon clean.

"Put the dog on the floor," Queenie said, pulling a clean spoon out of a drawer and scooping out some more peanut butter.

Summer obeyed and put Shortie on the floor. She had no idea what was going to be required of him. Shortie could not take his eyes off the spoon. He stood on his back legs in an attempt to reach it. Summer bit her lip in anticipation of how wrong this experiment might go.

"Sit," Queenie commanded.

Shortie lifted his paw for a handshake. Then he lay down. As the two women stared at him, he rolled over.

"Sit," Queenie said again, with more authority.

Queenie upping the authority quotient would get the attention of any creature. Summer found her heart starting to pound. She was about to apologize for Shortie, when the little dog got it right. He sat and whimpered.

"I could do without the whining," Queenie said. "But good enough."

She bent over and let Shortie eat the peanut butter. She looked at Summer.

"I probably should have asked this first..." Queenie said.

"Sometimes," Summer said, cutting Queenie off.

"Sometime, what?"

"Sometime, I let Shortie eat people food," Summer said. "Isn't that what you were going to ask me?"

"No," Queenie said, taking both dogs' spoons to the sink. "I was going to ask you if he was allergic to peanut butter."

"I didn't know dogs could be allergic to peanut butter."

"Why wouldn't they?" Queenie asked. "Allergies can strike people and animals anytime."

Had her grandmother become some sort of piano-playing animal-loving allergist since she'd seen her?

"Well, he's not," Summer said. "Although I do try to limit his junk food."

"Peanut butter is not junk food," Queenie said, rinsing off the spoons and putting them in the dishwasher. "It's a good source of protein, Vitamin E, and potassium. So there's no need to attack peanut butter."

"I'm not attacking peanut butter," Summer said, exasperated.

The kitchen door squeaked open and the bizarre peanut butter lecture came to an end. The dogs and Queenie turned toward the door. Keefe entered without knocking.

Summer looked at him. He seemed very comfortable breezing into Queenie's house. She wondered if this was business as usual, or if he was looking for an excuse to see her.

"Just checking in," Keefe said, picking up a peanut butter cookie and chewing thoughtfully. "These need something. They taste like peanut butter."

"That's because they're peanut butter cookies," Summer said fiercely, in defense of her grandmother.

Had everyone gone mad since she'd been here?

"I know," Keefe said, still chewing. "But if I want peanut butter, I'll just eat peanut butter. If I want a cookie…it's got to have….something else."

"I thought about raisins, but figured that'd been done to death," Queenie said.

"Maybe there's a reason," Keefe said, winking at Queenie.

Summer blinked in surprise. Keefe was *teasing* Queenie? As far as she knew, no one had ever teased Queenie.

"I'll try again tomorrow," Queenie said as she stared at the plate of cookies. "Back to the drawing board."

Summer reached for a cookie. She bit into it vigorously, to prove Keefe wrong, but as she chewed, she became aware that the cookie was…horrible. It was dry and crumbly…almost an impossible combination for something mixed with peanut butter. And yet, there it was.

Had Queenie lost her golden touch as the best baker in the Pacific Northwest? She caught Keefe's eye and noted the concern. He knew something was off.

Queenie gave each dog a cookie before Summer could stop her. It was too bad the dogs couldn't be customers, because they appeared to love the cookies, which disappeared in one bite (Andre) and three bites (Shortie).

Outside, lightning lit up the evening sky. Thunder followed, then the sky unleashed one of its Pacific Northwest dramatic downpours. Shortie ran to Summer and she scooped him up. He shivered in her arms. Andre, as a native Washingtonian, sat down on the kitchen floor and resumed his bored expression.

"I made a calamari casserole," Queenie said, pulling a glass baking dish from a corner of the counter, a dish towel covering it. "It should be heated in about forty minutes."

A lump rose in Summer's throat. Every year, when Summer arrived with her parents, Queenie would welcome them with a calamari casserole. There was nothing better than the fresh seafood of the Pacific Northwest, but somehow the calamari casserole had faded along with so many of Summer's fond memories of her childhood and teenage years.

"Sounds good," Keefe said. "Listen, Summer, I don't think you're going to be able to get your tiny house set up even if the rain stops. It's going to be muddy as hell."

"It can wait a day," Queenie offered, slamming the oven door. "She can sleep in her own room for one night."

Summer was about to protest, but who could argue with calamari casserole?

Keefe busied himself setting the table, while Summer stood watching them. Clearly, Queenie and Keefe had a rhythm to which Summer was not yet attuned. Her cheeks reddened as she thought back to her suspicion that Keefe was just looking for an excuse to visit. It was obvious now that Queenie and Keefe had dinner together often. Possibly every night! It was if Keefe were Queenie's family instead of her.

And who was to blame for that? She asked herself accusingly.

"Can I help with anything?" Summer offered, pathetically hoping to make up for lost time.

"We've got it," Keefe said.

"I guess I'll go up to my room then," Summer said.

"Do you need Keefe to run and get anything from your truck?" Queenie asked, peering out from the open refrigerator.

"It's pouring out there," Keefe said in mock horror. "What about my hair?"

Summer couldn't help smile. Keefe might be kidding, but he did have great hair.

"I have enough in my backpack to get me through the night," Summer said. She turned on her heels and headed out of the kitchen. She put Shortie back on the floor as they approached the staircase. As she reached for her backpack, she saw Shortie eyeing the staircase with suspicion.

"You can do it," Summer said. "You gotta get used to this, little man. This is nothing compared to the circular staircase that is your future."

Shortie eyed the staircase one last time than hurled himself at the first step. Summer laughed as he passed by her and scampered up to the first landing, He looked down at her, panting and wagging his tail in triumph. She caught up with him and they both looked over the bannister to see Andre looking up at them from the foyer.

"Do you want to come, too?" Summer said.

Andre took the steps two at a time and followed Summer and Shortie down the hall. Summer stood in front of her old room, flanked by her two sentinels. She touched the smooth dark wood of the door. It was ridiculous, but she felt all the defenses she'd built up over the last ten years were going to dissolve as soon as she went into the room. She wasn't going to lie to herself – the attraction to Keefe was as powerful as ever. She couldn't let herself be vulnerable – she didn't have the excuse of being a kid.

Her phone vibrated in her pocket.

It was Bale.

Her hands were vibrating as much as the phone as she tried to answer. She fumbled, almost dropping it over the banister. Her room was only steps away, but she wasn't sure her legs would get her there. She sat down on a lavishly upholstered bench in the hallway.

"Hello?" Summer said.

"Hey, it's Bale," he said.

"Hi!" Summer said as the dogs watched her.

"You sound out of breath," he said. "Everything okay?"

"Everything's great," Summer said. "I just…climbed a bunch of stairs."

"I guess that means you're not in the tiny house," Bale said.

"Far from it," Summer looked around her grandmother's opulent house and relaxed. "I just got to my grandmother's house."

"You made it," Bale said. "That's great! I've been thinking about you."

Summer paused. She wasn't sure what to make of this. Did he mean he was thinking about her as a client or as a friend or as a potential more-than-a-friend? She decided to go for broke.

"I've been thinking about you, too."

"That's nice to hear," Bale said. "Well, I'm glad you arrived safely."

That sounded ominously like the conversation was coming to an end. *Think of something to say!*

"Thanks for the purple sweater," Summer said, grateful for the surprising presence of mind. "When I finally get around to felting, it will be the first one I work on!"

"It was the least I could do," Bale said. "How's my buddy Shortie?"

Summer smiled. He didn't want the conversation to end either.

"He's great," Summer said, looking at Shortie, who stared at her, ears cocked. "He knows we're talking about him."

"Say hi for me," Bale said.

"I will."

There was another pause. Summer panicked. Except that she had everything to say, she had nothing to say.

"Listen, Summer," Bale said, his voice growing more serious. "I meant it when I said I was thinking about you."

"And I meant it when I said I was thinking about you," Summer whispered. Old habits of hiding romantic conversations from her grandparents died hard.

"I just wanted to make sure I wouldn't be intruding if I asked to see you when I'm up in Seattle for the tiny house show."

"I'd love that," she said.

"Okay," Bale said. "So I'll see you soon. I'll be in touch."

"Please do," she said.

Summer gripped the bench to keep from jumping up and down. She practically floated toward her room. She stopped in front of her closed door, as she came back to reality. It occurred to her that perhaps Queenie had given her room a makeover. Why keep a room ready for someone who hadn't set foot in the house, let alone the state, in a decade? Behind the heavy wood door, perhaps her demons had been vanquished by a new computer setup or second floor sitting room? Summer opened the door.

As the dogs scooted past her, Summer stood stock still in the doorway. The room looked as if she'd just walked out of it ten days ago rather than ten years. To give Queenie her due, the décor was actually suited more to an adult than a child. The walls were papered in sedate beige with tiny mint sprigs. The hardwood floor was covered by a Turkish rug in subdued pastels. The windows had dark grey fabric draped on finials. The fabric didn't close—there were shutters over the four windows for privacy—but cascaded to pool on the floor. Queenie's one nod to this being a girl's room was an enormous canopy bed, albeit a grey wrought iron with the same grey as the window treatments draping the corners rather than flouncing over the arc of the whole bed. The featherbed was covered in a muted sage and grey quilt. No girlie-girl pink for Queenie.

Shortie sniffed every corner while Andre made himself at home in the middle of the bed. As Summer stood back, determining if Shortie would be able to get himself up to the mattress, she saw him out of the corner of her eye as he took a running leap, up onto the sage-green and grey trunk at the foot of bed, before lunging forward toward the quilt. Summer closed her eyes as he overshot and sailed off the right side of the bed, landing with a yelp. She rushed to him as Andre peered over the side.

"Are you alright?" she asked as she scooped Shortie up.

She tested his little legs. He wagged his tail, signaling his hearty good health and squirmed to be put down. She put him gently on the bed next to Andre.

"Everything okay?" she asked him, but his attention had turned toward Andre, who sat impassively as the little dog sniffed at him.

"Everything okay?" Summer jumped at Keefe's voice in the doorway. "It sounded like you're rearranging the furniture."

"We're fine," Summer tried not to sound breathless. "Shortie doesn't know his limitations."

"He's a wise dog," Keefe said. "I'm not a fan of acknowledging my limitations either."

Keefe strode into the room. Summer willed herself to remain calm. Besides the nice furniture, there was a lot of history in this room.

"I haven't been in this room since..." Keefe's voice trailed off.

Summer was quiet. She was not sure what message she would like to convey. There were the lies: Nonchalance. World-weariness. Boredom. Sophistication. And the truth: Embarrassment. Hurt. Betrayal. Vengeance. She settled on: "Yeah."

Keefe wandered over to a corner of the room, which held a built-in reading nook. He ran his hand smoothly over the books. Summer remembered his hands running smoothly over her skin. He turned to look at her.

"The room is exactly the same," he said. "But you're not."

"No, I'm not," Summer felt a flush of anger. "How pathetic would that be, Keefe? If I were still that starry-eyed little teenager?"

"Oh, I don't know," Keefe said with a half-smile. "You weren't so bad."

Andre suddenly stood on the bed, towering above them. He yawned. Obviously the drama playing out in front of him was leaving him cold. He turned toward the door just as Queenie's voice came wafting up the stairs.

"Dinner's ready," Queenie called. "You got the dog?"

"Dogs, Queenie," Summer said. "There are two dogs here."

"We're on our way," Keefe said.

Summer tried to be annoyed that Keefe used the plural *we*, but decided that since it included the dogs, she really couldn't read too much into the statement.

"How big did you say your house was?" Keefe asked.

"I didn't," Summer said. "But since you asked, it's 220 square feet."

"Hmm," Keefe said as he darted a look into the empty closet at the far end of the room. "Your closet is bigger than that."

"And your point is?" she asked.

"You come back here with a house you could stash in your closet and still have room for more clothes than most people own. And you're seriously asking *me* what my point is?" Keefe said. "I think the question here is: What's *your* point?"

He stormed out of the room, Andre following closely at his heels. Shortie stood at the edge of the bed, making a show of attempting to jump off, but Summer seemed frozen in place.

"If Andre was on the bed, straighten the quilt," Queenie commanded.

Chapter 12

When Summer first decided to live in the caboose, it never even occurred to her that people—family, friends, and strangers—would have such outsized reactions to her tiny house. Most seemed to think it was whimsical; they'd chat about the house with small, lopsided smiles pasted on their faces as if humoring a small child. Others stared at the house longingly. They'd eye the caboose and say: "You know, I think I could live like that, one day." But Keefe's reaction was truly unnerving. He seemed downright hostile. What right did he have to be hostile about her life choices? If it hadn't been for his refusal ten years ago to see a future for the two of them, she might never have left, let alone returned with a tiny house.

Summer took a few deep breaths before scooping Shortie off the bed and following Keefe down to dinner. His outburst had come as a surprise. Was it possible the lack of closure about their breakup affected more than just her? It occurred to her for the first time that there was a distinct possibly it affected Grandpa Zach, too. But of course, she'd never know.

Summer could remember seeing the two men talking together as if it were yesterday. She was in her room, hiding behind the curtain, curled up in the window seat. Grandpa Zach and Keefe were standing in Queenie's rose garden below her window. She put down her book to listen. It was a favorite game of hers…listening in on the two men, who usually only chatted about flowers, the farm, or the bakery. But once in a while, she'd catch a piece of conversation that was a little more telling: A snippet about Grandpa's past or Keefe's thoughts about his future. She was especially keen on eavesdropping when the conversation turned to Keefe.

On that particular day, Summer was in the window seat reading when she was surprised to hear the men below her. It was extremely hot and they usually put off working in the rose garden until late in the afternoon. She peeked out and saw they weren't working. They were just standing there. It was clear by their body language something was very wrong between them. Summer's heart pounded. If Keefe and Grandpa were arguing, would Grandpa fire him?

"I don't see what would be so bad about Summer staying up here once she graduates. I think this farm is great. And the bakery is great, too," Keefe said. "I wouldn't mind staying here forever myself."

"Well, you've seen a bit of the world," Grandpa said. "You made the choice."

"I know she's still young..." Keefe asked.

"Don't forget what I told you," Grandpa Zach said. "She always says getting stuck on a farm can destroy a girl's dreams. You want that on your head if it turns out to be true?"

"I'm surprised she feels that way, honestly," Keefe said. "She never said anything like that."

"She obviously wouldn't say it to you," Grandpa Zach said.

Summer was shocked. Grandpa Zach was lying! Keefe was right, she'd never said anything like that! She'd never even thought it!

"Just don't encourage Summer," Grandpa Zach said. "That's all I ask."

Summer found it hard to breathe. Most of her friends had already had acceptance letters to colleges around the country, but Summer, who secretly thought she'd be making a life with Keefe, had put off applying until her parents forced the issue. And then, she only applied to Baylor University, sure she'd never make the cut.

But the gods of fate were feeling frisky that year. Her parents received the hefty envelope in San Francisco and mailed it up to Flat Top Farm without any announcement. Summer came in after a hot day in the bakery to find it sitting on the kitchen table. She was filled with dread when she opened it. She was accepted.

She didn't know it at the time, but the countdown to her broken heart had started.

The rain pelting against the windows brought her back to the present. She wondered: *Did Queenie know anything about Grandpa Zach's involvement in her unceremonious dumping by Keefe? Would she ever feel close enough to Queenie to ask?* It terrified her to think she might get close enough to Keefe again to actually ask *him.*

Summer put Shortie on the floor right in front of the staircase.

"Go on," she said. "You can do it."

Shortie took a step with one front paw. Then the other.

"Good boy," Summer said. "Keep going."

Trying to get Shortie to navigate the circular staircase in the caboose was not going well. Every night on the road, Summer lay flat in the loft, clapping her hands and begging Shortie to climb the stairs. Shortie would sit on the ground floor, tail wagging furiously but never moving an inch. Summer would finally give in, climb down the stairs, prop Shortie under her arm like a football and clamber up again.

"Come on, Shortie," Summer said, sitting on the step beside him.

He was never going to get the hang of this, she predicted.

Andre came into the hallway and looked up at them as if to say "Dinner is waiting. What's taking you so long?"

Summer was startled to see that competition lit a fire under Shortie's butt. She looked on in astonishment as the little dog took another step and then another, finally landing on the first floor hallway rug. Without a backwards glance, he and Andre walked together toward the kitchen.

"Are you coming down for dinner or what?' Queenie's voice floated up to the second-story landing, where Summer was still frozen to the top step.

As she headed toward the kitchen, Summer decided to give up predicting how this trip was going to play itself out.

Keefe was pulling a bottle of beer out the refrigerator.

"You want a beer?" he asked when he saw Summer. Whatever had him steamed upstairs seemed to have passed.

"No thanks," Summer said. "I'm not much of a beer drinker."

Keefe shrugged.

"Queenie?" he asked.

She'd almost forgotten that Queenie, not Grandpa Zach, was the big beer aficionado at the farm. Even when serving something as authentically Italian as calamari casserole, Queenie would drink a beer instead of a glass of wine. Of course, it was always served in a cut glass stein.

"The usual," she said, as she spooned mounds of steaming calamari casserole onto each plate.

Summer took a seat and was startled to see Keefe pull a bottle of hard cider out of the fridge and put it next to a frosted glass by Queenie's plate.

"Cider?" Summer asked. "I had one of those a few nights ago for the first time! Since when is cider your usual?"

"Since more than a few nights ago," Queenie said, as if she were discussing a fine champagne.

"Fine," Summer said. "It's not a contest."

"Would you like some wine?' Keefe offered.

She remembered that Keefe always had a way of defusing the tension between her and Queenie.

"Yes," she said. "Thank you."

She sat at the table, uncomfortably aware that she was being treated like a guest. As she watched Keefe pull a bottle of red from a wine rack, she realized she couldn't act like family even if she wanted to.

Acting being the operative word.

As Keefe expertly poured her a glass, filling her in about the local prize-winning wine, she snuck a peek at Shortie, who was mercifully being well-behaved. Summer hadn't exactly been keeping up with Shortie's manners while they'd been on the road. But he seemed to understand that her reputation was somehow at stake and he appeared to be content to just hang with Andre by the back door.

"You have a very good dog," Queenie announced, following Summer's gaze. "Ugly, but good."

"He is not ugly," Summer said, shocked. "He just has interesting proportions."

"That's one way to put it," Queenie said, returning to her dinner.

She could see Keefe duck his head. He was clearly going to steer clear of this. Summer thought about her phone conversation with Bale. She was sure he would come to the defense of her dog. She decided she was not going to let Queenie bait her. After all, Queenie had made calamari casserole. Summer looked forward to her first bite.

"This looks wonderful," Summer said, waving a sauce covered tentacle in the air before popping it in her mouth.

Queenie smiled, a rare occurrence. Aptly named, her smile felt like a royal benediction.

Summer tried not to feel self-conscious as she became aware of Queenie watching her. Really watching her. At the same time, Summer became conscious that the casserole didn't have exactly the same taste as she remembered. She chewed thoughtfully. No, the taste was the same, but the texture was different. She looked at Keefe, but he was fully engrossed in his food.

"Is there something wrong?" Queenie asked.

"No!" Summer said, a little urgently. "It's just…"

"Yes, dear?" Queenie asked.

"I don't know," Summer said.

It occurred to her what was different.

She continued, "You're using a different noodle. You used to always use elbow macaroni. This is…I don't know…penne?"

"That's rich, coming from Miss Thomas the Tank Engine." Queenie said.

"What does that mean?" Summer asked.

"Nothing," Queenie sniffed. "I just find it interesting that you of all people should criticize me for trying something new."

"I'm not criticizing you," Summer stammered. "I just wasn't expecting it."

"And I wasn't expecting you to show up in a steam engine when you've got a perfectly good house right here!"

"First of all," Summer said, wondering how the conversation had derailed so quickly. "It's a caboose and it doesn't run on steam. Secondly, I was planning on living in it before you called. It isn't personal, Queenie."

Both women turned to Keefe, who ignored them. Grandpa Zach used to do that. Summer wondered if there was any end to Grandpa's tutorials that Keefe didn't take to heart.

A deafening thunderclap startled them all and put an end to the conversation.

Summer hoped she and Shortie could escape to her room, but Queenie wasn't done with her yet.

"So where exactly are you planning on putting this caboose of yours?"

"I was thinking about taking it up to Flat Top."

"Flat Top Hill?" Queenie's fork clattering to her plate was worthy of an Academy Award for Best Performance by Cutlery.

Even Keefe looked up at this news.

"Yes," Summer said. "It has the best view. It's out of the way. Grandpa isn't using it."

"I might have plans for Flat Top myself," Queenie said.

"Do you?" Summer asked.

"No," Queenie said. "But I might have. I'm just saying, you might have asked me."

Summer caught Keefe's look. It may have been a decade since they'd looked into each other's eyes, but she could still detect the smallest hints of emotion. She could see he wanted her to let this go. There were certainly layers of mystery to unfold. She'd start in the morning, but right now, she just wanted to defuse whatever this was that was going on.

"You're right, Queenie," Summer said. "I should have told you I was bringing the tiny house and asked your permission to put it up on Flat Top Hill. May I have your permission?"

Queenie's eyes suddenly welled up with tears. Summer was horrified. She reached over to touch her grandmother's arm, but Andre beat her to the punch, poking his gigantic snout against Queenie's shoulder. Queenie rubbed the dog's head and reined in her emotions.

"Of course," Queenie said. "I swear, I don't know why I'm so cantankerous these days."

"*These* days?" Keefe asked, eyebrow raised.

Everyone laughed. The tension broke, even if the storm didn't.

After dinner, Queenie excused herself, leaving Keefe and Summer to clean up. Andre opted to stay in the kitchen with his new best friend, Shortie.

Summer had so many questions, but she didn't know where to begin. Queenie said the business was in trouble, but Keefe said it wasn't. Queenie, a fixture in the town as well as the bakery and famous for baking the most delicious confections in the entire Pacific Northwest, now stayed away from Cat's Paw and couldn't turn out a decent peanut butter cookie. She'd changed a family recipe that she'd once considered sacred. What was going on?

"Are you planning on coming down to the bakery tomorrow?" Keefe said.

Summer looked at him as he rinsed the dishes and stacked them in the dishwasher. Queenie obviously hadn't told him that Summer was coming to Flat Top Farm. Maybe he resented her being here.

"I hadn't really thought about it," Summer said, guardedly.

"I think you should," Keefe said. "I mean, there hasn't been a Murray at the bakery for many months now."

"I thought you said the bakery was doing fine."

"It is," Keefe said. "But I think it would be a good idea to let the town know that the family still runs the place. The tradition is part of the charm, you know."

It didn't sound as if he were resentful. But Keefe had surprised her in the past. She started scraping the leftover casserole into a plastic container.

"Don't forget to divide that," Keefe said.

"Pardon?"

"The leftovers," Keefe said. "One container stays here and one goes with me."

"That's a nice little perk," Summer said.

She meant it as a joke, but she saw a cloud pass over Keefe's features.

"What?" Summer asked.

"Nothing," Keefe said, busying himself.

"No," Summer said. "What is it?"

"Let's just say it used to be a better perk," Keefe said. He looked into Summer's eyes. "She's lost her touch, Summer. And what's worse, I think she knows it. She's always experimenting. The baked goods have been so bad that even Andre turns up his nose."

"He ate the peanut butter cookies today!"

"Are you seriously defending those cookies?" Keefe asked.

Summer shook her head.

"She's revising all the old recipes," Keefe said. "Nothing is working, but I can't get her to stop. Sometimes, only the ducks will eat the...experiments."

"This sounds really bad."

"It is," Keefe said. "She just won't leave it alone."

"Have you talked to her about it?"

"I've tried. She just says she's bored and looking to try new things."

"But you don't believe that?"

"Did you hear what I said? Even a dog won't eat her cookies. That's pretty damning testimony."

"Okay," Summer said. "I'll look into it."

"But go easy," Keefe said. "She's got a lot of pride."

"Are you telling me how to deal with my own grandmother?"

"Yes, Summer," Keefe said. "I am. You've been gone a long time."

The thunder and lightning reached a fever pitch. The lights flickered and went out, pitching the kitchen into total darkness. Summer felt unmoored standing in the middle of the floor. She took a step toward the sink but found herself stumbling. Shortie gave a squeak as he scooted out of her way. Summer was careening backwards. As sudden as she'd lost her balance, she was righted. The lights came back on. Keefe held her tightly in his arms.

"Are you okay?" he asked.

"I'm fine, she said as she pulled away. "What happened?"

"Just before the lights went out, I saw you were on a collision course with Andre," Keefe said. "Then, the lights went out."

Summer looked down. Andre was in his Sphinx position right next to her. He may have tripped her, but he hadn't budged.

"I'm a bit of an expert of tripping over that horse," Keefe said.

"I'll be more careful," Summer said, glaring at Andre.

"I better be going," Keefe said.

"I'm sure Queenie wouldn't mind if you waited out the rain," Summer said—meaning she wouldn't mind if he waited out the rain.

"I'll be fine," Keefe said. "We'd never get anywhere if we waited for the rain in Washington to let up."

"Okay, then," Summer said. "I guess Shortie and I will head upstairs."

Summer was rattled by the sensations that ran through her body. She could still feel the imprints of his fingers on her skin. Staying away from Keefe was going to be impossible. She scooped up Shortie and cast a glance at Andre.

Good dog!

Chapter 13

Summer awoke, sprawled on the queen-sized, wrought iron bed. She'd gotten used to sleeping in Wal-Mart parking lots on her little blow-up mattress in the caboose's loft, so opening her eyes to a twelve-foot ceiling was a little disorienting. She looked out the window. The rain had stopped during the night. It was barely dawn. Queenie would be up within an hour. Summer leapt quietly out of bed. She wanted to get the caboose up on Flat Top Hill with as little fanfare as possible. If everything went according to plan, by the time Queenie came down for breakfast, the caboose would be perched on the hill. As she pulled on a sweater, she wondered if Keefe came to the big kitchen for breakfast as well as dinner. Annoyed the thought even entered her mind, Summer brushed her hair furiously.

Then put on some lip gloss.

Shortie raised his head from a mound of blankets on the bed. He blinked sleepily as Summer headed toward the door.

"You stay," Summer said.

Shortie put his head down and was asleep in seconds.

That was easy!

Summer's feet crunched loudly through wet gravel as she dug through her felted purse looking for keys. After nearly two weeks using the bag, she realized she needed to make a few alterations to the design. Not only was the bag pulled out of shape (it folded in on itself, hiding keys, cell phone, wallet, and dog treats in waves of fabric), the straps were stretched so taut that they were more like ropes, which cut into her shoulder like a bra after a long day. When she finally located her keys, she was standing in front of Big Red and the caboose.

As she drifted off to sleep the night before, the thought of driving the truck up Flat Top seemed simple. But now, looking from the truck to the hill, the idea seemed preposterous. She knew it must be her imagination, but did the truck and the tiny house somehow get bigger during the night? They appeared absolutely enormous.

The sun was almost up. She stared at the truck, then walked around the caboose. She made sure the hitch was tight. Biting her lip, Summer couldn't think of any more stall tactics. She looked up at the hill. It seemed to have grown too.

Maybe I should go walk up the hill and see what I'm in for.

Pleased with her diversion, she headed toward Flat Top. She passed the garage, and Keefe's second-floor apartment. She crept quietly past. Bakers were always up before the sun. But his windows were dark. He must still be asleep.

Slacker.

Flat Top rose up behind the house and garage, a dark thumbprint smudged on the pink sky. Summer held her breath and headed up the hill that held so much of her past and her future. The lane that served as a road to the top of Flat Top appeared to be in good shape, much to Summer's relief. Although it was narrow, it was wide enough for the caboose. It also looped around the hill in a spiral, so the incline was not harrowing.

I can do this.

It was easy to keep the flames of outrage kindled three thousand miles away, but the familiarity of every step to the top brought pain and regret about the past as well as anticipation of the future. Even if Grandpa Zach had been instrumental in her breakup with Keefe, shouldn't she have given him a chance to explain himself? After all, even if his advice had been misguided, it came from love and a need to protect her, didn't it? And of course, Keefe could have ignored him. She would never be able to make amends with her grandfather now. She wiped away a tear. He felt so close.

Summer stopped in her tracks. A scratching sound was coming from the top of the hill. She hadn't crested the top, so she couldn't see what was making the noise. The sun would be up in a few minutes, but right now the world was still full of shadows. Washington remained a wild place. Her childhood was spent glimpsing bears, moose, wolves, and bobcats. She'd grown up with a healthy respect for animals and knew it was best to avoid any large animal that might be less than happy to have a close encounter with a human being.

She stopped and listened. She tried to identify the scraping noise. Claws? Very possibly. So…not a moose. And the sound was loud. That eliminated any of the cats. It was probably a bear—grizzly or black? It was important to know the difference in case a bear attacked. An unlikely occurrence, but to a child of the city, the wild creatures of the Pacific Northwest took some getting used to. Grandpa said fear and lack of understanding was what led to most bear attacks.

Her grandfather had drilled into her the difference in the bears: both breeds would rather avoid trouble than get into a battle with a human. But in the remote possibility a bear, surprised or defensive, decided to act aggressively, grizzlies and blacks reacted very differently to the stress of encountering a human. Summer knew she couldn't rely on identifying the bear by color. In that ironic way of Mother Nature, both breeds spanned the spectrum from light brown to black. The grizzly, usually larger, but not always. But there were distinctions: grizzlies had humped shoulders and a dished-in face, while the black bear had a more elongated nose. Summer was pretty sure she didn't want to get close enough to be making judgments on a bear's profile.

The important thing was to remain calm, but determine which kind of bear she was dealing with. If it is was a black bear, conventional wisdom suggested that you stand tall and make lots of noise. An aggressive stance was the best bet. On the other hand, if it was a grizzly, remain still and if things go really badly, play dead. Staring down at a bear was not the time to confuse them.

"And don't forget," Grandpa Zach had cautioned, "never underestimate a bear. Bears are the most intelligent of North American mammals."

The scraping suddenly stopped. Summer's heart pounded. She hoped the bear had read the literature about not wanting to confront humans and just go back into the trees. But black bear or grizzly, she knew she shouldn't run. The sun was coming up over Flat Top, to her disadvantage. She could see something move.

"Summer?" a voice called from out of the shadows.

For one terror-stricken moment, she thought the bear was calling her name. Talk about intelligent!

In an instant, she realized it was Keefe.

"What are you doing up here?" they asked at the same time.

As Summer made her way up the hill, the sun crested on Flat Top. Keefe was standing at the top, smiling down at her. She might have done better tangling with a bear.

"What's going on?" Summer said.

"I knew you were going to bring the caboose up here this morning and I wanted to get the slab ready," he said.

"Slab?" Summer asked.

She noticed he was carrying a rake, which accounted for the scratching noises. But that was the only part of this equation that made any sense.

"I'll show you," Keefe said.

Summer followed Keefe up the hill. Was he intentionally blocking her view? Was he deliberately being annoying?

"Check it out," Keefe said, stepping aside so she could see around him.

Summer gasped. She looked at Keefe in confusion. Two months ago, she would have had no idea what she was looking at, but the cement slab that greeted her now was the most beautiful sight she could imagine. Big, level, with a driveway at one end and full hookup—*full hookups, no more boondocking!*—on one side.

"I don't understand," Summer said.

"Your grandfather had this idea that he might buy an RV and put it up on the hill," Keefe said.

"Really?" Summer asked. "I know he always talked about building something up here, but he never mentioned an RV."

"Times change," Keefe said, not looking at her. "He was getting the itch to travel and thought he'd kill two birds with one stone. He and Queenie could take the RV around the country when they felt like it, and he could use it as a getaway when he was at the farm."

It broke Summer's heart that her grandfather never achieved his dream and it worried her that he might not want her to infringe on it now that she was here. Keefe appeared to read her mind.

"I think Zach would be very happy to pass this on to you, Summer," he said quietly.

Summer couldn't speak. She looked out over the farm. The view was as spectacular as she remembered. The peaks of the Victorian looked like a tiny mountain range from this vantage point. Morning fog still hovered over the lake. Queenie's flowers were waking with the sun. She wasn't sure her grandfather would have wanted to pass this on to her; after all, she'd abandoned the farm. Still, she desperately wanted it to be true.

"I won't pretend this isn't an amazing surprise," she said.

"Good," he said. "I was hoping that would be your reaction."

"What did you think my reaction would be?" Summer asked, taken aback.

"I had no idea," Keefe said. "I stopped guessing what you think about things a very long time ago."

"What are you doing up here, anyway?" Summer asked.

"I just thought I'd clean up a little," Keefe said. "Nobody's been up here in a long time."

"Thanks for that," Summer said, trying to get her emotions under control.

Why was every encounter with Keefe so damn hard?

"No problem," Keefe said, his tone softening.

He seemed to want to calm things down as well.

"Do you think the hookups still work?" She asked, looking down at the dirty-but-pristine electrical, water and sewer connections.

"I don't see why they wouldn't," Keefe said. "Only one way to find out."

"How?"

"Let's get the caboose up here and hook her up," Keefe said.

"Sounds good," Summer couldn't help herself, it was good to be partners in crime with Keefe again. "I've got my keys."

She reached in her pocket and pulled out a set of keys. Keefe put out his hand. Summer furrowed her brow.

"What?" she asked.

"The keys," Keefe said.

"What about them?"

"I can't very well move the truck unless you give them to me."

"I drove all the way from Kentucky, you know," Summer said. "I think I can—"

Stop! Stop! Stop! She willed herself to not say it, but she couldn't help it. She finished the thought: "I think I can drive it up a little hill."

"Suit yourself," Keefe said.

Summer turned on her heels and headed down the hill. She had no idea if she could drive the truck up the hill, get the caboose in place and line it up to the hookups. But thanks to her big mouth, she'd have to try. Given her history with Keefe, she'd have to succeed.

"I think I'll just stay up here," Keefe yelled to her retreating back. "Help guide you?"

Summer did not like the tone of his voice. Was he making fun of her? She turned around and looked at him. He threw up his arms in a gesture of surrender.

"Unless you can drive, look behind you and beside you while balancing a heavy load all at the same time," he said. "Then I'm good. I'll just go brush my teeth."

He *was* making fun of her! She wanted to tell him to go to hell. On the other hand, she probably could use some assistance.

Say it, Summer. Say it!

"Thank you," she said through gritted teeth. "I probably could use another set of eyes."

She was too far away from him to see the smirk that she just knew was spreading across his face. She trudged down the hill, checked the hitch and hopped in the cab of the truck. Summer glanced at the kitchen, hoping that Queenie wasn't witnessing the move. But there was no movement from the house.

She turned the key. The engine purred. Big Red was ready to give it her all.

Chapter 14

Summer gripped the steering wheel with such force, her knuckles turned white. She was going to get Big Red and the caboose up Flat Top Hill or die trying! She took a few deep breaths and started to drive. She went slowly, inching her way up. She felt as if she were climbing the Rockies while dragging the Empire State Building. She let out a sigh of relief as she rounded the last switchback. Keefe was standing on the slab with a somber look on his face.

He can't believe I did this!

She rolled down the window and said, in her breeziest voice:

"Is there a problem?"

"Yeah," he said, looking at her wheels. "I don't think you can get the truck over the slab at this angle."

Her breeziness blew away.

"What do you mean?" she said, pulling on the emergency brake and getting out of the truck.

"You'll need to back down the hill to the last curve and come up again," Keefe said. "Turn the wheels to the left as you approach and then straighten out."

What does that even mean?

There was no way she was going to put Big Red in reverse. Summer had avoided that dreaded maneuver on her entire trip across the country. She looked at Keefe. Perhaps he somehow knew she wouldn't back down, either down the hill or from this challenge. Maybe she didn't really need to start over at all and he was just calling her bluff.

Two could play at that game.

"I think I can get the truck up the slab," she said.

Keefe's eyebrows disappeared into his hairline.

"Yeah," Summer continued, as she walked around the truck. "I think I can just go for it. I've had a lot of experience, you know."

"Be my guest," Keefe said, backing away from the slab.

Summer got back in Big Red. She put the truck in low and slowly crawled up the slab. She snuck a look at Keefe, who was watching the wheels. He grimaced just before the passenger front tire slipped off the slab. Big Red shook dramatically, then settled, listing violently to the right. Keefe ran behind Big Red then whacked the back of the truck.

"It's okay," he called to her. "The hitch is holding. The caboose is still solid."

Summer willed herself not to cry in humiliation. If Keefe Devlin let her go ten years ago because she needed to mature and become a woman of the world, she could not give in to this insipid damsel in distress situation. She needed to save herself!

I'm going to have to put the truck in reverse.

The thought panicked her. But she had no choice. It was either that or admit failure and turn over the keys to Keefe. And turning over the keys was not an option.

"You were right," she said casually and graciously. "I probably should have started over. But I'll just, you know, throw this baby in reverse and head in again."

"Are you sure?" Keefe asked, doubtfully. "I can take it from here if you want."

Summer climbed clumsily out of the tilted truck. She faced him, hands on hips.

"You know what your problem is?" she asked.

"I didn't know I had a problem," he said. "You're the one with the sideways truck."

"Don't change the subject," she said, wagging her finger in the air. "I mean, you know exactly what's going on here, right?"

"What exactly is going on here?" he asked slowly.

"You're threatened by my competence."

Keefe looked again at the truck hanging off the slab. He shook his head. "I don't think that's what's going on here," he said.

Summer got back in the truck and in a fury, slammed Big Red into reverse. Miraculously, she got both wheels back on the slab. She backed off the slab and started over. She pulled forward and all four wheels sat squarely on the concrete. Summer exhaled. Maybe she should get angry more often! She looked at Keefe, waiting to see his stunned expression, but he seemed pleased, which took the edge off her victory.

"Nice work," he said, giving her a thumbs up. "Keep going!"

"Keep going?" Summer asked.

"The truck isn't going on the slab," he said. "The caboose is. Right?"

"Of course," Summer snorted dismissively, as if it had just slipped her mind.

But something had clicked in her. She knew she could do it.

And she did.

Having proven herself, she and Keefe worked together putting plywood under the wheels and blocking them; unhitching the caboose and connecting it to the electric, water and sewer hookups. After testing, all the hookups worked!

"That's about it," Keefe said, dusting his hands on his jeans. "Nice job!"

He put out his hands for a double high five. Summer raised her hands, but as their palms met, Keefe laced his fingers through hers. They stood frozen, not saying a word. The earth had no sound. A distant yapping brought them back. They released their fingers at exactly the same moment. Summer turned toward the noise—it was Shortie, barking his little brains out. He was following Andre, who was loping up the hill toward them at triple Shortie's speed. The distraction of the dogs was a godsend. Keefe tussled with Andre as they waited for Shortie. When the little dog reached the top, she scooped him up. Summer wanted something—even a writhing, slobbering dog—between her and Keefe.

Andre seemed to regain his regal demeanor after his dash to the top of the hill. He sat bolt upright next to Keefe, denying his frisky romp.

"I guess I better take Andre back down," Keefe said. "Let you get settled up here."

"That's..." Summer could feel the disappointment in the pit of her stomach. "That's a good idea. I have lots of unpacking to do."

She knew as soon as she said it how lame that sounded. She had one truck bed worth of stuff. She'd be unpacked in an hour.

"Oh no," Keefe said, his eyes focused on something in the distance.

Summer followed his gaze to Queenie, walking by the lake.

"Even the ducks won't eat those peanut butter cookies," Keefe said.

Summer squinted and could see Queenie scattering the cookies on the grass by the lake. The ducks assembled, stared at the beige lumps on the ground, then retreated to the safety of the water. Summer felt sorry for her grandmother, but couldn't really blame the ducks.

Keefe walked down the hill without a backward glance. Shortie tried to squirm out of Summer's arms and follow Andre, but Summer held him up and looked into his shiny black eyes.

"We need to stick together," she said. "I'd appreciate some support here."

She put Shortie on the ground. He took off down the hill, joining Keefe and Andre on their walk to the house. He didn't look back either.

Traitor!

Summer walked all the way around the caboose. She was finally going to make it into her *home*. She remembered Bale saying if she stayed in one place, she'd need to cover the tires, take the weight off them, put plywood under them and enclose the undercarriage. But she tried not to fantasize that this might be that place.

She had plans, after all. If Keefe and her grandfather thought she needed to see the world, she would still see it! One round of finger-lacing did not a future make.

Summer pulled a small step stool from Big Red. It was one of her first Wal-Mart purchases when she realized it was quite a big step up to the caboose on wheels. She stood on the top step, hand on the doorknob, and paused. Even though she had slept in the caboose for days now, she'd deliberately disconnected from the tiny house emotionally. For better or for worse, the caboose was going to be her home. She opened the door and walked inside.

Man, it was small.

Summer looked at the interior with new eyes. Exactly where was she going to put things? She tested the lights and the water in the kitchen. She was grateful for that small blessing. She walked into the closet and sat on the circular staircase, the only seating in the place. She realized she had one more essential to check before she could call this place home: Wi-Fi. If the Internet gods were with her, Queenie's signal from her house would reach Flat Top. She used her thumbprint to activate her phone and scrolled through the settings till she found Wi-Fi, then smiled triumphantly. There, among the networks was *Queenie*. Summer attempted a few passwords: Queenie (nope), Zach (no), DoughZDough (negative). She was about to give up and just call Queenie for the password, when it occurred to her that Queenie wouldn't know it. There was no way in hell either she or Grandpa Zach knew enough about computers to set up a password. Grandpa never went near the computer and Queenie was always insisting the computer was broken every time she couldn't figure something out. It hit Summer like a thunderbolt: Keefe was the computer guy around the farm. He had to be.

With technological advances seeming to sweep across the globe every few seconds, ten years ago was practically the Stone Age in technology. Even then, Keefe was interested in the field. She thought back to one of their many conversations about where technology was going. Keefe predicted that cell phones would one day be multi-functioning devices and remote businesses around the world would start doing business on the Internet. Facebook had just appeared on the scene, but was only being used by college students. He used to tease her that she would be using Facebook when she started college and he'd lose track of her. When she arrived at Baylor, students were in a delirium over Facebook. She refused to use it. And he lost track of her anyway.

She knew she shouldn't attempt to guess Keefe's password for the farm, but she couldn't help herself. She tried "Summer." If technology was just a little more advanced, the password-rejection notice might have read: You're pathetic...and no, that's not it. This game was lose-lose and Summer knew it. But she couldn't help herself. She tried again, this time typing "SummerofLove." She was embarrassed for herself, let alone the poor database that was having to put up with her. Besides, Keefe wouldn't have come up with SummerofLove even if things had worked out between them. He wasn't that kind of guy.

Summer remembered reading an article that said it was good to use symbols and numbers in any password. She had a hunch that if she knew a techno-tip, Keefe knew it too. She told herself she'd try one more time: $umm3r.

She was in.

She stared down at the phone. There was so much she could read into this. He regretted letting her go was her favorite scenario. Her least favorite was, since it was the farm's password and not his, the whole thing might just be an innocent homage to the past.

The good thing about being logged on was Summer could always lose herself online. It had worked in the early days of trying to forget Keefe, and it worked now. She logged into Instagram to check on the tiny house community. People who bought into the tiny lifestyle were fanatics about posting pictures. Summer smiled—she would now start posting pictures herself, maybe even start a blog. Yet from her own research, she knew that the world didn't need another tiny blogger. Maybe a blog about running a purse-making venue out of a tiny house. She hadn't seen that before. And she could have used a blog or two in her early days as a felter. Catching a glimpse of her purse, now stretched out to the point it hugged her knees, she decided maybe she needed more purse-making practice before offering tips to the world.

She clicked on Facebook. Summer was never a huge fan of this site in her other life as a risk management specialist. She was more of a Twitter girl. But life on the road changed all that. She'd doubled her friends since heading across the country. The tiny world was bigger than she could have imagined. She was about to check on Margie and Alf when she was distracted by a familiar photo on the right side of the screen. It was an ad announcing that *Bale's Tiny Dreams* would be featured at the Tiny House Road Show in Seattle. She had seen the ad many times before, but now she took in every detail. She knew tiny houses caught people's imaginations and sometimes wouldn't let go. That's what happened with her. But now, there was more to it.

Bale Barrett would be in Washington, and he was coming to see her.

Chapter 15

Summer's head was about to explode. There was so much to think about at the farm: the caboose, Keefe, Queenie, the password. And now Bale was coming to Washington! She took a few deep breaths and put everything out of her mind. She was going to move into her tiny home, free of distractions. She went out to Big Red, hauled in the first box to the minuscule living area, and opened it. She looked down at her seventy-two articles of hangable clothing. Heading for Kentucky and *Bale's Tiny Dreams,* she'd lived in jeans, yoga pants, Tieks, and assorted T-shirts. Living on Flat Top Hill and working at the bakery might involve a change of footwear. Buttery leather ballet flats would have to give way to Doc Martins, but other than that, she didn't see a need for a pair of dressy dove-grey linen pants or a 1940's vintage floral blouse with a sweetheart neckline. They seemed like costumes from another life.

Unless Keefe takes me on a date, I won't be needing this, she thought, as she dragged the box into the walk-in closet. She hung up a simple black dress with a lace hem. She shook her head. A little black dress would look ridiculous at the one small Cat's Paw café.

But if Bale were to take her to dinner in Seattle…

Her thoughts were interrupted as Queenie's voice attacked the space.

"Hello?" Queenie called, noisily stomping around the front of the caboose. "Summer?"

"Yes, Queenie," Summer said, sidestepping the box and the circular staircase. "I'm in here."

She met Queenie in the miniscule hallway between the kitchen counter and the closet. Queenie was looking around the caboose, dipping her head into the closet behind Summer, and darting her eyes toward the bathroom at the far end of the caboose. Summer swelled with pride. You couldn't help but be impressed with the workmanship and the brilliant use of space.

Even Queenie could see that.

"My dear," Queenie said. "You're not seriously going to live in this thing?"

Or not.

"Where are you going to do your laundry?" Queenie asked, spreading her hands to indicate that she saw no washer or dryer in the place.

"As a matter of fact, there's a combination washer-dryer in the bathroom," Summer said, trying to hit the perfect tone between nonchalance and unbridled triumph.

"And there's no *oven*," Queenie said, practically daring her to produce one.

"I don't need an oven," Summer said.

"What are you talking about?" Queenie asked. "How can you bake without an oven?"

Summer instinctively knew that "I wasn't planning on baking" was a statement sure to enrage her grandmother, but that was the truth. She should just tell her that.

"I can use the oven at your house," Summer said carefully.

Shortie isn't the only half-weenie in this family.

Summer expected this statement to meet with huge approval, but Queenie only looked sad.

Summer knew better than to pry into her grandmother's business. Even now, with Queenie's cryptic demands that she come save the business, it was clear that events would unfold on Queenie's timetable, not hers.

Summer noticed a box from Big Red sitting in the living area.

"How did this get in here?" Summer asked.

"I brought it in from your truck," Queenie said. "I saw you moving boxes and thought I'd help."

"Oh," Summer said, startled that her life on the hill was not going to be as private as she imagined. She wondered how she was going to sneak a man—Keefe? Bale?—into the caboose if her grandmother could see everything from the house. Maybe she could turn the caboose around, but she'd lose the fantastic view. The entrance would just face the huge evergreens. That was a lot of work for an imagined love affair, especially when she couldn't decide on the leading man!

She returned her attention to her grandmother, who pulled a Leatherman multi-tool from her pocket. Summer smiled. It was her grandfather's. He never left the house without it. Now that he'd left the planet without it, it was still working hard for Queenie. She opened the box cutter and zipped it across the packing tape. The box contained the sweaters Summer had collected before heading across the country. She'd packed them as tightly as possible and they sprang, panting over the ridge of the box as if gasping for air. Queenie picked up a particularly hideous red, pink, and purple wool sweater and stared at it.

"This is a look," Queenie said.

Summer toyed with the idea of not telling her grandmother anything about her plans. Two could play the taciturn game. But she knew she was no match for her grandmother.

"I'm planning on starting a business," Summer said, taking the ugly sweater and holding it closely.

"You're about a hundred years too late to be a ragpicker," Queenie said, pulling an orange cashmere out of the box.

"I'm going to make purses."

The surprise on her grandmother's face was worth giving in.

"Out of these?" Queenie asked.

"Yes." Summer tried to hide her excitement, but it felt good to be talking about her dreams. "I'm going to felt the wool and make them into ..."

She ran to the kitchen and opened the narrow cabinet that would hold her broom and mop, the ones she would eventually buy, where her purse was hanging on a peg. The weight of the contents in the bottom strained against the handles. The purse was now twice as long as it was when she'd designed it. It was twisted and distorted; the Quasimodo of purses.

"You're going to make them into..." Queenie prodded.

"This..." Summer said in a tiny voice. She held up the revolting bag, and said in a quavering voice, "It's not supposed to look like this."

"Obviously," Queenie said, taking the purse and studying it.

Summer sniffed, which caught Queenie's attention. Her grandmother looked up from the purse.

"Why do you want to make purses?" Queenie asked.

The question surprised Summer.

Why did she?

"I just loved the idea of doing something unpredictable."

"Living in a train car is not enough?" Queenie asked.

"It was going to be a whole thing." Summer tried not to wail. "A whole new life!"

Queenie perched against the kitchen counter and stared at Summer.

"So I guess that made it twice as hard returning to your old life," Queenie said.

Summer waited. Was her grandmother going to tell her what this summons was all about? Queenie studied the purse. The silence was stretching as painfully as the handles on the bag. But Summer could feel a real bonding moment was upon them. She would wait for her grandmother's next move. Finally, Queenie jumped down from the counter and handed the purse back to her.

"Lining," Queenie said.

"Pardon me?"

"You can't make a purse out of wool and hope for the best," Queenie said. "You need to make a lining for each bag, so the outside of the purse doesn't have to bear any of the weight."

"Do you really think that will work?"

"Would I be telling you this if I didn't think it would work?"

Clearly, their bonding moment was over.

Both women turned toward the door as Andre bounded in. Shortie yapped from the stepladder. Summer went to retrieve him. She had to thread her way between her grandmother and the Great Dane. The three of them took up the entire living space – and this was before Summer furnished it!

"You shouldn't baby that dog," Queenie said as Summer lifted Shortie into the caboose. "He's never going to learn to do anything if you'll do it for him."

"You used to say that to Grandpa Zach when you thought he was spoiling me," Summer said.

"Good advice never goes out of style," Queenie said as she headed out of the caboose.

"Do you mean, *And look how well you turned out?*" Summer teased.

Her grandmother was silent.

"Well?" Summer said, pleased to have the upper hand.

"I'm ignoring you," Queenie said as she swept out of the caboose.

Summer smiled. She knew that was exactly what her grandmother meant.

"Come on, Andre," Queenie called from outside the caboose.

Summer stood in the tiny house looking out at Queenie, who was framed in the doorway. Behind her, the view from Flat Top Hill was stunning. Whatever misgivings Summer had about returning to the farm, the view from her tiny house helped soften them. Andre nudged Summer's arm, waiting for a pat. Summer wondered if she should pet him, now that her grandmother had commanded him to follow her.

"Andre!" Queenie called into the caboose, giving her hands one sharp clap. "Did you hear me?"

Summer was impressed. Queenie might have cowed everyone in the town of Cat's Paw, but Andre was holding his own.

"Don't make me come get you," Queenie threatened.

Summer felt as if she were back in middle school, waiting to see a fight was going to break out. She looked at her grandmother and then at Andre. Suddenly, Andre skittered across the hardwood floors and leapt out of the caboose, ignoring the stepladder all together.

Smart dog, Andre. I wouldn't test her either!

Summer watched her grandmother march down the hill with Andre walking beside her, his giant tail swinging like a furry metronome. Summer turned her attention to the box of sweaters and sighed. How was she ever going to fit all of these in her house? The box was only the start of her stash. All the sweaters she'd collected along the way were tucked into Big Red's every corner. Summer realized with a jolt that the orange sweater was gone. She looked out the window at the speck on the horizon that was her grandmother. Queenie was carrying the orange sweater.

Her grandmother was getting weirder and weirder.

The next few hours flew by. Summer put away everything from Big Red and discovered there was still room to grow. Several of the cubbyholes in the bathroom were bare, there were still two vacant shelves in the kitchen and even an empty drawer in the loft. Of course, there was no food or furniture in the place. But the feeling of spaciousness was a relief. On the other hand, the walk-in closet was a disaster. It looked like the remains of a neighborhood after a cyclone, randomly filled with clothes, shoes, sweaters, two sewing machines, dog paraphernalia, and everything else that didn't have a rightful home in the caboose. But Summer had left a path from the closet door to the circular staircase and decided to call that a win.

From the closet window, she could see Keefe leaving his apartment and heading toward Queenie's house. She looked at her watch. It was almost dinnertime. She started for the front door. Eventually, she'd start cooking at the caboose, but that was a few days away, at least. She caught sight of her reflection. She was a wreck!

She sprinted into the bathroom and ran a brush through hair. As she headed out of the bathroom, she thought about the electricity between herself and Keefe. She pivoted back to the sink and added lip gloss. Her closet called to her as she passed by. She heeded its call, changing out of her jeans and into the dove-grey linen pants.

She opened the front door. The sun was going down and the vista took Summer's breath away. Shortie stood at the small stepladder and wagged his tail, waiting for Summer to pick him up. Summer gauged the stairs. They were wide and flat.

"You can do it," she said to Shortie.

Shortie barked. Then whined. Summer put her hands on her hips.

"You're never going to learn to do anything if I do it for you," she said. "Come on Shortie, get with the program. Things are different up here."

If Queenie can stare down a Great Dane, I can stare down a half-wiener dog.

Just as Summer was about to cave, Shortie lightly stepped onto the ladder and trotted down the three stairs as if he had been doing it all his life. Maybe Summer should have followed more of her grandmother's advice.

She grabbed Shortie's leash, then stopped herself. She needed to take her own advice: "Things are different up here."

"Come on, Shortie," she said, putting his leash away. "You're going commando from now on."

Chapter 16

Shortie ran into Queenie's kitchen as if he'd been living there his entire life. Summer laughed as she watched him invade Andre's personal space. Shortie jumped all over him, demanding attention by pulling on Andre's long ears with his tiny teeth. The big dog bore the intrusion like a champion. But the laughter caught in Summer's throat. Something was wrong. She knew it as soon as she stepped through the kitchen door. Queenie was at the stove and didn't turn around when Summer walked in. Keefe was sitting at the table, the ice-cold beer and hard cider bottles sweating and ready to be poured. There was a basket of homemade biscuits on the table. Although blocked from view by her grandmother. Summer recognized the aroma drifting up from the stove. It was another of her favorites. Summer knew her grandmother was not a demonstrative woman, but always proved her love by making Summer's favorite foods whenever she arrived. Summer was touched that her grandmother seemed to remember these dishes even a decade later. Stew wasn't usually on the menu until winter, but Queenie was making a fuss over Summer's arrival in her own way.

Summer caught Keefe's eye and saw nothing but misery. What was going on? He looked down at a sad-looking biscuit sitting on his plate. It had one bite taken out of it. Summer may not have grown up to be a master baker, but years around her grandparents' business had given her a critical eye. She knew a good biscuit when she saw one, and she knew this wasn't one.

Queenie finally turned around, carrying a huge earthenware bowl laden with the fragrant stew. She put the bowl in the center of the table, ignoring the discarded bread on Keefe's plate. Keefe and Queenie had an easy rhythm. Keefe poured the drinks while Queenie served up the stew into individual bowls. Summer looked at the stew. She was confused. It smelled the same but looked very different. The sauce was a richer brown. Summer speared a carrot and held it up to the light. The rich sauce clung to it, but it was unusually translucent.

"Is there something wrong?" Queenie asked.

"No," Summer said, embarrassed to be caught examining dinner. She popped the carrot into her mouth.

Much like the calamari casserole of yesterday, it was delicious but different. Summer smiled at her grandmother and gave her a thumbs up. It was obvious the positive reinforcement meant a lot to Queenie. She visibly relaxed. If only Queenie were more...approachable. Summer couldn't imagine saying: "So, Queenie, isn't it bad enough that you've given up going to work in town and you've obviously lost your touch with baking? Do you have to mess with everything?"

Her eyes stole a peek at the basket of the limp biscuits. Was there ever a smaller elephant in a room?

"How are things going up at the train, Clarisse?" Queenie asked.

"You could just ask how things are going up at my house," Summer said. "It's my home, you know."

"This whole tiny house thing that's sweeping the country is just crazy. I can't believe my own flesh and blood is buying into it," Queenie said, then gestured around the kitchen. "This is your home, too. Why do you need another three hundred square feet?"

"Two hundred and twenty square feet," Summer said.

Summer deliberately did not look at Keefe. His comment about the caboose fitting in her closet upstairs still stung.

"Everybody's making interesting choices these days," Keefe said. "We don't always understand what's going on with another person. Isn't that right, Summer?"

Summer nodded, but didn't say anything. If Keefe's observation was an opening for Queenie, she did not walk through it. She did not even walk up to it.

"More stew, anybody?" Queenie asked.

Summer looked at Keefe as he passed his bowl back to Queenie. It occurred to her that he might not have been talking about Queenie, or perhaps not *just* about Queenie. He might have been talking about himself!

"How *are* thing going up there?" Keefe said, smoothing out the accusation in Queenie's query.

"So far, so good," Summer said. "I've got water, electricity, and Wi-Fi."

Keefe reddened. Summer tried not to smile. He obviously figured out that if she had Wi-Fi, she'd figured out the password. Not exactly the same as stumbling across a treasure trove of love letters, but at the very least, a twenty-first century "gotcha."

"We've got water, electricity, and Wi-Fi here, too," Queenie groused.

"Thanks for dinner," Keefe said abruptly. "I have some work to do this evening, so I'm afraid I'll have to leave the cleaning up to Summer."

Had everyone in this house gone insane?

"I can clean up," Queenie said. "You've had a long day."

"Oh, no, Queenie, that's fine!" Summer protested. "You made dinner, I'm happy to clean up."

Queenie gave her one of her imperious stare-downs that helped her get her name. Summer shrugged. She went to the door and called Shortie. Sleeping curled in the hollow of Andre's legs, Shortie looked up sleepily and closed his eyes again.

"Shortie," Summer said, imitating Queenie's commanding manner with Andre. "Don't make me come get you."

Shortie's ears shot up. Untangling himself from Andre, he flounced to the door like a sullen teenage boy. Summer could barely make out the silhouette of the tiny house on the hill. No matter what Queenie said, it was home.

Summer fed Shortie and decided that was her final chore of the day. Tomorrow, after she'd worked at the bakery, she'd check out some of the new antique stores on Main Street. She thought back to furnishing her apartments over the years; even a dorm room required more inventory than this place! Summer stretched and hit her knuckles on the wall. Every gesture was going to have to be rethought. In the loft, she couldn't stand up straight. In the kitchen, she had to keep her elbows tucked in or risk hitting the wall beside her. But the bathroom was luxurious. It was the one room in the house where no compromises had to be made. Even with the washer/dryer, the trough bathtub, the toilet, sink, and storage, there was still room to walk around. She knew it wasn't fair to the other rooms, which still needed decorating and furnishing, but the bathroom was her favorite place in the house—although she would never let the walk-in closet get wind of that.

Summer prepared the bathroom for her first bath. She turned the taps on, fingers crossed that there would be enough hot water to fill the trough. While water splashed into the trough, she ran to the kitchen to get a baggie. She'd learned the hard way that if she wanted to use her iPad in the tub, she needed it to be waterproof. She poured a capful of bubble bath into the trough, turned down the lights using the dimmer switch, and lowered herself into the water.

It was heaven. She was so grateful Keefe had helped her with the hookups.

Do not think of Keefe right now.

Shortie stuck his nose in the bathroom.

"You can come in," Summer said, feeling guilty she'd spoken harshly to him down at the big house.

How quickly had Queenie's place become "the big house?" She wondered if that moniker would catch on in town.

Shortie hesitated for a few seconds, then trotted into the room. Summer watched him as he looked around. She could practically see him mentally claiming a bottom cubby as his own. He sniffed at it, then curled up on a fluffy yellow towel, circling a few times before settling. He looked at Summer as if to say, "You have your place and I have mine."

Summer leaned back and closed her eyes. The warm water enveloped her and the lavender-scented bubbles soothed her aching limbs. She would have to tell Bale what a great bathtub a horse trough made. He should put them in all his dream homes.

Do not think of Bale right now.

Summer distracted herself with the iPad, making a mental list of the furniture she needed: two small chairs to use around the hinged dining room table, a small coffee table, and a small sofa or futon. *Small* was the operative word. She realized, at the moment, she only needed one dining room chair, but she couldn't help but put either Bale or Keefe in the other chair, serving either one of them a gourmet meal. Queenie's stew and gross biscuits popped into her mind. Summer really needed to get to the bottom of her grandmother's unusual behavior.

Do not think of Queenie right now, seriously!

She determinedly linked to a few websites, browsing living room furniture. Many of the pieces were too large to even consider. She suspected even the love seats might be too big. She made a mental note to measure the space before she went into town tomorrow.

The washer/dryer caught her eye, turning her imagination to her sweater purses. Maybe eBay would be a good source for a few interesting finds, since she was clearly moored up on Flat Top Hill for the foreseeable future. The first sweater to catch her eye made her laugh. It looked exactly like one she owned and rejected. She moved on. The next sweater was also a spitting image of one she'd discarded.

Why was everything so strange these days? Had she somehow moved to the Twilight Zone?

She clicked on the second sweater and zoomed in on the right sleeve. There was a tiny moth hole in exactly the same spot as the one Summer had put in the GIVEAWAY box.

Summer opened the drain, got out of the tub, wrapped herself in her blue bathrobe and scrambled up to the loft. Shortie squeaked in outrage at the bottom of the circular stairs. Summer let out a deep sigh, clomped back down the stairs, stuck the dog under her arm, and climbed back up again. They both settled on the mattress, Shortie going right back to sleep. Summer began looking up the listings of the seller called M'Laitest: Mary-Lynn Laite, AKA Lynnie, her neighbor in Hartford, who was so kindly going to dispose of Summer's possessions for her.

Summer gasped as she scrolled down listing after listing. Every single offering was Summer's. Clothes, knickknacks, furniture, even that damn black cavalry jacket was for sale! And Lynnie was asking forty bucks more than Summer had paid for it! Summer thought about contacting M'Laitest.

Summer was not sure what to do. She was outraged that Lynnie would be so duplicitous. Of course Lynnie didn't say she *wasn't* going to sell Summer's stuff, but it was just bad form. Summer plotted her next move, turning on her side to look out at the farm in the bright moonlight. She had to admit, it was a gorgeous sight. If she had landed here by accident, with no history, she would be congratulating herself on finding such a perfect place for her tiny house. The back porch light at Queenie's suddenly went on. Summer sat up and squinted, trying to make out what was happening at the big house. Andre came out leaping out of the house, burning off some energy before bed by racing around the yard. Summer could barely make out the tiny dot on the porch, but she knew it was Queenie. Queenie probably wasn't aware how bright the porch light was and Summer felt as if she was invading her grandmother's privacy. But she couldn't look away. She watched as her grandmother sat heavily on the top step and put her head in her hands. It was too far away to tell if Queenie was crying, but no one could mistake, even from the distance of the hill, that this woman was defeated.

You can keep everything, M'Laitest. There are bigger problems to solve.

Chapter 17

Summer woke before the sun, turning off her phone alarm before it sounded. Looking out the loft's window, she could see a tiny light glimmering in the darkness. Keefe was already up. Even though it had been years since she'd stepped foot in the bakery, an entire childhood of training kicked in: bakers rose before dawn. She was planning on going to Dough Z Dough. She'd hoped to stumble upon any clue that might help to explain Queenie's unusual behavior.

Shortie showed no interest in getting out of bed, so Summer made her way down the circular staircase and into the kitchen. The counter space was prime real estate, but she'd given Bale instructions to build an appliance garage in the corner that adjoined the bathroom wall. It was a wide cabinet where she'd stowed her Keurig coffeemaker, KitchenAid mixer, Cuisinart toaster, and Vitamix. When she was researching what to dump while downsizing, most online articles counseled tossing the big kitchen appliances. But Summer used hers. Thumbing her nose at the advice, she packed them all.

The idea that Lynnie would have made a boatload selling these on eBay if Summer had left any of these treasures at home flitted into her mind. She shoved the thought away. Lynnie was the past and there was too much on Summer's plate to worry about her.

Summer slid the Keurig from the cabinet and inserted a hazelnut coffee K-Cup. She slid one of her two coffee mugs into place. When she was fourteen, Grandpa Zach had introduced her to the wonders of coffee. She had forgotten that until just this moment. So many memories tickled her brain up here on Flat Top Hill. Unlike the outsized thoughts of heartbreak and betrayal that had dominated her thinking in years past, these remembrances were different—as sweet and tiny as her new house.

Summer turned toward the bathroom, almost tripping over Shortie. She looked at him, stunned.

"Did you get down the stairs all by yourself?" she asked, scooping him up and kissing his needle snout. "Who is the smartest dog in the whole world?"

The smell of coffee made her mouth water, and the sound of it trickling into the mug made her bladder roar.

"I'll be right back," Summer said to Shortie, putting him on the floor.

When she got back to the kitchen, teeth brushed and hair wrestled into a ponytail, she started looking through the cabinets. Any dog who would brave a circular staircase needed a reward. Shortie was going to get the wet dog food this morning.

After opening and closing all four cabinet doors, Summer realized she hadn't gone shopping yet.

"Sorry, dude," she said in a bright tone, as if a treat were on its way. Looks like it's dry dog food for you."

She was glad Shortie didn't speak English.

A sandy cloud rose over the doggy-dish as she poured out the brown pellets. Shortie attacked the bowl, hungry as a mountain climber after his historic descent. Summer gave him a pat, which he ignored; there was food to devour. She sipped her coffee, leaning against the counter. She really needed to buy a chair.

Summer took the few steps to the walk-in closet. She'd had her doubts if it made sense to give up so much square footage to storage, but she was glad she'd gone with her instincts. While still a novice when it came to the tiny house experience, she could tell storage would always be the greatest challenge of her new lifestyle.

She tried to convince herself she needn't look cute for Keefe, so she settled on needing to look cute for the townspeople. They were sure to be full of questions now that a Murray was working at the bakery again. In her old life, getting dressed in the morning could result in ten or more wardrobe changes, but her options here were limited. Should she go with the dark jeans or the light jeans? The white V neck T-shirt or the soft, dark blue T-shirt with the rounded neck? She settled on the light blue jeans and the dark T-shirt. Even with the closet as packed as it was, Summer knew where everything was. She laid her hands on her lace-up boots and was tugging the first one on when she heard a sound at the door. She hopped out of the closet, one shoe on and shoe off. Shortie was standing at the door, front paws on the door, tail wagging with such ferocity that Summer wondered how he stayed upright.

"Some watchdog you are," Summer said, smiling.

She knew it had to be either Keefe or Queenie on the other side of the door. Once again, the differences between living tiny and living in her apartment revealed itself. Before she could collect her thoughts, she was across the entire room. There was no time to overthink in a tiny house. She swung the door open, ready to greet her early morning visitor.

"Andre?" Summer said in surprise.

She looked down at the large dog, whose back paws were still on the ground with his front paws balanced on the top step of the pudgy ladder. She was just about to ask him what he was doing here, when Shortie scooted past her and the two dogs took off down the hill.

"Shortie!" Summer hissed in a whisper. She pulled on her other boot in a panic. "Shortie! Come back here."

"Shortie will be fine," Keefe's voice startled her in the darkness. "Andre knows the ropes."

"Oh! I thought Andre came up here by himself," Summer said. "You brought him."

"More like he brought me," Keefe said. "Now that Queenie isn't coming to the bakery, I let Andre out of the house in the morning."

"That's very nice of you."

His voice boomed in the predawn light. She kept her voice pointedly low.

"Why are you whispering?" Keefe said, lowering his voice to match hers. He looked around the hillside. "There's nobody else here."

"Sorry," Summer said, turning up her volume with effort. "I guess I've been living in the city too long."

"Or long enough," Keefe said. This time it was his voice that was barely a breath on the wind.

Summer wasn't sure what to make of that statement. It was dark and she couldn't really see more than his shadow standing outside the tiny house. Memories of talking to Keefe in the dark came flooding back. Her heart beat faster.

She snapped on the porch light, snapping herself out of her dangerous walk along memory cliff.

"Want some coffee?" she asked brightly.

Keefe followed her into the caboose. For the first time ever, Summer was sorry her coffeemaker was so convenient. She could stand some frittering time in order to gather her thoughts. But once she'd put the K-Cup in the coffeemaker, there was nothing to do but face him. She couldn't even offer him a place to sit.

"This place is insane," Keefe said, looking around. "I mean, in a good way."

"Thanks," Summer said. "I know it's not for everybody, but I think it'll be great for me."

"Yeah," Keefe said, smiling. "A house on wheels. Ready to roll out at a moment's notice."

She was about to protest, but had to admit, that was a pretty accurate description.

The coffeemaker sputtered to a stop. She knew he took his coffee black. Should she pretend she'd forgotten? While she was deciding, Keefe reached around her and took the cup himself. He was so close, she could see a small nick from his morning shave. She was dizzy with him standing so close. She closed her eyes, and by the time she opened them, he was looking out the front window.

"I'm really glad you're here," Keefe said, without turning from the window.

"You are?"

You are?

"Yeah," he said, facing her. "Zach would be so happy you were living up here on the hill. He loved it up here."

"I know," Summer said. "And I hope you're right. I hope Grandpa would be happy I'm here."

"Why wouldn't he?"

"I guess because..." she wasn't sure what to say. "Because when he died, so many things were...unresolved."

"I don't think Zach was unresolved," Keefe said. "He understood you were starting a new life. He was proud that you went out and made something of yourself."

"I hope you're right," Summer said, looking into her inky coffee.

Especially since the two of you made me go.

"Sun's almost up," he said, finishing his coffee and putting his cup on the counter. "I'd better be heading out to work."

"I'm going with you," she said.

Keefe looked so surprised, she found herself stuttering.

"I mean," she continued, "Queenie did call me to say there was trouble at the bakery."

"I told you there wasn't."

"But it's Queenie's bakery."

"Meaning it's *your* bakery?"

"No!" she said. But then, upon reflection, said, "Well, yes. I guess."

"I don't understand why we're even discussing this," Keefe said. "Let's just go ask Queenie what she was talking about."

"That's fine with me," Summer said.

Neither wanted to confront Queenie, especially when she was acting so weird. They glared at each other.

"Do you want to go with me to town," Keefe said. "Or drive in yourself?"

Just the thought of riding behind Keefe on his motorcycle made her dizzy. Memories came roaring back. She remembered riding behind him on his ancient Honda Nighthawk 450, flying through town and into the hills. She relished everything about those trips: the wind, and this being Washington, the rain on her hair; the disapproval of the older townspeople; her arms around Keefe's waist. She would think: *I'm such a badass!*

Queenie had never liked the idea of a motorcycle.

"Those things are dangerous," Queenie said as Summer raced off the porch to meet Keefe. "You're going to get hurt!"

Queenie proved right, even though it had nothing to do with the motorcycle.

Summer told Keefe that she really wanted to bring Shortie to town, so she couldn't possibly hop on the back of his bike. She'd take her truck and meet him at the bakery. It wasn't easy to hide behind a seven-pound wiener dog but Summer managed.

As she headed into town, she shot a look at Shortie, strapped in his car seat. He looked back at her, the tip of his tongue hanging out, the picture of innocence. She didn't feel like a badass now.

I'm such a coward!

Chapter 18

It was disconcerting to be back in town before dawn. In the daylight, it was clear the town had moved through time, but the building silhouettes looked just as they had the day she left. The shadows seem to have memories all their own. Big Red's tires crunched loudly on the asphalt, the only sound on the street. As Summer got Shortie out of the back, she could see a light coming from the bakery. She looked through the window. The front of the shop was empty, but the sweet, promising smell rising like yeast meant Keefe was already at work in the kitchen. She stood still, holding onto Shortie, afraid if she lost her grip on him she'd be sucked back in time. She wondered if that would be so bad—to discover love and have her grandfather back.

To have all that heartache ahead of me? No thank you!

"This is why I stayed away!" she hissed at Shortie, as if he had asked.

She wondered if the door would be open. As a teenager, she's begged her grandparents for her own key. Queenie refused.

"This is a business, Summer," Queenie said. "Keys can't be handed out to everybody who wants one."

"That's right," Grandpa Zach would chime in. "We turn away thousands of people demanding keys to the bakery. A croissant and a key, please!"

Queenie won, as always, but Keefe managed to get around the rule by leaving the door open for her once he got to work. She shook her head at the thought. Queenie might have been a little too prudent refusing to give her own granddaughter a key, but leaving the place open before business hours was just crazy. Still, she couldn't resist. She took a deep breath and tried the knob. The door was open.

Keefe had remembered.

Summer wondered if she should turn around and go back to the caboose. She didn't owe Keefe Devlin anything. But then, why was she even in Washington if not to sort out what was going on at the bakery? She put Shortie on the ground, feeling rebellious that she'd forgotten his therapy jacket, and pushed open the door to the shop. If driving into town brought back memories, stepping through the threshold felt like stepping into her past.

Everyone said places that were important in your childhood looked smaller than you remembered. It was true. Summer felt like Gulliver as she looked around the café and counter section of the bakery. It had loomed so large in her life and had taken on an almost mystical aura over the years. The glass cases, the assortment of small tables and wrought iron chairs, the white towers of paper boxes behind the counter, all seemed shrunken.

But the pastries…they were still the foodstuff of which dreams are made. When Summer walked out the door ten years ago, Queenie was still the monarch of the pastry shelves. A tray of Napoleons, stuffed with clouds of whipped cream and thinly sliced strawberries had already been set in a place of honor in the front display case. Keefe had obviously been a good apprentice.

What was going on with Queenie? No matter how hard it was going to be, she needed to find out what was going on. While she wasn't quite ready to confront her formidable grandmother, perhaps she and Keefe could be civil enough to each other long enough to figure out a game plan or an approach.

The case was still mostly empty. It was a Murray tradition that all baked goods be made daily and it was still very early. Summer could hear the oven doors opening and closing in the back of the store. She sniffed the air—French bread and something with cinnamon was being created back there. As hesitant as she was to work alongside Keefe in such a small space, there was no resisting the sweet temptations of the kitchen. It suddenly occurred to her that Keefe must have been holding down the fort completely alone since Queenie bailed on the bakery. Summer's heart went out to him; running a bakery by yourself was nearly a super-human feat!

A knock on the front window startled her. It was barely dawn! She whipped round to see Mrs. Pendergrass, from Pendergrass's Coffee Shop standing at the window. Mrs. Pendergrass waved and opened the door.

I should have locked the door behind me.

Mrs. Pendergrass was as nosey as Mr. Caleb, without the excuse of being a reporter. Summer realized she needed to smile. Like it or not, Summer was a representative of her family. Coming across as a scowling teenager would not do. What if Queenie heard? Summer had to keep reminding herself that she was an adult. That image of herself kept slipping.

"Hi, Mrs. Pendergrass," Summer said, bending over to receive the older woman's hug.

It was difficult, not only because Mrs. Pendergrass had shrunk at least four inches since Summer had been in Cat's Paw, but she was balancing two mugs of coffee.

"How have you been?" Summer said, as Mrs. Pendergrass pushed her way into the room.

"I don't know if your grandmother told you, but I have bursitis, and osteoporosis and a touch of arthritis," Mrs. Pendergrass said. "Can't complain."

Can't complain?

"I brought you a cup of coffee from the shop," Mrs. Pendergrass said, looking around the bakery.

"That's very sweet of you," Summer said, reverting against her will to the eighteen-year-old who left Cat's Paw. "But you know, we have coffee right here."

"Oh, I know," Mrs. Pendergrass said, putting the steaming mug in Summer's hands. "But I didn't want you to go to the trouble of brewing it on your first day back."

"That's very kind of you."

Now please leave.

Mrs. Pendergrass took a seat at one of the café tables and sipped at her coffee. Apparently, she was going to settle in for a chat. Summer didn't know what to do. She knew Grandpa Zach would have just sucked it up and humored her, and Queenie would have thrown her out. Summer thought it would be best to emulate her grandmother. Summer needed to let the town know that she was no pushover. And she should start with Mrs. Pendergrass.

Who am I kidding?

She sat down at the table. Summer wanted to smack the triumphant look off Mrs. Pendergrass's face.

Maybe Queenie was ornery for a reason.

"I was so surprised when I saw that tiny house being pulled into town yesterday," Mrs. Pendergrass said. "You could have knocked me over with a feather when I saw it was you driving that thing! Of course, I couldn't even get near you, you drew such a crowd. You surprised the whole town!"

"I don't even know the whole town anymore," Summer said, not sure if she was deflecting a compliment or a complaint.

"I guess Keefe is already hard at work," Mrs. Pendergrass said, looking at the kitchen door.

"He is," Summer said, not believing her luck. She had the perfect out! "And I really need to go help him. We've got a big day ahead of us."

"Why?" Mrs. Pendergrass asked.

"Why?"

"Yes," Mrs. Pendergrass said. "Why is this a big day?"

"Because..." Summer was at a loss for words. "Because, as you just said, this is my first day back. I'm probably rusty."

"You probably are," Mrs. Pendergrass agreed. "But that doesn't really matter. Keefe has it covered. He's a hard worker."

"He is," Summer agreed, although she really wasn't in a position to know this, not to mention she didn't want to be singing his praises.

He dumped me!

"He's such a good boy," Mrs. Pendergrass continued.

"He has his moments," was all Summer could muster.

"He's been just great running the place since Queenie..." Mrs. Pendergrass's voice trailed off.

"Since Queenie what?"

"Since Queenie stopped coming to town a few months ago."

"It's been *months*?" Summer asked.

"Didn't you know?" Mrs. Pendergrass's eyes widened in mock surprise. "Of course you didn't. You didn't stay in touch."

Summer needed to remain calm. Perhaps Mrs. Pendergrass knew what was going on.

"I'm here now, aren't I?" Summer said.

"So you are," Mrs. Pendergrass said, patting Summer's hand. "So. You. Are."

Mrs. Pendergrass continued to look around the bakery, shooting her eyes toward the kitchen from time to time, whenever Keefe so much as rattled a pan. Why was she so interested in the goings on at the bakery? Surely there was more interesting gossip in town.

"Are you going to replace Keefe as manager?" Mrs. Pendergrass asked suddenly.

Keefe was manager? Of Dough Z Dough? Summer bristled. She knew it was a knee-jerk response. What was her grandmother supposed to do? Make her the manager from three thousand miles away?

"Nothing has been decided yet," Summer said. "I think right now, we'll just work together."

"Oh, that's sweet," Mrs. Pendergrass giggled. "Just like the old days."

Summer breathed in. This old bag really knew how to get under her skin. Suddenly, Mrs. Pendergrass let out a squeak and leapt out of her seat.

"Something touched my leg!" she shrieked.

Mrs. Pendergrass and Summer looked at the floor. Shortie was standing beside Mrs. Pendergrass, waiting for attention.

"What is that?" Mrs. Pendergrass said, pointing at the dog.

"That's Shortie," Summer said. "He's a Dachshund-Chihuahua mix."

"He's not supposed to be in the store," Mrs. Pendergrass said. "There are rules..."

"He's a therapy dog," Summer said, grateful she'd made Shortie legal. "I just forgot his paperwork and vest. I can bring them over to the coffee shop tomorrow. Shortie and I would love to come visit."

"That won't be necessary," Mrs. Pendergrass said, visibly paling at the thought of a dog in her shop. "Welcome back, Summer."

Mrs. Pendergrass gathered up the coffee cups and headed to the door. Summer watched her go. For an old woman with bursitis, osteoporosis, and a touch of arthritis, that woman could *move*!

"You know she's going to be telling all her customers that she spent the morning with you, right?" Keefe's voice interrupted her thoughts.

She turned to face him. He was standing in the doorway, a crisp white apron covering his clothes, pulled tautly over his waist. His shirt sleeves were rolled up. Summer could see he'd developed the muscular forearms of a serious baker.

A man who used his hands.

"Why would anybody care that she spent time with *me*?" Summer asked, turning around to face him.

"Bragging rights," Keefe said. "For all the changes, this is still a small town. Everybody's pretty curious about you."

"I think I'll keep my distance," Summer said. She smiled. "Keep the mystery alive."

"Why change now?" Keefe said.

Summer's smile faded. She realized there still seemed to be activity in the kitchen.

"Have you gotten some help?" Summer asked.

"Yes," Keefe said, furrowing his brow. "It would have been impossible to do all the morning baking by myself."

"I'm not criticizing you," Summer said. "I was just asking!"

"Hi Summer," Evie said, sticking her head out of the kitchen.

Summer tried not to gasp.

"Evie. This is a surprise."

Truer words were never, *ever* spoken. It was obvious that Mrs. Pendergrass did know where the hot gossip was in Cat's Paw.

"Oh, I've just been lending a hand," Evie said, wiping her hands on a Dough Z Dough apron and coming into the bakery. "I need cookies for my ice cream sandwiches and cake for my ice cream cakes, so you could call it self-preservation."

That's not what I'd call it.

"That was very thoughtful of you," Summer said. "But I'm here now. We'll make sure you get your cookies."

"And cake," Evie said.

What was it Evie had said? "Cake and ice cream, natural allies?" But Summer preferred to keep her ice cream and cake separate.

The two women stared at each other, but one of them was trespassing. Without a word, Evie took off her apron, handing it to Keefe.

"I'll need two dozen extra-large chocolate chip cookies and a full vanilla sheet cake by noon," Evie said to Keefe.

"Uh...thanks," Keefe said, looking at the apron in his hand as Evie stormed out of the shop.

"What just happened?" Keefe asked.

"Shall we get to work?" Summer said, suddenly all business.

"Sure," Keefe said, standing back so Summer and Shortie could precede him into the kitchen. "Do you remember how to make Nanaimo Bars?"

Summer smiled to herself. The Nanaimo Bar was a complex layered bar named after the west coast city of Nanaimo, British Columbia, and was a favorite across the Pacific Northwest. Time consuming and consisting of a lot of ingredients, the bar required skill in the kitchen. When done correctly, the Nanaimo Bar was a wafer crumb-based layer topped by a lavish spread of custard icing which in turn is covered with melted chocolate. She knew Keefe was testing her, but what *he* didn't know was that Summer had made the bars for the Christmas party every year at the insurance company to much acclaim.

"I haven't thought about those bars in years," Summer said, pulling a white apron from a shelf and tying it rather aggressively around her waist. "But I think I can handle it."

Game on!

Chapter 19

Summer and Keefe worked side by side for a few hours without saying a word but were aware of each other's every move. Summer wondered if Keefe really needed to touch her waist as he slipped by her to retrieve the butter. She wondered if *she* could have scooted past him on the way to the whisk without touching his arm.

Summer remembered seeing an interview online with a singer who was publicizing her ubiquitous "duets" album. The singer said she loved doing duets because it made you competitive in the very best way: each of you trying to outdo the other. The results were usually inspiring! By the time Keefe was ready to flip over the OPEN sign, Summer was fairly certain it had been years since the glass display cases held such an assortment of perfect breads, cookies, and pastries. The Napoleons held the place of pride, but Summer nudged them over to display her Nanaimo Bars.

"Too bad Queenie is giving this place the cold shoulder," Keefe said. "She'd be impressed with those Nanaimo Bars."

Summer took that to mean *he* was impressed with them.

"We'll…I mean…*I'll* take one home to her," Summer said.

"Won't matter," Keefe shook his head. "She won't eat it. She throws away anything I bring from town."

Summer pursed her lips. She'd been doing online research about personality changes in seniors. Of course, there were the terrifying possibilities: cancer, dementia, a brain injury. All risks, but Summer was hoping for a more benign diagnosis. One interesting report stated that people reaching their senior years tended to reevaluate what's important in life. They worked on changing themselves instead of other people. This was the sort of evaluation to which Summer could cling. But she had to admit, Queenie didn't seem to be giving up working on others, especially Summer.

Celia Bonaduce

Maybe she could poke around Queenie's computer and see if there were any medical records or current searches offering clues. She might even try some old-fashioned sleuthing: looking in the medicine chest or speaking to Queenie's doctor.

Anything but ask her.

Summer felt lost without her grandfather. Grandpa Zach would know what to do. Another twinge of remorse struck Summer. She had wasted so much time. She stole a look at Keefe as he went to open the front door. She used to wonder if she should have let her grandfather come between them. Should she have intervened as soon as she knew there was an issue? Now she wondered if she should have let Keefe interfere with her precious relationship with her grandfather.

It was too late in any event. Summer snapped back to the present as the bakery doors swung open. The entire town seemed to turn out. She was greeted by old-timers singing the old refrain of "You've grown up" and newcomers who were curious about the tiny house. All of them were sorry that Queenie was not back at the store. Summer was touched by their concern, although their expressions of concern were transparent.

"I don't see your grandmother," said a man Summer didn't know but who obviously knew Queenie.

"She's up at the house," Summer said.

She realized this man might not know anything about Queenie. Just because someone bought bread at your store didn't mean he had any insight into your life.

"We have a little farm over…" Summer began.

"Flat Top Farm" the man said. "Everybody in town knows about Flat Top Farm. Your grandmother is an institution around here. Don't tell her I said that. She thinks that makes her sound old."

"I won't," Summer said. "I promise."

Especially since I don't know who you are.

"Did you make these?" asked Mrs. Dodson, eating a butter cookie (which Summer *had* made). Mrs. Dodson owned the general store – and had for as long as Summer could remember. "You've got your grandmother's touch. Where is she?"

"I thought Queenie would be here to see her granddaughter take over the helm," Mr. Caleb said.

"I'm not sure I am taking over the helm," Summer said as she bagged two Nanaimo Bars, a loaf of French bread, and twelve chocolate meringue cookies for him.

She was aware Keefe was listening to every word. Was that why he was being so testy with her? Was he afraid she was going to take over the bakery, which he saw as his? She tried to work up a killer outrage, but in all honesty, he had been doing the bakery's heavy lifting for years.

She'd never really thought about the succession of the bakery before. Summer had always assumed it would go to her father, who had no interest in the bakery, and then to her, who did have an interest in the bakery but more of an interest in Keefe. Her grandfather had to have used some sort of supremely enticing bait to make Keefe turn his back on her. Or did he? Keefe seemed to be doing just fine with the younger women in Cat's Paw, who seemed to lingering at the cash register, where Keefe was stationed. She had to admit, he was more at home here than she was.

And whose fault was that?

By noon, the shelves were so bare, they would have disappointed an ant colony. Summer was happy she'd put away a few chocolate meringues for herself. Keefe turned the sign back to read: Closed. With a bakery the size of Dough Z Dough, hours were irregular. Summer was used to her grandparents returning to Flat Top Farm in the early afternoon many times, but she couldn't remember ever selling out before lunchtime. But she'd been gone a long time.

"Is it always like this?" she asked.

"We stay busy," Keefe shrugged. "But today was crazy. I'm not sure if more people were interested in getting the scoop on Queenie or getting the scoop on you and your tiny house. But whatever it was, it worked for us."

For us?

"I didn't know Evie was back in town," Summer said.

"With a vengeance," Keefe said. He headed out the back door with a bag of trash.

What did that mean?

Summer went back to the kitchen. She gave Shortie a few doggie treats and the remains of a slightly burnt sugar cookie. He'd been very good about staying in the kitchen. She realized with a start that she hadn't checked her phone in hours—a rarity for her. But she'd been so busy, it hadn't even occurred to her. She tried to Facebook-stalk Evie, but Evie had a private account. Nothing very important to be read on Twitter or seen on Instagram. She tried to resist searching eBay, but couldn't help herself. She logged on and typed in: M'Laitest. A new crop of her own possessions popped up. She had to give it to Lynnie, she was making some serious money on these hand-me-downs. The nerve! Summer logged off the website and was scrolling through her contacts to find Lynnie. That's when she heard the back door slam. She stuffed her phone in her back pocket as Keefe came back into the room.

"It's good to have you back, Summer," Keefe said. "I've missed you."

She looked at him. He said it so casually. If he'd meant it in any meaningful way, would he be smiling like that? She had no idea where she stood with him or where she wanted to stand with him. And what about Evie?

For that matter, what about the fate of the bakery? And her grandmother? There was so much to wade through right now.

Keefe walked toward her, his look very serious.

"I mean it, Summer," he said. "It just feels right having you back."

"Really?" Summer said. "You seemed to be getting along just fine with Evie."

"I could never have kept the bakery going without her," Keefe said. "You know this is not a one-man job."

Summer knew she was in no position to ask what Keefe's relationship with Evie was. She could read the intent in Evie, but when she looked in Keefe's eyes, she saw something else entirely.

Summer's heart was pounding. Shortie seemed to realize something was up, because he started barking. She looked down to tell him everything was okay. The last thing she needed was for her dog to attack the man of her long-ago dreams.

But Shortie was not barking at Keefe. He was barking at the man standing in the doorway of the kitchen.

It was Bale.

Chapter 20

"I hope I'm not interrupting anything," Bale said.

"Bale!" Summer said. "No, of course you're not interrupting."

"Hey Shortie," Bale said as the dog came over to check him out. "Remember me?"

Summer's feet finally started to move. She met him at the doorway and gave him a hug.

"What a surprise," she said, keeping her back to Keefe. "I thought the Tiny House Convention wasn't till next week."

"It isn't," Bale said. "But these shows don't produce themselves. Vendors need some time to set everything up. My tinies are all at the fairgrounds, but I had some time to kill so I came up to Cat's Paw. You made it sound pretty interesting."

"Did I?" Summer stammered. "I mean, I did! It is!"

Keefe cleared his throat. Summer and Bale turned to him.

"It's a great place," Keefe said, heading toward them with his hand outstretched. "So, by process of elimination, I'm guessing you're the guy who made the caboose?"

"That would be me," Bale said.

The men shook hands.

Summer hadn't thought the two men would burst into some sort of fertility dance, but there didn't seem to be the slightest sign of a struggle for male dominance. Summer was disappointed. One minute she thought both men craved her, the next, she worried that neither of them did.

"Can I get you some coffee?" Summer asked. "We had a busy morning, but I have a few burnt sugar cookies left."

"How could he refuse an offer like that?" Keefe said, gesturing that they should all go back into the bakery's showroom. "I'll make the coffee."

All the men, Bale, Keefe, and Shortie went into the bakery while Summer scratched off the offending edges of the sugar cookies. The bakery phone rang. Summer looked to the wall where the phone had always hung. It wasn't there.

Just another little cosmic sign that everything changes.

She looked around for the source of the ring, finally locating a small, inexpensive cordless phone. She knew she was a technology snob, and made a note to get a new phone soon.

"Hello?" Summer said, the words her grandfather taught her to say coming back without her realizing she hadn't said them in over a decade. "Dough Z Dough. What's cookin'?"

She cringed. She had never realized what horrible dialogue that was! Not to mention, they were *baking* at Dough Z Dough, not *cooking*!

"Summer?" a voice said from the other end of the phone. "You might not remember me. Gina?"

Gina? Just Gina? But then she realized she did know Gina. She was a woman about her grandmother's age. If you could say that Queenie had a best friend, Gina would have the designation. Summer had always called her...

"Aunt Gina?" Summer said.

"I didn't want to introduce myself as Aunt Gina," Gina said. "I mean, you're a grown woman now."

Summer wasn't sure what to say. Did she not want to be called "Aunt" by a grown woman? Or did she not want to force the moniker on Summer? Why was everything so complicated in this small town?

"I stopped over this morning, but the bakery was packed," Gina said.

"I guess you were hoping to see Queenie," Summer said, knowing this phone call was just another attempt by a concerned friend to figure out what was going on.

"And to see you," Gina said. "I was so happy when I heard you were back. Are you staying?"

"Yes," Summer said, surprising herself. "I mean, no, well, yes—for a while. But I've got places I need to be."

Catching a glimpse of her distorted bag, she decided not to go into details about her future in felted purses.

"It's good to have you back for any amount of time," Gina said. "I'm sure Queenie is thrilled. By the way..."

Here it comes.

"How is she doing up there at the house?"

Summer didn't know what to say. She couldn't say Queenie was fine; she obviously wasn't. But she wasn't sick. Should she tell Queenie's closest friend that Queenie seemed healthy but weird?

"She's…" Summer began, "she's Queenie."

"Ain't that the truth," Gina chuckled.

The call ended with promises of getting together soon. Summer stacked the cookies on a white dish, arranging them as best she could to hide the brown ends, and carried them into the bakery. No one, not even Shortie, was there. She could smell the coffee, and could see a drop of spilled cream and two torn sugar packets, so she knew they'd been there. She looked out the window. Bale had brought one of his tiny houses with him. At least she thought it was a tiny house. He was standing in front of an apparently converted school bus. She watched him as he fielded questions from interested onlookers, finally opening the door and letting people step inside. If the attention he was getting, not to mention the curiosity the country had shown her in her trek across America, was any indication, the Tiny House Convention was sure to be a big hit.

Summer put the cookies down. Queenie would throw a fit if she thought Summer would let less than perfect Dough Z Dough cookies out of the bakery. She closed the door behind her and stood by Keefe, who was sitting on his motorcycle with Shortie in his lap, sipping his coffee and watching Bale.

"Do you guys draw a crowd everywhere you go?"

"Actually," Summer said, "we do."

Summer studied the school bus. This was a new design. She'd only seen tinies on trailers at his lot. She was impressed Bale didn't go the clichéd psychedelic-flowers route. The bus was painted a deep green. She thought the color could only be described as shiny olive. Bale did keep things interesting.

"I'll watch Shortie, if you want to go check it out," Keefe said.

"That's okay," Summer said, shoving her hands in her jeans pockets.

She hoped the gesture said: "I'm a woman of the tiny-world and a converted school bus is no big deal." She felt at home by Keefe's side. If she went to see the bus, would that signal her solidarity with Bale? Did she have solidarity with Bale? Would Keefe be threatened? Would that be a bad thing?

"You sure?" Keefe asked.

"I'm sure," Summer said, smiling at him.

"Okay," Keefe said, handing Shortie to her. "Then I'll go. I think you guys are all nuts, but…"

Keefe's voice trailed off as he walked toward the crowd surrounding the bus.

Summer didn't need him to finish his thought. The idea of living in less than three hundred square feet seemed to ignite the imagination of so many people. There were some who looked longingly at the caboose and said, "I think I could live like this." They did so in almost a whisper, as if to say the words out loud would be daring the cosmos to take away all their hard-won stuff. Almost everyone she met on the road had a love-hate relationship with their stuff; even people already living in tiny houses were trying to figure out how to declutter. The appeal to others was the concept of getting out from under debt. Life without an insanely huge house payment would be so much simpler. Of course, Summer also met a lot of people like herself, who saw the tiny house on wheels as a gateway to a new life.

No matter what the motivation, a tiny house signaled one thing: freedom.

As she watched Keefe disappear into the bus, she wondered, *What about this lifestyle appeals to him?* Her heart started racing as it occurred to her that he might be just like her, seeing the mobile existence as a way to start a new life. Although she'd done a valiant job of boycotting Cat's Paw for years, she never pictured the town without Keefe. Even as she wrapped her head around the idea that Grandpa Zach was gone, Keefe remained a constant.

Did Keefe want his own freedom?

Was freedom just escape in disguise?

Was it possible Keefe wanted out of the bakery?

Questions came at her fast and furiously. Had he discussed this with Queenie, and that was the trouble the bakery was in? Was Queenie staying away to prove to him how valuable he was? Was she just pretending to have forgotten how to bake to guilt him into staying? Summer would not put that past her grandmother. She almost dismissed the notion. Why would Queenie be reconfiguring old family recipes if she was pretending to have lost her touch? The answer came to her in an instant. Boredom! Queenie was a woman of perpetual motion; staying at the house must be driving her crazy. Summer thought of another possibility: Queenie asked Summer to come back because she wanted to signal the bakery could move on in spite of Keefe's impending desertion.

It was only a theory, but the pieces fit.

If she were right, it meant Queenie wasn't sick. Summer was warming to this idea more and more.

Summer blinked as she realized Keefe and Bale were walking toward her, a ribbon of townspeople still pulling themselves up and into the bus.

Shortie squirmed in her arms and she put him on the ground. When he was excited, the dog would wag his entire frame. As he ran, his long body would curve in the middle, so his tail was almost parallel with his ears. It was quite a form of locomotion, but he still managed to propel himself toward the men. Summer wondered to whom he would run. Shortie barreled into Keefe's legs. He barked and Keefe picked him up.

If only it were this easy to make a choice.

"The bus is pretty cool," Keefe said.

"I'm unveiling it at the road show," Bale said, looking at Summer. "You should come to the show."

He wanted her to come to Seattle with him! She could feel her cheeks turning pink. The fact that he was asking her in front of Keefe was too tasty. This was a fantasy she wouldn't dare have dreamed, it was so perfect.

"I'd love to," Summer said.

"And you too," Bale said to Keefe, reaching into his jacket pocket. "Here's a ticket for the road show."

Summer felt she'd been slapped. When would she learn? She really needed to give up on fantasies.

"I think you'll get some ideas," Bale said to Keefe.

Ideas? What kind of ideas? Did Keefe confide to Bale he was planning on leaving?

"Sounds good," Keefe said. "We'd have to come in the evening after the bakery closes."

"No problem," Bale said. "Floor is open till nine."

"Alright then," Keefe said. He turned to Summer. "Bale was going to the campground for the night, but I figured he might as well park up at Flat Top Farm. We've got plenty of land."

"It's no problem to head over to the campground," Bale said.

"I told him I couldn't really invite him myself, since it's not my property," Keefe said, scowling at Summer's perceived lack of hospitality. "But I figured it wouldn't be a big deal."

"No, of course it's fine," Summer said. "We've got plenty of room and I'm sure Queenie would love to see the bus."

Would she?

Evie sashayed up to Bale.

"That bus is just awesome," she gushed.

"Thanks," Bale said. "I'm still road testing it, but it's getting there."

"I'd be happy to help you road test it!" Evie giggled. "I could give you lots of feedback."

Summer rolled her eyes. Keefe might be a local boy, but Bale was a man of the world. Evie would have to up her game if she hoped to get his attention.

"Hey," Bale said, again reaching into his jacket and pulling out another ticket. "I was just telling these two that they should drive down for the show. You should come, too."

Or not.

Chapter 21

Keefe, Summer, and Bale caravanned to Flat Top Farm. Keefe, the most nimble on his Fatboy, led the way. He was followed by Summer in Big Red with Bale's school bus bringing up the rear. People along the road waved to them as if they were their own parade.

Summer chewed on her bottom lip. It occurred to her that perhaps she should have asked Queenie if Bale could park on the farm. It was, after all, her property.

She shot a look in the rearview mirror. Bale had the window rolled down, his left arm casually propped on the window ledge. *Queenie isn't shy*, Summer thought. *She'll just throw Bale out if she doesn't like the looks of him.* This thought did nothing to reassure her.

The cavalcade pulled into the winding driveway. Keefe drove on to his apartment over the garage, but Summer pulled up in front of the Victorian. She didn't think it fair to leave Bale on his own while she retreated to Flat Top Hill. Queenie came out on the porch immediately, pulling open Big Red's door.

"You have a visitor," Queenie said.

"I know," Summer said. She shouldn't have been surprised that news of Bale's arrival had preceded her. It was a very small town. "I'm sorry. I should have asked if he could stay."

"He?" Queenie looked puzzled.

Bale had walked up and extended his hand.

"Hi there, you must be Queenie," Bale said. "I'm Bale Barrett."

Summer released Shortie from the back of the cab as Queenie looked over her shoulder at the Shiny Olive.

"You live in that thing?" Queenie asked.

"Yes. It's a long story," Bale said, "but a tiny house."

"How many times have you used that line?" Queenie asked.

Summer gasped.

Bale laughed.

"Now, about your visitor," Queenie turned to Summer, ignoring Bale.

"I…" Summer started, more confused than ever.

Shortie started barking and ran toward the front of the house. A woman came out onto the porch, Shortie's tail wagged furiously as he crab-walked toward her. Shortie seemed to know this visitor, but because the woman was in shadow, Summer couldn't make out if it was someone she knew.

"Hey, Shortie," came a voice Summer knew instantly.

"Lynnie?" Summer squeaked.

Queenie arched one eyebrow.

Summer was gobsmacked. How did Lynnie have the nerve to show up after stealing all Summer's possessions?

Well, okay, not stealing…

"Admit it," Lynnie commanded as she came off the porch, Shortie at her heels. "You can't believe your eyes!"

"I admit it," Summer said, grateful for a polite way to phrase her feelings.

"I was just telling your Grammaw," Lynnie said.

"Queenie," Queenie said, adding in a stronger voice, "please."

"I was just telling *Queenie*," Lynnie said, "that I took all the stuff you left at the apartment and put it on eBay!"

Summer wasn't sure what to make of this confession. Lynnie was beaming smugly, not acting contrite. Was Lynnie asking forgiveness or bragging?

"What do you know about that?" Summer responded.

"I thought to myself, I'm going to sell all this crap online and buy myself a plane ticket to Washington." Lynnie looked at Queenie, who was glowering at her. "I thought you might need to see a friendly face."

It was quiet as everyone looked at each other. Lynnie broke the silence.

"Surprise!" she said, but her voice lost its confidence.

Summer realized Lynnie's heart was in the right place, even though it was a very weird gesture.

"I'm Bale Barrett," Bale said, joining the conversation.

He put out his hand to shake. Lynnie took it excitedly.

"The man who builds the tiny houses?" Lynnie gasped, as if meeting a rock star. "What are you doing here?"

"Same as you," Bale said, smiling. "Coming to visit without an invitation."

Lynnie seemed to think this was funny, rather than an awkward truth. She slapped at him playfully. Bale turned to Queenie.

"Summer was kind enough to offer my rig and me a place on the farm," Bale said. "But it looks like your hands are full. I can head down to the campground..."

"Don't be silly," Summer said, surprised that she found her voice. "We have plenty of room. Don't we, Queenie?"

Bale, Lynnie, and Summer all turned to the matriarch of Flat Top Farm. She stared back at them defiantly. While Queenie was a stickler for niceties such as table manners, etiquette often went right out the window if she felt she was being challenged. Summer held her breath.

"Over five acres," Queenie said. "I'm sure we can spare a patch of earth."

"That's very kind of you," Bale said. "I keep a small footprint, I promise."

"Not with those monster bus tires," Queenie said. "But you're welcome to stay anyway."

Summer exhaled.

"Is that the caboose?" Lynnie asked.

Everyone's attention turned toward Flat Top Hill. The sun was just setting. The tiny house perched on the plateau with the blazing orange sun behind it looked like something out of a postcard. Bale took out his phone and snapped a picture of it. Even though he'd designed it, Summer felt a swell of pride.

"Let's go look at it," Lynnie said, pulling at Summer's arm. "I can't believe I'm finally here!"

"Me either," Summer said, looking sheepishly at Queenie.

"I'm going back in the house," Queenie said. "The *real* house. There's not enough room up there for all of us anyway."

"You can leave the bus here for now, if you want to see the caboose," Summer said to Bale.

Bale shot a look at Queenie, as if for permission. Queenie nodded slightly. Summer saw Queenie trying to suppress a smile. Bale clearly was going to fall into line.

Queenie certainly had a way with people. Not a winning way, but she definitely had her own style.

Summer left Big Red in the driveway and ushered Bale, Lynnie, and Shortie up the hill. Lynnie was out of breath by the time they'd reached the caboose.

"We must be pretty high in the mountains." Lynnie gasped. "The air is so thin!"

"We're only about six hundred feet above sea level," Summer said.

"That's 550 feet more than Hartford," Lynnie said, leaning against the caboose and gasping.

Summer studied Bale as she waited for Lynnie to catch her breath. He ran his hand along the side of the caboose in a way that made Summer almost agree with Lynnie; the air seemed very thin.

"Okay." Lynnie's chirpy voice broke into Summer's thoughts. "Let's see what you've got here."

As Summer approached the front stairs, Shortie shot in front of her. He may not have learned how to navigate the circular staircase inside, but he was a champ at getting in and out of the tiny house. Summer opened the door.

"Wow," Lynnie said as she followed Summer inside, "it's tiny."

"That's why they're called tiny houses," Bale offered.

"I know," Lynnie said, looking around. "But still..."

"The grand tour doesn't take very long," Summer said, without moving from her spot. She pointed out the kitchen area, the bathroom, opened the door to the walk-in closet and the staircase to the loft. "Feel free to take a look."

Lynnie went into the bathroom.

"It feels strange giving someone a tour of this place," Summer said to Bale as Lynnie looked around. "It seems as if you should be doing the honors."

"Not anymore," Bale said. "I relinquish all claim to the tinies once they're off the lot."

Summer was vaguely disappointed in this answer. She was hoping they would bond passionately over the caboose. She wondered if all the women who bought one of *Bale's Tiny Dreams* felt that way.

"That bathtub looks like one of those things horses drink out of," Lynnie said as she squeezed by them on the way to the walk-in closet.

"It is," Bale and Summer said together.

They grinned at each other.

"That's just gross," Lynnie said. "Why would you ever want to take a bath in a bucket slimed by a horse?"

"It's called a trough," Bale said. "And it's new."

"Then what's the point?" Lynnie asked absently as she disappeared into the closet.

"You either get it or you don't" Bale said to Summer.

"This closet is amazing!" Lynnie's voice came drifting out. "Can I go up the staircase?"

Bale opened his mouth, then shut it again.

He gestured for Summer to field the question.

"Sure," Summer said.

"Sorry," Bale said. "Old habits die hard."

Summer shrugged her shoulders and smiled. She was secretly thrilled he hadn't relinquished ownership completely.

"You've done a great job," Bale said. "Usually it takes a while to find your stride. Most people pack too much stuff into the place and it becomes claustrophobic."

"I did my research," Summer said with some bravado.

She didn't remind him she'd been on the road and hadn't really settled in. Let him be impressed with her restraint.

Shortie had curled up in the bottom kitchen cubby which he'd made his own. He'd figured out early how to stay out of the way. Summer could hear the sound of Lynnie winding her way down the circular staircase.

"Pretty tight up there," Lynnie said, rubbing her forehead. "I hit my head."

"You get over that," Summer said.

Summer's phone vibrated in her pocket. She picked it up. There was a text from Queenie.

"It's from my grandmother," Summer said. "I didn't know she even knew how to text."

"I showed her this afternoon," Lynnie said. "She's a pretty fast learner for a senior."

"It's a very long text! She says..." Summer said. She started reading out loud: "I spent ten minutes trying to text this there should be a comma here but oh well period dinner is ready, and I should invert both of you."

"I think she means invite," Lynnie said, looking at the text over Summer's shoulder. "I taught her how to use that little microphone thingy."

"It's called voice recognition," Summer said.

It annoyed her when people didn't have the proper respect for technology.

"You can count me in!" Bale said. "Everybody in town said Queenie is the best baker in the Pacific Northwest."

Summer's heart ached. She didn't want Bale to get his hopes up, considering what was going on. She switched gears.

"Lynnie," Summer said. "I forgot you're gluten free! I have no idea what—"

"We covered that too," Lynnie said, waving her hand dismissively. "She said she'd make a nice enchilada pie. Corn chips are my new best friend."

Summer texted back that they would be down in a few minutes. She kept the text short, so her grandmother didn't have to reply. Why tempt fate?

Shortie, with his keen sense of smell, was the first at the door. Summer led the two guests down the hill. Lynnie stumbled a few times and Bale took her arm. Summer tried not to be jealous. She was fairly sure Bale had no interest in Lynnie, who was probably old enough to be his mother, but she envied Lynnie's easy coquettishness. This was not a skill one would pick up spending summers with Queenie.

Andre met them at the porch.

"There's my big boy," Lynnie said, giving the dog a resounding smack on both ribs.

"This is Andre," Summer said.

"Oh, we're old friends," Lynnie said. "Aren't we, Handsome? I just love big dogs."

"Me, too," Bale said, giving the Great Dane's head a tussle. "Hello, Andre. You are one fine looking dog!"

Summer felt defensive. She scooped Shortie up and kissed him on his needle nose. Even through the eyes of love, Shortie could never be described as fine looking.

Keefe was already in the kitchen, the table set and the wine decanted.

"Smells awfully good in here," Bale said. "Anything I can do to help?"

"I think we're all set," Keefe said, while Queenie pulled the casserole out of the oven.

"Beer?" Keefe asked Bale, as if these two newcomers came to dinner every night.

"Sounds good," Bale said.

"Queenie says you can't have beer," Keefe said to Lynnie, as he handed Bale a beer and a glass stein. "We have cider or wine…"

"Bless your heart," Lynnie said. "Wine is just perfect."

"I'll have wine as well," Summer said, feeling suddenly shy having a hard cider with Bale in front of others.

"Everybody sit," Queenie ordered.

If Queenie had lost her mojo at the bakery, she sure still had it going on in the kitchen of her own home. The enchilada pie was perfection. Queenie had also fried up fresh tortilla chips and served them with homemade salsa and guacamole. Conversation flowed as smoothly as the wine. Summer was happy to see Queenie enjoying herself.

"I think Bale and I should clean up," Lynnie said. "I mean, all of you have been working so hard."

"Good idea, Lynnie," Bale said.

"Oh, that's alright," Summer said. "I don't mind. Bale and I can do it."

Out of the corner of her eye, she saw Keefe put down his fork. She couldn't read his expression. Had she hurt his feelings? She only meant to give him a night off. She knew Queenie had taken in the subtleties and turned to her imploringly.

"I never have my guests clean up," Queenie said.

Summer thought back. Was that even true?

"Summer and I will do it," Queenie continued. She stood up. "I wish I had some dessert, but I didn't get around to it."

"That's okay," Lynnie sighed. "Being gluten-free, I don't eat much dessert any more. There's flour in almost everything."

"But not in chocolate meringue!" Summer said, popping up from the table. "I forgot, I have a bag of them in the truck!"

Summer stood up and headed out to Big Red, Andre and Shortie at her heels. She came back with a large white bag. Queenie shot a withering glare as Summer almost put the bag on the table. She'd forgotten Queenie never allowed beer bottles, soda cans, milk cartons, or bags from the bakery to be plunked down on the table. Summer put the meringues on a plate and presented them with a flourish. As the plate made its way around the table, Summer took pride in the looks on everyone's faces as they bit into them. Summer knew she'd done a great job. The victory was bittersweet as she thought how proud she would have made her grandfather. And of course, Queenie now wouldn't touch anything from the bakery.

Summer watched her grandmother take a meringue from the plate and take a bite.

Chapter 22

Summer tried not to stare at Queenie as her grandmother chewed thoughtfully on the chocolate meringue. Didn't Keefe say her grandmother never ate anything from the bakery?

"Did you make these?" Queenie asked Keefe.

"Summer did," Keefe said.

Summer noticed that Keefe said it proudly, without a hint of competition.

"Not bad," Queenie said.

Summer smiled. That was high praise from Queenie.

"Not bad?" Lynnie sounded astonished. "These are to die for! How many gluten-free desserts do you have down there?"

"Gluten-free?" Bale asked. "That's without flour, right?"

"Right," Lynnie said. "There's more to it than that, but that's the big one. I'm still getting used to it. When Summer was in Hartford, she made me..."

"We really don't have much call for gluten-free stuff," Summer said, cutting Lynnie off.

God forbid Queenie should hear about the automatic bread maker.

"I've noticed more and more people come in asking for it, though," Keefe said. "I don't see how we'd ever get a decent Napoleon without wheat. Not to mention the cakes and breads. We might figure out a way to make a few decent cookies. But I think this is one trend we're going to have to sit out."

"It's not a trend," Lynnie said, a chill creeping into her voice. "It's helping people all over the world feel better."

Summer looked at Queenie. She was hoping a discussion about the bakery would awaken something in her, but her grandmother remained quiet. Summer once again missed Grandpa Zach. Without him to interpret Queenie, Summer was at a loss.

"It's been a long day," Bale said. "Thanks for everything. Any special place you'd like me to park the bus?"

"You can take it over by the garage," Queenie said. "Or leave it where it is. Whatever suits you."

Summer couldn't believe her ears. Queenie giving someone an option on her property was unheard of.

"I'll just stay where I am," Bale said. "Why make life complicated?"

Summer looked to Bale, to Keefe, to Lynnie, and then to her grandmother. Life couldn't *be* more complicated.

Keefe was the next to say goodnight. He was unusually subdued. Summer wanted to apologize. She was hoping for a chance to explain that she didn't mean anything by her offer to help Bale with the dishes. As Keefe stalked out of the kitchen, her mood shifted from one of remorse to annoyance. She certainly didn't owe Keefe Devlin any explanation of her actions.

Of course, he hadn't actually asked for any.

"We better get going on these dishes, Queenie said to Summer. "I'll rinse, you put them in the dishwasher?"

Summer nodded. It suddenly occurred to her that Lynnie was still sitting at the table. Summer looked on as Lynnie took the last meringue, making no move to leave. Did Lynnie expect to stay with Summer in the tiny house?

"Are you sure I can't help?" Lynnie said as she chewed.

"No, we're fine," Queenie said.

"I guess I'll turn in then," Lynnie said, getting up from the table and stretching. "I hope I was a big surprise, Summer."

"The biggest," Summer said, truthfully, still wondering how the sleeping arrangements were going to play out.

"Goodnight, then," Lynnie said, leaving the kitchen.

Summer stared after her.

"I told her she could stay here," Queenie said, rinsing a dinner plate and handing it to Summer. "As you know, I've got plenty of room."

"You didn't have to do that," Summer said.

"Oh?" Queenie said, turning off the faucet and looking at Summer. "And what was I supposed to do? She came all this way to see you."

"I know," Summer said, surprised by her grandmother's accusation. "But I had no idea she was on her way here."

Summer thought her own argument sounded pretty lame. But she had no idea what her grandmother wanted from her.

"I think Lynnie is very resourceful," Queenie said.

"Really?" Summer said, hands on hips. "She financed the trip selling my stuff."

"She said you gave it all to her."

"You think that's resourceful of Lynnie," Summer said, a tremor in her voice. "But you think me arriving with a tiny house is silly."

"I didn't say that," Queenie said.

"But you think it!" Summer said.

"I think it's silly," Queenie said, turning the faucet back on. "*And* resourceful."

At least that was something.

"I don't want to fight with you," Summer said.

"Since when?" Queenie said, but there was the slightest tug of a smile on her lips.

The feud was over.

"Oh, I have something for you, before I forget," Queenie said, snapping the faucet off. "I've done some experimenting today…"

Summer's breath caught. Was Queenie baking again? Were they on the road back to Dough Z Dough?

"Here," Queenie said, thrusting the folded orange sweater she'd snagged from the caboose into Summer's hands.

As soon as Summer touched it, she knew it was felted! She unfolded it and stared at the amazing workmanship in the bag. It was a perfect oval, with a knitted piece that folded over the opening, helping to keep the contents from spilling out. She looked inside. The bag was lined with an old orange and white linen dishtowel—a perfect complement to the funky purse. Queenie had even sewn an interior pocket. But the greatest addition to the bag was the handles. They were knitted out of orange yarn, exactly the same color as the sweater. Where could Queenie have gotten matching yarn…especially in a day?

"I unraveled the sleeves before I felted the sweater." Queenie said, as if she'd read Summer's thoughts. "Then I made circular handles and threaded some of the fabric from the dishtowel through the hollow tube, so the handles won't stretch."

"It's amazing," Summer said. "I can't believe you know how to do this?"

"Why is that, Summer?" Queenie said, shooting Summer a reproachful gaze. "There are many things about me that might surprise you."

But you won't let anyone get close enough to find out what they are.

Lynnie's voice floated down from the second story landing.

"I'm turning in," Lynnie said. "Good night."

"Good night," Queenie and Summer called back in unison.

"Thanks for letting her stay here," Summer said by way of an olive branch.

"No problem," Queenie said. "I don't mind. She's lonely. I understand that."

Summer felt Queenie kept trying to open doors, but slammed them before Summer could wedge in a toe. Perhaps Summer could pry the door open enough to start a real conversation. Her thoughts were interrupted by scratching at the door that was followed by an intense shake. Summer jumped in surprise. Queenie smiled.

"It's just Andre," Queenie said, heading to the kitchen door. "We'll never get those dishes done."

"Oh my gosh," Summer said. "The dogs went out when I was getting the meringues out of the truck! I forgot all about them."

Queenie opened the door. Andre bounded in. Queenie looked out onto the back porch.

"Shortie, come here, boy," Queenie called.

Summer stood by her grandmother. Her heart started to beat faster, but she willed herself not to panic.

"Here, Shortie!" Summer called.

Her grandmother gave a shrill whistle, which brought Andre to her side, but no sign of Shortie.

Summer ran out to the back porch and down the stairs. She could hear nothing but the croaking of frogs and the chirping of crickets. Queenie came out and put her hand on Summer's arm.

"Maybe he's visiting Keefe or Bale," Summer said, hysteria sneaking into her voice.

Chapter 23

Summer grabbed a flashlight.

"Do you want some help looking?" Queenie asked.

"Thanks, but I think you should stay here in case he comes back," Summer said, trying not to let the mounting panic show in her voice. "I've got my cell phone. Call me if you have news."

"Alright," Queenie said. "And you call me."

Queenie looked worried, not a common expression on her regal features.

"You're not scared, are you?" Summer asked.

If Queenie was frightened, they really were in bad way.

"No," Queenie said, too quickly. "It's just that…"

Queenie hesitated, but Summer pressed.

"What?" Summer asked.

"He's so small," Queenie almost whispered.

Summer shot off the back porch.

"Shortie," she called. "Come here, boy!"

Summer swept the flashlight right and left as she went toward Bale's bus in the driveway. Maybe Queenie was right and Shortie was just visiting one of the men.

Bale opened the bus door and was on the ground before Summer could knock.

"What's up?" Bale asked.

"Shortie is missing," Summer said. Trying to steady her voice, she added, "He's not used to being on his own."

Summer was afraid she sounded childish, but Bale looked concerned.

"Okay. It's still pretty early," Bale said, looking up at the sky. "And the sky's clear. That should help."

"That could change on a dime up here," Summer said, blinking back tears.

The thought of Shortie being gone was bad enough. Adding a chilly rain would just make it worse. She heard gravel crunching. It was too heavy a sound to be Shortie, but she turned toward the sound. A tiny circle of light was bobbing toward them.

"Queenie just called me," Keefe said as he approached. He was wearing a headlamp. "Let's get out there."

"What can I do?" Bale asked.

"You don't know the farm," Keefe said. "But you could go down the road—check it out? See if there's any sign of him?"

Bale disappeared into the bus. He returned with a lantern and headed down the driveway toward the road without a word.

Summer had forgotten how dark it was on the farm. The moon was bright enough to make out the outline of the caboose on Flat Top Hill, but that was all she could see.

"Maybe he went up to Flat Top," Keefe said, following her gaze.

"Maybe," Summer said, her hopes lifting.

"I'll head around the back of the house and..." Keefe said. But stopped himself.

Summer knew why. He was going to say he'd go down by the pond. A tiny dog with only city smarts might find himself in trouble if he fell in the water. The thought went unspoken.

"Thanks," Summer said.

She climbed the hill, calling for Shortie every few seconds. She could make out the sounds of the night creatures and of Bale and Keefe whistling and calling. She checked her phone, hoping she had somehow missed a call from Queenie saying Shortie was back at the Victorian. The moon slipped behind a black cloud, making the landscape as foreboding as the moon.

Shortie wasn't at the caboose. Summer sat down on the step, numb with fear. Her eyes swept over the view she always loved, seeing it for the first time as terrifying rather than comforting. She saw the sweeping tiny orbits from Bale's lantern and Keefe's headlamps. They converged on the driveway, the men obviously comparing notes. Maybe there was good news? The lights continued in unison toward Queenie's house. Summer jumped up and headed down the hill.

Keefe and Bale were already in the kitchen when Summer burst through the door. She was met with four sets of sorrowful eyes. Besides Queenie, Keefe, and Bale, Lynnie had joined the group in the kitchen.

"Nothing?" Summer asked.

No one spoke.

"We need to go back out," Summer said, looking out the window at the quickly darkening sky. "It looks like rain is coming."

"Come on, Andre," Keefe said to the Great Dane. "Can't you give us a clue?"

At the sound of his name, Andre pulled himself off the floor, but seemed to be having trouble getting over to Keefe.

"Is he limping?" Queenie asked, getting up from the table.

Keefe and Queenie settled on the floor with the huge dog. Summer wanted to scream. Whatever was wrong with Andre could wait! They had an emergency! But Andre seemed to really be in some distress and she remained silent.

Andre put his huge head in Keefe's lap. Queenie, fishing her reading glasses out of her pocket, examined his foot. She pulled her hand away. There was blood on it. Summer, alarmed at the blood, turned her attention to the dog.

"Andre, what were you two doing out there?" Queenie said, rubbing the dog's flanks.

"It sounds like it's starting to rain," Lynnie said.

Bale put a comforting hand on Summer's shoulder and squeezed. She was about to head outside, when she heard Andre give a little snort.

"Sorry, dear," Queenie said as she massaged the paw. "But you have something in there…"

Andre looked soulfully at Summer, then blinked up at Keefe while Queenie worked on the toughened skin between his toes. Andre suddenly jerked his head up. Keefe comforted him and he settled back down.

"Got it," Queenie said.

"It looks like a thorn of some kind," Keefe said. "Rose bush?"

Queenie shook her head.

"This isn't from any of my plants," Queenie said.

Queenie held it up for inspection. Summer studied it.

"Oh my God," Summer said, staggering back. "I know where Shortie is!"

She raced into the rain, followed by Keefe and Bale.

Summer ran blindly, hindered by the rain and not sure exactly where she was going. She swung her flashlight wildly, but only saw sheets of rain.

Think! She commanded herself. She ran toward the creek, trying to remember her last outing with her grandfather. She stopped in her tracks. Bale and Keefe caught up with her.

"What the…." Keefe started, but Summer put up her hand for silence.

"Listen," she whispered.

"I don't hear anything," Bale said.

Summer put her finger to her lips, quieting him. For a moment, all they could hear was the driving rain. The storm suddenly paused, and they all heard it: a faint, distant barking. The three ran toward the sound. The rain started again and Shortie's cries were once again lost in the wind.

"Be careful," Summer said. "Somewhere around here, there's a—"

"Holy—." Keefe said.

He staggered. In the darkness, it appeared he went down on one knee. He leapt up, reaching for some invisible handgrip.

Summer and Bale turned toward him as he regained his balance.

"There's a hole here!"

"It's an old well," Summer said as she pushed past him. "It's a long story…"

Summer pulled branches out of the way, ignoring the thorns which bit into her palm. She thrust the light down and illuminated a perfect, bricked-in cylinder. The light traveled down to the bottom of the well.

Shortie barked, ran in a circle, and wagged his tail.

"He's okay," Summer called, choking on the words.

At the sound of Summer's voice, Shortie put his front paws on the side of the well and started to whimper.

"Hang on," Summer cooed. "Poor little guy."

Bale and Keefe stood over Summer, all three of their lamps pointing down at the little soaking-wet dog in the bottom of the well, which was slowly filling with rain. Shortie's tail made little splashing sounds in the water.

"We've got to get him out of there," Bale said. "Who knows how long the rain will last or if this well will fill up. Do you have a ladder?"

"I'm not sure any of our ladders will fit down there," Keefe said. "It looks like it's about nine feet deep but only about three feet wide. Our ladders are all too short or too wide."

"No time to shop for one that does fit," Bale said, "and it's too high for one of us to pull the other one out."

"I could get the truck," Keefe said. Summer patted her pockets for the keys, but realized Keefe must mean the farm's truck. "One of us could go down there for Shortie and the other could use a rope attached to the truck to get up."

"Ascend the wall?" Bale asked.

Summer had done some rock climbing at her gym, so she knew about repelling and ascending, but never thought she would ever have to do any real climbing in anything but a controlled environment. Keefe nodded.

"That could work," Bale agreed, looking down the well.

Summer didn't think. She tucked the flashlight into her waistband and jumped into the well. She landed with a splash, miraculously avoiding Shortie. The two men looked down at her.

"We didn't mean you!" Keefe called.

"Just go get the truck and the rope," Summer said, grateful that she didn't seem to have broken any bones on the way down.

Shortie scratched rapidly at Summer's leg, begging to be picked up and enjoy their reunion to the fullest. As improbable as it was, it seemed he hadn't sustained any injuries either.

When she tried to bend over to pick him up, she hit her head on the bricks less than a yard away.

"Ouch," Summer said, rubbing her head.

The only way she could pick him up was to slide down the wall, brace her feet on the rounded bricks opposite her, and hover above the slowly mounting waterline long enough for Shortie to climb into her lap. Once she got a firm grip on him, she planted her feet back on the ground and stood up again. She still didn't know how they were going to get out of the well, but at least Shortie had had another five feet of air before disaster struck.

It was dark and cold in the well. Cradling a shivering Shortie on one arm, she reached for her flashlight. She fumbled and felt it slipping out of her hand. She could hear the water at her feet.

"Everything okay down there?" Bale shouted.

Things have been better.

Summer could hear Bale clearing salmonberries away from the opening of the well. She covered Shortie's head to protect him from the thorny debris that showered down on them.

"Sorry," Bale called down.

"Any sign of Keefe?" Summer called up.

There was a pause.

"Not yet," Bale said. Shining his lantern into the well.

Summer followed the beam coming through the raindrops. She lifted one foot and then the other.

"The water is up to my ankles," she said, surprised how much water the well had taken on.

"My guess is this well was abandoned when it dried up," Bale said, sweeping the beam over the bricks. "But that doesn't mean it can't fill up in a storm."

"Maybe the well will fill up and I can just climb out," Summer said.

There was an unearthly silence up on earth, where Bale was sitting.

"I wouldn't count on that," he said.

He suddenly swung the lantern out of the well. Summer's stomach lurched. Were she and Shortie going to drown? The lantern appeared over the edge again.

"I see the truck," Bale said. "Just hang on."

The well went dark again. She could hear voices murmuring and heard the tailgate open and close. The lantern appeared again. She blinked through the rain dripping in her eyes, trying to make out the shapes at the top of the well. Bale, Keefe, and Queenie all looked down at her.

"Dear heavens," Queenie said. "You really are down a well."

"Without a paddle," Summer said, trying to make light of the worsening situation.

"Okay, hang on," Keefe said.

"I don't think there's room for another person down here," Summer said, remembering Keefe and Bale's plan to get Shortie back up. "You'll just have to throw me the rope."

"I brought your purse," Queenie said.

Summer was stumped. Did Queenie think she was going to do some Internet shopping while down a hole?

"Thanks?" Summer said.

"I emptied it," Queenie said. "I thought you could put Shortie in it. We could pull him out first. God knows that felted bag could hold anything at this point."

Summer wasn't in a position to take offense. Bale held the lantern while Queenie tossed the felted bag into the well. It bounced off Summer's head into the rapidly filling basin at her feet. Summer managed to fish the bag out of the water. Luckily, the thick felting kept the bag from taking on too much water. She loaded Shortie into the bag as Keefe tossed down a rope. Summer grabbed the end of the rope and tied it to the straps of the purse. She was grateful her grandfather had taught her several sound sailor's knots.

Summer had confidence the rope wouldn't give. She gave the rope a little tug, kissed Shortie on the nose, and watched as he made his way very slowly up the well. The purse spun and knocked against the bricks, but Shortie was getting closer and closer to safety. She could see Queenie reaching into the well, which meant Bale and Keefe must have been hauling the rope. Queenie must have been lying in the mud as she stretched toward the ascending rope. The rain poured down in a torrent. Summer could see her grandmother's hands close in around the straps of the purse and haul Shortie out of the well.

"I've got him," Queenie's voice echoed into the well. "Now let's get you out of there!"

Bale and Keefe's heads appeared over the side, Bale shining the lantern once again into the depths. The water was at Summer's waist.

"Do you know what to do?" Keefe called down.

"Of course," Summer said, with more confidence than she felt.

When she was at the climbing wall at the gym, there was an instructor at the other end of her rope as well as a four-inch rubber pad on the floor.

"I've got the rope tied to the truck hitch," Keefe said, letting down the rope again.

Summer stood back as the rope splashed into the water. Someone had made a slipknot at her end. She held it up.

"Put your foot in that," Bale said. "Queenie is going to drive the truck. Keefe and I will be here to pull you over the top."

"Be careful," Keefe said. "You all set?"

All set might be a bit strong.

Summer couldn't speak. The rain was pouring into the well so fast it was getting hard to breathe. She positioned the rope under the arch of her foot and realized she was almost underwater when she bent over. She pulled on the rope, signaling she was ready.

The rope gave a powerful lurch and Summer rose out of the water. Her hands crashed against the bricks, scraping her knuckles. She realized that she had to somehow work with the rope, work with truck, and work with the people who were trying to save her. But she had no idea how to do that and there was no Internet research that could give her the answer. She would have to work on trust, which was not her strong suit. She put her back against one wall and used her legs to climb up the other side. She gave herself over to instinct, and knew everyone involved was doing the same. With a few more bumps and bruises, she finally felt strong hands latching on to upper arms: Bale and Keefe were pulling her the remaining few feet out of the well.

Queenie came racing from the cab of the truck. Shortie, even in the driving rain, barreled toward Summer at Queenie's heels.

Summer was grateful Bale and Keefe continued to support her. She wasn't sure her legs would hold her.

Chapter 24

They all piled into the truck, Keefe driving, Queenie riding shotgun. Bale, Shortie, and Summer perched on the back bench of the cab. Unlike Big Red, with every upgrade known to Detroit, the farm truck was a workhorse; no upholstered back seats here. Summer put her head against the window, eyes closed, as they drove back to Queenie's house. She absently stroked Shortie's wet fur. She could feel the muscles in his tail moving as he wagged. She couldn't help but smile. All the humans involved in the drama were spent. But now that Shortie was out of the well, it was business as usual for him.

She had almost drifted into an exhausted twilight sleep when she felt a pressure on her hand. She opened her eyes, Bale was squeezing her hand. She stared at him.

"Sorry to wake you," Bale said, not letting go of her hand. "Keefe just asked if you wanted to be dropped off at the caboose."

"I thought you might want to get some dry clothes," Keefe said, looking at her through the rearview mirror.

Summer wondered if Keefe could see Bale's hand on hers. She wondered if he cared.

"That would be great," Summer said.

Keefe changed course and headed up Flat Top Hill.

Summer and Shortie got out of the cab. Summer was surprised that Queenie got out of the truck, too.

"How did you know about that well?" Queenie asked. "I've lived on this farm for forty years and never knew anything about it."

"Grandpa and I found it," Summer said. "It was the last time I was here. He said he was going to fill it in."

Summer could see Queenie shaking her head in the darkness.

"He kept so much to himself those last few years," Queenie said. "I'm sure he meant to fill it in, but his health was failing and he didn't want anyone to know. He was so full of secrets at the end."

Summer knew that now was not the time to point out that Queenie herself had become secretive. She also knew that all of them were cold, tired, and hungry. Nothing much was going to be settled tonight. Queenie seemed to read Summer's mind.

"I better get back to the house." Queenie said. "I can send some hot chocolate up here if you want to skip all the hoopla."

Summer tried not to yawn. As much as Summer wanted to get into some dry clothes and curl up with Shortie, she knew it would not be fair to leave Queenie to contend with Lynnie and Bale, who were *her* guests.

"Oh no," Summer said, mustering all her energy. "I'll come down. Shortie and I will be down after I get a quick shower."

Summer watched the truck head down the back side of Flat Top Hill. She and Shortie went into the caboose. She let out a deep sigh. The thought of packing up all her belongings again so Bale could show the caboose at the convention made her tired to the bone. She shrugged out of her wet clothes, and tied on a warm bathrobe. She was dying for a shower but felt it only fair to get Shortie some food. He'd had a rough day. She poured out some dog food, placed it on the floor, and sat down on one of the built-in benches.

Summer woke, disoriented. There was a knocking sound. It took her a moment to realize she was in the caboose, and a few seconds longer to remember she was at Flat Top Farm instead of a Wal-Mart parking lot. She had no idea how long she'd been asleep, but considering how creaky she felt as she stood up, it must have been awhile.

Rubbing her eyes, she went to the door. She cringed when she saw she was still wrapped in her old tartan bathrobe, and prayed it was Queenie or Lynnie coming to check on her. She snapped on the outside light.

It was Keefe, carrying a plate covered with a napkin.

"I fell asleep!" she said.

"We guessed," Keefe said. He held up the plate, but made no attempt to come inside. "Queenie sent some leftover casserole and hot chocolate."

"Oh! That's great," Summer said, realizing she was starving. She knew she looked like hell, but her manners and curiosity got the better of her. "Do you want to come in?"

In three steps, Keefe was in the middle of the caboose. He handed Summer the plate.

"Have a seat," Summer said.

"Okay," Keefe said. He looked around. "Where?"

She pointed to the bench she had just vacated.

"Then where will you sit?" Keefe asked.

Summer perched on the kitchen counter, motioning Keefe to take the bench. She was mastering the concept of making people feel at home in her tiny house. Shortie also played host and jumped in Keefe's lap.

"How is Andre?' Summer asked between bites.

"No worse for wear," Keefe said. "What a night!"

"Seriously," Summer said.

It felt like old times reliving farm life with Keefe.

"I somehow expected Andre would lead us to Shortie," Keefe said. "I think I've watched too much TV."

"He might have pointed," Summer said, getting into the spirit of things. "If he didn't have a thorn in his paw."

"Thank God for that thorn," Keefe said, turning serious. "I'd hate to think what would have happened if you hadn't remembered..."

"Let's not even go there," Summer said, finding her appetite suddenly gone.

They both turned and looked at Shortie, who knew he was being discussed. He raised his head and wagged his tale.

"I heard you telling Queenie that you and Zach found that well together," Keefe said. "I know he had his pride, but if he'd just told me about it, I could have filled it in years ago."

"I don't think it was personal," Summer said.

"I know," Keefe said. "But he was pretty direct with me at the end."

Summer knew this was the perfect opening to put the past behind them.

"I don't think forgetting to mention the well was his only bad decision," Summer said, going for broke.

Keefe looked into her eyes. Neither one of them moved, but the current buzzing between them said it all. He knew exactly what she was talking about. She looked down at her shabby bathrobe and realized she still hadn't showered. The good news was, she was naked underneath the robe. The bad news was, she probably smelled like an old well. This was not how she pictured their big confrontation and possible reconnection.

Keefe might have watched too much TV, but Summer had read too many romance novels.

Shortie started barking. He jumped off Keefe's lap and ran to the door as he heard a knock. The spell was broken. Summer went to the door. Why was her timing always bad with Keefe? She swung the door open. Bale stood outside. He smiled.

"I saw the light on and thought I'd come see how you were doing," he said.

She stood back and Bale strode past her, smelling like lime aftershave. Summer could not believe her bad luck. She looked like hell in front of not one, but two desirable men.

"I guess I'll head back," Keefe said.

Summer savored the idea that both men had come to check on her. Maybe the bromance was over and the two of them would end up fighting over her. She looked around the caboose. There was nothing breakable in sight.

Definitely too many romance novels.

Keefe stood up and grabbed the plate off the counter. Getting through the caboose with three people and a dog in it was like trying to navigate the aisle of a plane with the beverage cart in the center. After much maneuvering, Keefe stood at the front door.

"Before you leave," Bale said to Keefe, "I just wanted to let you both know, I'm going to head up to Seattle in the morning to get my houses set up at the show. I know you two have to work tomorrow morning, but I was wondering if we could set a time to get the caboose down to Seattle."

Both men looked at Summer.

"She's been through a lot tonight," Keefe said.

Summer bristled. Keefe had no right to speak for her.

"I'll totally understand if you want to back out," Bale said.

"No," Summer said. "I'm happy to bring the caboose. As a matter of fact, I can be finished at the bakery by midafternoon, and I can get everything out of here and back into the truck in an hour."

"Hold on," Bale said, smiling at her. "I appreciate the offer, but you really don't have to get the caboose to me tomorrow. In the next day or two will be fine. I'll hold a platform for you."

"She can get it to you tomorrow," Keefe said. "I'll call Evie. She can come in and help with the bakery. Summer can get the caboose ready and drive down tomorrow. Evie and I will come down before the show closes. How does that work for everybody?"

"Sounds great to me," Bale said. He turned to Summer. "But only if you're sure."

If Keefe wanted to be back in the bakery with Evie, why didn't he just say so?

"That sounds fine," Summer said, irritated with Keefe.

No punches thrown, but Bale had certainly come out the winner.

"Okay," Keefe said. "Well, I've got an early morning, so..."

He didn't finish the sentence. It amazed Summer how fast you could disappear from a tiny house.

She turned to Bale, who was still standing in the middle of the caboose looking around. She could see how much of an interest he took in the place. He seemed at home here.

"Would you like some tea?" she asked.

"That's okay. You must be tired," Bale said. "I should go."

"No," Summer said, sounding a little hysterical. She calmed her voice. "No, I'm fine. I'd be happy for the company. Chamomile okay?"

"Perfect."

Summer stretched to reach the tea in the cupboard above the sink.

"Let me get that for you," Bale said.

He easily reached over her head and pulled down the box of Chamomile tea.

He took a step back, but their bodies almost touched. As he handed her the box, their fingers brushed against each other. Preparing a cup of tea had never been so exciting.

Bale took the seat recently vacated by Keefe. Shortie took this as a sign for a new lap to sit in and took advantage. Summer heated water in the microwave, making a mental note that she needed to get an electric tea carafe. Microwaved water might be hot, but it was not sexy.

"I have honey," Summer said, looking through the one cabinet she'd unpacked. "I'm not sure what else I have."

"Do you have feelings for Keefe?" Bale's voice came from behind her.

Summer froze. She couldn't bring herself to turn around.

"I'm sorry," Bale said. "I have no right to ask that."

Summer forced herself to turn around.

"Keefe and I... have a history," Summer said.

She leaned against the counter, gripping it for support.

"Everybody has a past," Bale said. "I was thinking more along the lines of the future."

Gently putting Shortie on the floor, he was standing in front of Summer in two strides.

Bale took her face in his hands. Summer lifted her eyes to meet his. He pulled her close and gently kissed her lips. She put her hands over his and closed her eyes. If anyone could make her forget the pain of Keefe Devlin it was going to be Bale Barrett.

"Hey, I just talked to Evie," Keefe said as he burst into the caboose.

Bale and Summer jumped apart.

"Oh! Sorry," Keefe said, looking sheepish. "I didn't realize you were still here," he added to Bale.

"What about Evie?" Summer said, all business.

"She's happy to take the morning shift at the bakery," Keefe said sharply, looking at Summer. "So you can go to Seattle tomorrow with a clear conscience."

"That's very good news," Summer said in an equally sharp tone. "I'll do that."

She snuck a look at Bale, and her fears were realized. Bale, as a salesman was probably used to reading the room and the tension in the tiny house could fill a stadium. Even if she threw Keefe out, Summer couldn't think of any way to rekindle the sweet moment they'd shared.

But there was going to be Seattle! With no Keefe to barge in.

Summer turned to Bale.

"I'll have the caboose ready to roll by noon," she said.

"Sounds good," Bale said. "You can follow me in the bus."

Without a word, Bale was gone. Keefe stood in the doorway watching Bale head down the hill. He suddenly turned to Summer.

"Why did you come back here?" Keefe said.

"You know why," Summer said. "Queenie asked me."

"But you always have one foot out the door, don't you?"

Summer opened her mouth to respond, but Keefe was gone.

Chapter 25

Lying in bed, awake before dawn as the bakery demanded, Summer found herself reliving the night before. She stretched out her hand to make sure Shortie was safe. Now that everything had turned out okay, she found herself shaking at the endless possibilities last night presented for disaster. She was sure her grandfather was guiding her back through the years to the memory of the abandoned well.

In her years away from Cat's Paw, Summer had become quite disciplined at averting her thoughts whenever they turned to Flat Top Farm. Now that she was back, so many emotions were at the surface. Her grandfather had been gone ten years, but to Summer, the pain of losing him felt very new. Everywhere she looked, there were reminders of her grandfather's goodness, kindness, and attention. If she hadn't been so stubborn, perhaps she could have patched things up. Now, she would never be able to tell her grandfather she forgave him. A tear ran down her cheek as she realized perhaps this was not entirely one-sided. What if her grandfather had not forgiven her for turning her back on Flat Top Farm?

Closing her eyes, she thought back to the drama in the caboose: Bale's sweet kiss and Keefe's annoying interference. She struggled to concentrate on the kiss, but Keefe kept popping into her mind. She wondered if there was such a thing. It was pretty clear Keefe was just as inclined to have Evie by his side. She swallowed hard as it occurred to her that he might be more inclined to have Evie by his side. She needed to do some Internet research about putting feelings for an old flame to rest.

Unfortunately, she was finding Wi-Fi reception less than consistent up here on Flat Top Hill. She was on her own.

Summer shimmied down the loft with Shortie draped over one arm. She put him on the floor, stepping seamlessly around him while he devoured his breakfast in the middle of the narrow walkway that separated the kitchen from the walk-in closet. Summer had mastered the choreography required in living tiny. Two steps to the Keurig, pivot. Three steps to the K-Cups, pivot back. A lunge to the refrigerator for the cream. And a stretch to the coffee cup.

She sipped her coffee and looked down at the Victorian at the bottom of the hill. The house's outline was just shimmering in the predawn mist. Summer could see the lights in Queenie's kitchen. Her formidable grandmother looked tiny from this distance, and vulnerable. Summer knew she needed to stop avoiding the situation and confront Queenie about why her grandmother had summoned her. Of course the words *confront* and *Queenie* had never been used in the same sentence by anyone in her family, as far as she knew. Searching her brain for a way out, Summer wondered if she should call her parents and let her father handle it. But Queenie clearly wanted Summer up here, or she wouldn't have made the call. Perched on her elbow, wondering how her life had become so insanely complicated, she noticed another figure enter the kitchen.

It was Lynnie.

Summer shot up in bed, hitting her head on the ceiling.

Holy shit!

She had forgotten all about Lynnie! In all the uproar of the night before, she'd never said anything about going to Seattle with the tiny house.

Summer couldn't go to Seattle and leave Lynnie in Cat's Paw. That would be completely unfair to both Lynnie and Queenie. As she rubbed the bump on her head, it occurred to her that if anybody could find out what was going on with Queenie, it would be Lynnie. Was that cowardly?

Yes, but effective.

Summer was relieved to see the orange felted purse her grandmother had made. Shortie's rescue had left her without a bag. She piled her phone, money, cables, earbuds, and lipstick into the new bag, which swallowed the items like a greedy frog. She picked it up and examined it. The bag didn't sag an inch. It occurred to her that the cosmos might have sent her here to save Queenie, but Queenie might just save Summer's dream in the process.

She cleared out the caboose in less than an hour. She'd originally thought she'd repack all her belongings in the truck and cart it to Seattle. But with thoughts of seeing Bale again, she wanted everything to be perfect. It was the tiny-house-living equivalent of shaving her legs. Instead, she piled everything into the back of Big Red. She opened the passenger door and helped Shortie up.

"Don't get your hopes up," Summer said. "I'm only letting you sit up front because we're not leaving the property."

She ignored the fact that he fell down an abandoned well on the same property. Everything in her life was topsy-turvy and she just needed to go with her instincts and not overthink things. She drove down the hill to a storage shed on the property, and unceremoniously tossed everything inside. She decided to take a shower before heading over to Queenie's to explain she needed to go to Seattle. The thought of this impending conversation made her break out into a cold sweat.

Maybe she should shower afterward.

She and Shortie made their way into Queenie's kitchen. The heady aroma of coffee, bacon, and eggs filled the room. Queenie took a quick look at Summer carrying the orange purse, then nodded at her to take a seat at the table. Lynnie was already there, eyes closed in ecstasy over Queenie's hot coffee.

"That was quite a night you had," Lynnie said. "Your grandmother filled me in this morning. Who said life was boring in Cat's Paw?"

I don't know. Who?

Shortie seemed to hold no grudge against Andre for deserting him at the well. The two dogs tore through the house like long lost friends.

"We could learn something from dogs," Lynnie said. "Just go with the flow."

Queenie and Summer looked at each other. This was clearly something each felt the other had not learned.

Queenie was always in her element when she was serving food. Everything was simple and elegant. Summer gulped down a final cup of coffee and steeled herself for the conversation ahead.

"Do you have plans for today?" Queenie asked suddenly.

Time for the big-girl panties.

"Ummm, yes," Summer said.

This wasn't the brave start she'd envisioned.

"I thought so," Queenie said. "Since you didn't go to the bakery this morning."

"Keefe said Evie would be happy to cover for me," Summer said.

Summer couldn't believe she was hiding behind Evie of all people!

"So I guess these plans have something to do with that darling Bale," Lynnie said in a teasing tone.

"Actually, yes." Summer said.

"Good for you! I looked for the bus this morning. You know the old saying, "If the bus is a'rockin', don't come a'knockin'." But the bus was already gone. I thought you let him escape."

Summer was shocked. Tasteless, opposite-sex jokes in front of Queenie were just not told.

"I'm taking the caboose to Seattle," Summer said. "Bale wants to feature it in the Tiny House Show."

"But you'll be back, won't you?" Queenie said.

There was a note of fright in her voice that startled her. Summer wanted to reach out and pat Queenie's hand but feared she'd lose a limb with such impertinence.

"I'm not going anywhere," Summer said. "I'm just dropping off the caboose at the show and might do some sweater shopping."

"Oh, honey," Lynnie said holding up Summer's orange bag. "This is stunning! You've made so much progress."

"Actually, Queenie made this," Summer admitted.

The pride she had in Queenie's work outweighed the slight sting of the unintended insult to her own expertise.

"Now don't you worry," Lynnie said to Summer. "You have other skills."

Summer heard Queenie make a little noise that sounded like a suppressed giggle. Not that Summer had ever actually heard Queenie giggle.

"Maybe you should be taking Queenie with you to Seattle then," Lynnie said. "She obviously knows more about this sweater felting thing than you do."

Everything that annoyed Summer about Lynnie came flooding back.

"That's alright," Queenie said as she poured more coffee. "We already made plans for today."

"Who's we?" Summer asked

"I thought Lynnie and I could go take a drive to Vancouver," Queenie said.

"That sounds nice," Summer said, rejoicing that Vancouver was the opposite direction of Seattle.

Hospitality to strangers was not known to be one of Queenie's strong suits. Summer wondered where the Queenie of old had gone.

"Thank you," Summer said warmly.

"Well, I thought you'd be at the bakery this morning," Queenie said, in her most passive-aggressive injured tone.

Oh, *there's* the old Queenie. She hadn't gone far at all.

"I better be going," Summer said, deciding to bail before the conversation turned against her. "You guys have fun today. I'll see you…"

She was going to say, "I'll see you tonight," but she paused. Depending on how things evolved in Seattle, she had no idea if she'd be coming back to Flat Top Farm this evening or not.

Keefe will be perfectly happy to ask Evie again, I'm sure.

Summer called into the house, "Come on Shortie."

In ten minutes, Summer, with Shortie relegated to his car seat, was heading down the highway to whatever adventure lay ahead.

Chapter 26

It was nearly eleven when Summer pulled the caboose down Flat Top. Last night's rain made the journey down the hill a little tricky, but she was proud of herself for tackling the challenge on her own. She felt she was still earning her stripes as a tiny house owner, but every test gave her more confidence.

Summer told herself that she was annoyed there was no way to get out of the area without driving through Cat's Paw. But if she were being honest, she secretly wanted Keefe to see her heading out to Seattle. As luck would have it, he was on the sidewalk in front of the bakery wiping down the outdoor tables as she drove by. It had taken Summer awhile to get used to the attention every time she went somewhere with the caboose, but now she almost took it as the caboose's due. She felt as if she were her own parade as she waved to everyone on Main Street. She put on her most casual smile as she sailed past Keefe. She caught his eye. He looked troubled.

Isn't that what you wanted? For him to be jealous that you were going to see Bale?

She almost put on the brakes, but Evie was suddenly at his side, resting her hand on his shoulder while engaging him in conversation. Neither looked up as Summer waved. She drove out of town.

Summer looked in the backseat at Shortie.

"He's coming to the Tiny House Convention with his good pal, Evie," she said defensively. "He'll be fine."

As she drove out of town, a man with bright red hair gave a small nod. She did a double take. It was Shy Sherman, heading into the *Cat's Paw Chronicle* office. She made a mental note to check on the paper when she got back; maybe she made the front page with her caboose!

The trip to Seattle went smoothly. Summer was perfectly comfortable driving Big Red and towing the caboose. Other drivers saluted her and some of their passengers took pictures. Summer felt strongly that the tiny house movement was going to explode, but it was fun being at the foreground of the revolution.

Especially when there was a good-looking man like Bale helping to lead the charge.

It was easy getting back into the swing of constant Internet connection. The satellites led her directly to the road show. Summer pulled up to the vast hotel parking lot where the event was being held. She sat in Big Red, staring at the entrance, disappointed because she had somehow pictured the event as being more elegant. Summer had been to several conventions in her day, from baking industry trade shows with Queenie to boat shows with Grandpa Zach, and car shows with her parents.

A uniformed guard rapped at her window.

"May I help you?" he asked.

"I'm here for the Tiny Road Show," Summer said.

"I wouldn't have guessed," he said, glancing back at the caboose.

"I'm supposed to deliver this house to Bale Barrett."

The man looked down at his iPad, swiping past a few screens at dizzying speed.

"I don't have a Bale Barrett," he said.

"That's impossible."

"People living like hobbits," the guard replied. "*That's* impossible."

"But it's happening, isn't it?" Summer said. "So maybe it's possible there's a Bale Barrett, too. Could you just take another look, please?"

The man looked down at his screen as Summer peeked over his shoulder. Even reading upside down she could see *Bale's Tiny Dreams*.

"Right there," she stabbed at the screen.

"That says *Bale's Tiny Dreams*, Miss. You said to look for Bale Barrett."

"How many Bales do you think are here?"

"It's not my job to guess how many people named Bale are at the convention, Miss. It's my job to keep out unauthorized personnel. Of which, you, apparently, are one."

"It's okay, Chester." Bale's voice seemed to come from nowhere. "She's with me."

"Okay, Mr. Barrett," Chester said. "Just doing…"

"Your job," Bale said affably as he jumped in the passenger seat. "I appreciate it."

"He knows you?" Summer asked, outraged. "He was giving me the third degree."

"You have to learn to go with the flow when you're in the land of tiny," Bale said, directing her to go through the gate Chester was opening. "It's a whole new world."

"That's true," Summer said, looking around at the array of tiny houses being assembled on site. "Thanks for coming to the gate."

"I'm happy you're here! I've kept my eye on that gate all day."

She was pleased to know Bale was keeping his eye out for her.

"Got a space for you right on the edge over there," Bale said, pointing to an open spot by the exit sign. "Quick escape route."

"Do I need an escape route?"

Bale looked at her with a lopsided grin. He shrugged but didn't say anything. Instead he turned to the backseat and ruffled Shortie's head. A few weeks ago, Summer could not have imagined she would be threading her way through a parking lot studded with tiny Victorians, gypsy wagons, steel and glass miniatures. But she pulled up to Bale's shiny olive-colored bus without a problem.

"You go, girl," Bale said as she cut the engine, the caboose perfectly in place.

She was disappointed to receive only a high five for her efforts.

Bale jumped out and uncoupled the caboose from Big Red. He directed Summer to park her truck outside the gated area and come back on foot.

"The trucks are a distraction," he said.

"Do I have to go through Chester again?" she asked.

"No. Just park around the side of the hotel. You're one of us now."

Summer warmed to the thought of being one of anything that included Bale.

"Sorry, dude," Summer said, as she put Shortie on his leash.

It had been a while since Shortie had to be tamed.

Summer could not believe her luck, being behind the scenes at a tiny house show. She'd done all her research online. Seeing so many of them in person was like seeing Main Street Sleeping Beauty's Castle at Disneyland for the first time. By the time you got there, you knew it by heart, but somehow, it was even more magical than you'd dreamed.

"Is that my blacktop boondocker?" called a voice from the crowd.

Summer didn't need to see the face; she knew exactly who it was. She spun around to see her Wal-Mart guardian angels, Alf and Margie, beaming at her.

"What are you guys doing here?" Summer asked as she was enveloped in hugs.

"Margie's been dragging me to these tiny house shows since we met you," Alf said. "Can't say I'm ready to take the plunge, but..."

"But we're having a ball looking around," Margie added, giving Shortie a kiss. "There are so many styles. I mean, I keep telling Alf, you've seen one RV, you've seen 'em all."

"Which is not true," Alf said defensively.

Summer laughed. She had been so new to everything when she met Alf and Margie, she'd let then escape without getting any contact information. Back at Wal-Mart, she'd been afraid she'd never learn the ways of living outside the box, but she had. Now, she was the one in the position to be the voice of experience. They exchanged phone numbers, Instagram handles, and Facebook information.

"If you have any questions about tiny living," Summer said, "I'm practically an expert. "

A tiny Swiss Chalet caught Margie's eye. Summer waved as she watched Margie pull Alf inside.

As Summer surveyed the parking lot, she had to admit, the caboose was the showstopper. Even the tiny veterans were gathered around Bale as he went into salesman mode. Summer looked down at Shortie and nodded toward Bale.

"He's frickin' adorable. Isn't he?"

At that moment, Bale looked up and winked, apparently thinking the same about her. When there was a break in the crowd, Bale escorted her and Shortie into her own house. It was an odd sensation. Empty again of all her belongings, it felt more like Bale's showpiece than her home. But the concept of home was turned on its ear at the moment anyway. She had no idea where she was headed, emotionally or physically.

"I hope you can hang around for a couple days," Bale said. "I think people would be very interested to talk to an actual human being who lives in one of these things, instead of just a salesperson. Of course, that's not the only reason I want you to stay, but it's a hell of an excuse."

He pushed a strand of hair behind her ear, then caressed her cheek. Was she where she belonged? Could she turn her back on Flat Top Farm and all its unfinished business?

"I'm not sure I..." Summer started, when a potential customer knocked on the door and stepped through without waiting for an invitation. The woman carried an enormous messenger bag, which didn't strike Summer as the wisest choice for touring tiny houses. Some of the hallways in these home would require her to turn sideways to get from one end of the place to the other. Summer had to remind herself that this was a public forum.

"Hi there, I'm Mindy," the woman said. "This little train car is the cutest thing ever."

"Thank you," Bale and Summer said in unison.

"Can I poke around?" Mindy asked.

Bale and Summer parted, Summer going toward the dining area and Bale into the square that was the living area.

"It's really small," Mindy said. "I mean, wow-small."

"It takes a certain discipline," Summer said, proud to be an authority.

"This walk-in closet is amazing," Mindy said, making her way inside. "I could really use something like this."

Bale gave Summer a thumbs up.

"I have a dog," Mindy said, jerking her thumb toward the staircase. "I'm not sure he could navigate those stairs."

They all looked at Shortie, who, on cue, ran up the stairs, looked down on everyone, and ran back down.

"Oh!" Mindy said. "Well, if that little wiener dog can do it, my schnauzer could do it."

"When did he learn to do that?" Summer whispered to Bale as Mindy climbed the stairs.

"Who knows?" Bale said. "Maybe following Andre? In any case, I'd like to hire him to be a Tiny Dreams salesperson, if you don't mind."

"I get a finder's fee," Summer said.

They found themselves drawn to each other like magnets, but Mindy came down the stairs and they moved apart.

Mindy was noisily chewing as she came back from inspecting the bathroom.

"This place might just be a little too weird for me," Mindy said. "I think I'll check out something that looks more like a house."

"Be my guest," Bale said cheerfully.

Summer tried not to look resentful.

Mindy rummaged in her bag and pulled out a white bag with the Dough Z Dough logo. Summer and Bale exchanged a look of surprise. Mindy opened the bag and offered it to Summer.

"Want one?" Mindy asked. "They are from a destination bakery in Cat's Paw."

"Destination bakery?" Bale said teasingly, sounding very impressed. Summer blushed.

"Yes, they're amazing," Mindy said. "I found out I had to be gluten-free about a year ago, and I stopped going for a while. I didn't even want to be around baked goods. Then one day I was walking by Dough Z Dough and I thought, *I'm just going to check it out and see if there's anything I can eat.* I really missed the place."

"So they had these meringues," Mindy said. "They're GF and perfect. I'm a regular customer again."

Summer grabbed the bag and stared into it as if she'd never seen chocolate meringues before, let alone made this very batch.

"My God," Summer said.

She looked up. Mindy and Bale were both staring at her.

"I have to go," Summer said. "I'm so sorry, but I have to get back to the farm."

"So go," Mindy said, gingerly retrieving her bag.

"Is everything alright?" Bale asked.

"Yes," Summer said. "No. I don't know."

Mindy tiptoed out of the caboose.

"I have to go check on something," Summer said as she kissed Bale on the cheek. "But I'll be back."

"Will you?" Bale asked as she scooped up Shortie and ran toward the front door. "Will you be back, I mean?"

"Of course," she said, trying to make light of it. "You've got my house."

"It's a start," Bale said.

Chapter 27

Summer hurried up the highway toward Cat's Paw, her head spinning. Thoughts of Keefe and Bale seemed almost like a luxury. She was completely focused on Queenie. Like dominos, everything started to fall at a dizzying pace.

Summer was sure Queenie had been diagnosed with celiac disease. So many of the pieces fit. Refusing to go work at the bakery, eating none of the goodies except the chocolate meringues, trying out cookie recipes and failing, adjusting family recipes that called for pasta, never having beer. The only problem with Summer's theory was it didn't make any sense to keep it such a deep secret. It wasn't as if society would shun her for being gluten-free.

Summer drove through Cat's Paw. She spotted Keefe's motorcycle, but did not even glance at the bakery, which still had an hour until closing. She could only stand one drama at a time.

She pulled into Flat Top Farm. Andre came rushing out the kitchen door to meet his best friend, Shortie, who was just getting paws on the ground. The dogs tore back into the kitchen. Summer, charged as she was with her suspicions, was losing her nerve with every step. Confronting Henry VIII would have taken less finesse.

It didn't matter if Summer was right or wrong. It was time to have it out with her grandmother. She took a deep breath and forced herself to step into the kitchen. Queenie and Lynnie were at the kitchen table. A loaf of bread, several varieties of cookies and some sort of lopsided confection Summer could not identify sat on the table between them. Lynnie looked guilty and Queenie looked annoyed. No one spoke. Finally, Queenie broke the silence.

"You used an automatic bread maker, Clarisse?"

Chapter 28

Summer looked accusingly at Lynnie, who shrugged helplessly.

"I don't think that's the point, Queenie," Summer said, regaining her footing.

"And what *is* the point?" Queenie asked.

Summer gripped the counter. She could not back down. She needed to be firm.

"The point is, you've been hiding the fact that you're gluten-free and that's just infantile."

Summer never used words like *infantile*, but Queenie did. Summer had to play on Queenie's level if she was going to stay in the game. They'd escalated from Dominos to Wrecking Ball in less than a minute.

"Really?" Queenie said icily, arching an eyebrow. "And what would you suggest? That the only living artisan of Dough Z Dough should announce to the world that she suddenly can have nothing to do with *flour*?"

"Would that really be such a big deal?" Summer asked.

"Ask Paula Deen!" Queenie said.

"Paula Deen?" Summer said.

"Yes. Paula. Deen." Queenie enunciated every word. "Even if you didn't have any interest in the food world at the time…"

"Guilting me isn't going to work," Summer countered at her grandmother's dig at Summer's long absence.

"As I was saying," Queenie went on, "Paula Deen hid her diabetes from fans for three years."

"So what?" Summer asked.

"So, she was right," Queenie said. "You've heard nothing about her since she gave up the fried chicken and her bacon-wrapped macaroni and cheese."

"I don't think that's the reason Paula Deen is out of favor," Summer said.

"Just an unfortunate coincidence?" Queenie asked.

"I don't think so," Lynnie shook her head in agreement with the conspiracy theory.

"Besides, since when has Paula Deen been your role model?" Summer, ignoring Lynnie, asked Queenie.

"I happen to have thought the hamburger patty and fried egg between two glazed donuts was genius," Queenie sniffed.

"Oh, that was a good one," Lynnie said. "I loved those until I had to be…" Lynnie had the good sense to trail off.

"I think I'll go take a nap," Lynnie said, pushing back from the table.

Summer couldn't believe Lynnie had the discipline to remove herself from such a trove of potential gossip.

"No need," Queenie said. "Summer and I were just going for a walk."

Going for a walk with Queenie was never good. But Summer was powerless to resist. Queenie grabbed her jacket and took Summer by the arm. They were out the door before the dogs even had a chance to join them. Summer knew the drill. They would walk in silence until Queenie lulled her victim into complacency. Then, and only then, would she speak. Summer tried to convince herself that she could open the conversation herself, but years of training held her tongue.

Summer could not look at her phone, but they must have been walking for a half hour in silence. Summer's mind drifted to Bale. She'd left him with no word about when she would be back. The sky was darkening quickly and she was exhausted. She probably would spend the night in her old room and go back in the morning. Her mind wandered to Keefe and Evie, but she resisted the thought. She had enough problems.

"Here we are," Queenie said, invading Summer's thoughts at last.

Summer hadn't really been paying attention to their route and was startled to find themselves, at sundown, in front of the cemetery.

Summer had been terrified of the cemetery when she was little. As she grew, she found herself drawn to the serenity of the place, often going and sitting under the large saucer magnolia and reading for hours, at first dreaming of Keefe and later, bringing him with her. Intimate memories of her days with Keefe made her shy in her grandmother's presence.

"W…w…what are we doing here?" Summer stammered.

"I realized you haven't had a chance to visit your grandfather yet," Queenie said.

If guilt-tripping me didn't work, maybe unnerving me will?

They stopped in front of a gravesite. The headstone, simple and elegant, read:

Zachary George Murray
1932–2007
Beloved Husband, Father, and Grandfather

Tears pricked at Summer's eyes. That was the perfect word to describe him—he was beloved.

Man, it was hard staying angry at him up here.

Queenie led Summer to a bench opposite Grandpa Zach's grave, which had flowers on it. Summer looked at her grandmother.

"Times are tough," Queenie said with a small smile. "I've gotten in the habit of coming here and just...sharing my thoughts."

"You can share your thoughts with me now," Summer said softly.

"When I was deciding to ask you to come back up here to Flat Top," Queenie said, ignoring Summer's overture, "I came up here every day, hoping for an answer."

"Did you get one?"

"I'm not crazy," Queenie said as she shook her head. "I knew your grandfather wasn't going to hand me a cell phone and tell me what to say...."

"He didn't do that when he was alive," Summer smiled.

"But I sometimes think I was to blame for the fact that you went away," Queenie said. "And I just wanted to get a....a sense...of whether I should try to explain."

If Queenie was trying to get Summer off the gluten-free thing, she was doing fine.

"That's not true," Summer said emphatically. "You had nothing to do with me staying away, I promise."

"I heard rumors, of course," Queenie said.

"You of all people know you shouldn't listen to rumors!"

"Why don't you tell me why you left," Queenie said.

"I left to go to college!"

"All right, if you insist," Queenie said patiently. "Then why didn't you ever come back?"

It was a simple request. Or it would have been from anyone else. Nothing was simple coming from Queenie. This was a command, no matter how politely couched. Summer sighed. She would have been the worst in an inquisition.

"I overheard Grandpa Zach and Keefe talking about me."

"Never good."

"No," Summer said. "Grandpa was trying to talk Keefe into...well... into making sure I didn't stay at Flat Top. He thought I needed to see the world or something. And he lied to Keefe to make his point."

"Do you remember exactly what Grandpa said?"

Summer snuck a look at the grave. She hadn't seen Grandpa Zach in a decade and she found it unsettling bagging on him at his grave.

"Of course I remember," Summer said with more vehemence then she intended. "He acted like he talked to me about it. I heard Grandpa say, 'She said getting stuck on a farm can destroy a girl's dreams,' and I never said that! I never even thought it!"

Queenie sighed. It took her a few moments before she spoke.

"That's the unfortunate thing about pronouns, isn't it?"

"Pardon me?" Summer said. From gluten to a graveside chat about the past to grammar? Summer's head was spinning. "What do *pronouns* have to do with anything?"

"Everything," Queenie said. "Just...everything."

Summer looked at her grandmother. Was Queenie wiping away a tear?

"I don't understand," Summer said.

"The *she* Grandpa was quoting was me, not you."

"That doesn't make any sense," Summer said. "You love the farm. And the bakery. And the town."

Queenie gave her a bitter smile. "That's a lot of love you're subscribing to me."

"Well, don't you?"

"Yes," Queenie said. "But I grew to love it. That was after years of hating it. I resented the fact that I didn't have any choice about my life. I got married and I did what your grandfather wanted me to do, which was to become part of the farm and part of the third-generation bakery. That's what women did in those days. I just wanted you to have choices I didn't have. I didn't want you to make a mistake."

"I need a minute," Summer said as she sprang off the bench.

Summer stood up and walked down the path. She needed to absorb all of this. Ultimately, did it matter that it was her grandmother or grandfather who put the idea in Keefe's head that he should turn his back on her? Would it have been a mistake to stay? If she'd stayed, she and Keefe would have been happily married almost ten years by now.

They might have had a family. It occurred to Summer now that this was the polar opposite of what would be termed a good risk in a risk-management exercise.

Eighteen-year-olds think they are so smart.

She and Keefe would have kept the bakery going. Life would have been simple and perfect.

Or not.

Perhaps Queenie was right. Perhaps Summer would have felt restless. But could anything good be obtained by going down this line of reasoning? Just as there was no predicting the future, there was no predicting the what-ifs of the past.

Summer knew one thing: Her family needed to be more forthcoming. If her grandparents had talked to her instead of Keefe, maybe she would have seen their point and gone off to college anyway. The secrecy led to her estrangement with her grandfather, and that could never be repaired. She knew she would regret it for the rest of her life. But she was going to suck up this lesson. She would make Queenie come to terms with having celiac disease. No more secrets or misunderstandings. They would face this one as a family.

Was Keefe family?

She came back and sat with her grandmother, who looked pale and tired.

"I know that wasn't easy," Summer said. "And I won't lie, it's going to take a while to process this."

"I know," Queenie said. "But let's put at least a few thing to rest."

"Like what?" Summer asked.

"You and your grandfather loved each other," Queenie said. "If I somehow came between you, I'm sorry."

Summer swallowed hard.

"That's now the past. Can we agree that we need to live in the present and work on the problems that are in front of us now?" Summer asked.

Queenie nodded.

Summer had never felt so grown-up. Maybe she'd made the right choices in life after all.

"That's fine with me. Although I will tell you one thing," Queenie said, looking down at the gravestone. "I'm pretty sure your grandfather agrees with me about Paula Deen."

Chapter 29

Summer was caught off-guard as she held the kitchen door open for Queenie. Keefe was inside with Lynnie. The table was set for dinner, a large chicken salad at the center. Summer spent the walk back thinking about everything Queenie had told her. It was a surprise to return so abruptly to the present.

Summer wasn't hungry. All she wanted to do was have a moment alone with Keefe. No matter what the outcome, she needed to put the past to rest.

But Lynnie was gunning for the spotlight. Nothing but gluten was going to have center stage tonight.

"Since the secret is out," Lynnie said. "I've filled Keefe in."

"Being gluten-free wasn't a secret," Queenie said. "I just hadn't told anybody yet."

"I think that's the definition of secret," Keefe said with a teasing tone.

Summer was surprised at Keefe's reaction. She felt slighted that Queenie hadn't told her, but Keefe seemed fine with the news.

Maybe he was relieved it wasn't something more urgent.

"The chicken salad is gluten-free, Queenie," Lynnie said, seating herself at what was now her place at the table.

"I know that," Queenie said. "I made it."

When everyone had been served and compliments given to the chef, Keefe finally addressed the issue.

"Here's what I don't understand," Keefe said to Queenie. "Why is everything you're baking so bad?"

"That's right to the point," Queenie said.

"Learned from the best," Keefe countered, toasting her with his beer.

"I was wondering that myself," Summer said, hoping to show some solidarity with Keefe. "I mean, you know the science of baking better than anyone. Lynnie made fine gluten-free cookies right away."

"How were the cookies?" Queenie said.

Summer wondered if Queenie didn't hear her.

"They were fine," Summer said again.

"Exactly," Queenie said in triumph.

Summer and Keefe exchanged a concerned look.

"I don't mean to brag, but I'm known as one of the best, if not *the* best, pastry chefs in the entire northwest," Queenie said. "What do you suppose would become of my reputation if I suddenly started making fine cookies as opposed to the best cookies? I was experimenting. I think they call it pushing the envelope."

"How's that working for you?" Keefe asked.

"Well, the ducks are coming around again," Queenie said.

"Now don't you be so hard on yourself," Lynnie said, going to the old-fashioned bread box and pulling out a loaf of crusty bread. "Check this out!"

Lynnie sliced the loaf and passed it around. Summer caught a glimpse of her grandmother's anxious face, but knew Queenie could read insincerity a mile away. Summer took a bite.

The bread was delicious!

Lynnie clapped her hands.

"Club soda!" Lynnie said. "Your grandmother is so smart! You know how so many gluten-free breads taste like cardboard? Well, Queenie figured out club soda would add some lightness to the texture! She could take over the gluten-free world, I tell you!"

The rest of dinner went by effortlessly. Summer knew her grandmother was on her way to figuring out her life.

Now, if only Summer could do the same. Now that she knew what was going on with Queenie, it just made one more tough decision she had to make. Could she leave Flat Top and the bakery to pursue her felting and purse-making? Should she? She needed to talk to Keefe. She needed to talk to Bale.

"I'm going to bed," Summer suddenly announced. "Okay if I take my old room?"

"It's not your old room," Queenie said. "It's just your room."

"I need to get back to the road show tomorrow," Summer said to Keefe. "But I can come take the morning shift at the bakery."

"Don't bother," Keefe said, testily. "I wouldn't want to hold you back—again."

Keefe stormed out, the women and dogs looking after him in surprise. Summer stood up, but Queenie put her hand on Summer's arm.

"It's been a long day." Queenie sighed and shook her head. "Leave it till morning."

Since Summer wasn't sure what it was she wanted to say to Keefe, she took her grandmother's advice. She scooped up Shortie, much to the confusion of Andre, and climbed the stairs to her room.

A storm woke Summer during the night. She reached out and pulled Shortie close, remembering the well. She thought about Bale and Keefe, and how they were both so dedicated to rescuing Shortie. Summer had always lamented that there didn't seem to be any good men left, and here she was, deciding between two. It occurred to her that neither had pledged any sort of undying love for her, but knowing where she stood herself would probably be a big help in sorting out her life.

Step one: talk to Keefe and put the past to bed. With that settled, Summer drifted back to sleep on a lullaby of raindrops.

Summer woke before dawn. The rain had stopped and she could just make out the taillights of Keefe's motorcycle leaving the farm. She hurriedly dressed. She tiptoed down the hallway and stairs, grateful that Shortie's nails made no sound on the carpet. She fed Shortie, drank a quick cup of coffee and lathered some jam on the gluten free bread, which was still wonderful in the morning! Summer almost make a second cup of coffee, but realized she was stalling.

Summer needed to get on with her life and she needed to start now. She and Shortie got in the truck. Heading out of the driveway, she looked up over to Flat Top Hill. It looked forlorn without the caboose in the predawn light. She put Big Red in drive and headed to town.

The light was on in the bakery. She tried the front door, it was open. She heard voices in the kitchen. A man and a woman. Evie was here! Since Shortie had no sense of keeping quiet, Summer picked him up and tiptoed closer to the door. She tried to listen, but couldn't decipher what was being said.

It sounded as if Evie was crying.

Summer's mind raced. Was it possible Keefe was breaking up with her? Summer's stomach flipped. Did she really want that? If she and Bale decided to give romance a spin, would it be fair to ruin Keefe's relationship? She chided herself. Evie could be crying for any number of reasons. Shortie suddenly started squirming. Summer put him on the ground. He shot through the kitchen door. She tried to grab him, but the kitchen door swung open. She caught a glimpse of Evie in Keefe's arms.

That could still mean anything.

"Oh, sorry," Summer said, as Keefe let go of Evie. "I didn't know you were going to be here, Evie. I thought I'd..."

"Oh, don't apologize," Evie said.

There was no malice in her voice. Summer tried not to feel disappointed.

"I'm just a little overwhelmed," Evie continued.

You and me both.

"Oh?" Summer said.

She wasn't prodding. She wasn't sure she wanted to know.

"We're having a baby," Evie said, bursting into tears again and resumed crying into Keefe's chest.

There was more, but Evie's voice was muffled in Keefe's bakery apron. Summer thought Evie said, "We've wanted this for so long," but Summer wasn't sure.

"Congratulations," Summer said automatically.

Summer felt sick. She knew she couldn't burst into tears, but she felt bereft. She chided herself for being so egotistical as to think Keefe might be considering returning to her when and if she decided the time was right. Maybe she'd read Bale wrong, too. Maybe no man but Shortie loved her.

"You'll just have to excuse me," Evie said, trying to collect herself.

"It's okay," Keefe said. "Perfectly understandable."

Perfectly understandable? Wow, Mr. Romance.

"I just couldn't wait to share the news," Evie said, wiping her eyes. She turned to Summer. "I can't stand the smell of the bakery in the morning right now, so I'm not going to be much help for a while."

"That's okay," Keefe said. "We'll...I'll manage."

"I better be getting home," Evie said. "Sherman is starting to think I live over here."

"Sherman?" Summer asked.

"Yes," Evie said. "Sherman Caleb, my husband."

"Sherman Caleb is your husband?" Summer asked. "Shy Sherman?"

"He's not so shy anymore," Evie said, patting her still flat stomach.

Was Evie leering?

"So, he's the father of your baby?" Summer said, before she caught herself.

"Of course, he's the father of my baby," Evie said. "Who else?"

Summer wished she'd never come into the bakery. Keefe was looking at his shoes as it dawned on Evie what Summer was implying. Summer's cheeked burned with embarrassment.

"Oh!" Evie said, looking at Summer. "You thought...."

Evie looked over at Keefe and started laughing uncontrollably.

"I'm sorry," Evie gasped between bursts of laughter. She turned helplessly to Keefe. "I just...I mean, you've been like a brother to me for years. So...you know...*ick.*"

"It's not you," Evie said affectionately to Keefe. "It's just the hormones laughing."

Evie kissed Keefe on the cheek and laughed her way out of the store. Summer was mortified. Keefe stared after Evie.

"It wasn't *that* funny," Keefe said.

Summer smiled.

"Sorry," Summer offered.

"It's not even six in the morning and two women have already apologized to me," Keefe said. "You here to help?"

"Do you *want* help?"

"I wouldn't turn it down."

Summer grabbed an apron and started to work. There was so much she wanted to say, but had no idea where to begin.

Keefe put a tray of breads in the oven. He slammed the door harder than advisable, which made Summer face him.

"Why did you come back?" he asked.

"I told you," Summer said. "Queenie asked me."

"Well, now the Queenie mystery is solved, are you staying?"

The hostility in his voice shook her to her core. It didn't sound as if he was saying, "please stay," as much as it sounded like, "please leave."

"I don't really know," Summer said honestly. "There's a lot to think about."

"Well, think fast," Keefe said. "I don't have the luxury of waiting for you to decide if you're going to be part of this operation or not."

"I didn't realize this was all about you," Summer said. "I'm the one who packed up her whole life to move here, you know."

"If I remember correctly," Keefe said, "You stopped by here on your way to ....God knows where, to do God knows what."

She couldn't really argue with that. Even her so-called solid vision of making felted purses needed to be rethought, especially since Queenie obviously knew a lot more about the process than she did.

"Do you want me to stay?" Summer asked. She lost her nerve and quickly added, "To help around here, I mean."

Keefe started whipping cream with a vehemence that did not bode well for the éclairs. Summer started rolling out dough for sugar cookies.

"In all seriousness, Summer," Keefe said, sounding tired, "I can't run this place by myself. If Queenie comes back, fine, but if she can't deal with...what's it called..."

"Airborne flour," Summer said, parroting Lynnie.

"Yeah, that," Keefe said. "If Queenie is out of the picture, I'll have to hire somebody if you decide to flake out on me again."

"Flake on you again?" Summer slammed the dough on the counter.

Clearly the quality of the baked goods was going to suffer this morning.

Shortie scooted under one of the baker's racks as Summer and Keefe squared off.

"You just disappeared," Keefe said.

"You didn't seem to want me around," Summer said.

"You know that's not true."

"You didn't put up much of a fight to get me to stay."

"I didn't want you to stay because I fought you or pressured you," Keefe said. "I still don't. Life in a small town isn't for everybody. I wasn't sure if was best for you ten years ago, and I'm not sure now. That's all on you."

Summer felt she'd been slapped.

"I think I better get down to the road show," Summer said. "Come on, Shortie."

"Fine," Keefe said.

Summer picked Shortie up and headed for the door. She turned to Keefe, not wanting to leave things in such turmoil.

"Will I see you later at the show?" she asked quietly.

"I gave my ticket to Evie, so she could take Sherman," he said without looking up.

"Why did you do that?" Summer asked, astounded.

Keefe looked at her.

"I've lost my taste for tiny houses, I guess."

Chapter 30

Summer stopped for tea twenty miles from the road show. She'd cried so hard she'd scared Shortie, not to mention her eyes were almost swollen shut. She ordered two cups of hot water and gratefully accepted the tea bags, which she dipped in the hot water and then placed on her tender eyelids. Shortie sat in her lap, his tiny paws on her shoulders. He licked her salty cheeks.

"It's okay, Shortie," Summer said. "Your mom is just a jerk."

Her harsh assessment of herself made her start crying again. She took a few deep breaths. She should be grateful to Keefe, she thought. At least the handwriting was on the wall. She should concentrate on Bale.

Bale never criticized her!

Summer looked at herself in the rearview mirror. The tea bags had done a world of good. If she could keep herself from bursting into tears again, she might fool Bale into thinking everything was fine. She added two coats of mascara—waterproof, just in case—and a swipe of melon flavored lip gloss. She settled Shortie in his car seat and gave him a quick kiss, which she instantly regretted as several sticks of his fur stuck to her gummy lips. She laughed, grateful that life with Shortie always managed to put things in perspective.

Arriving at the road show, Summer drove to the gate and waved to Chester, who was zealously safeguarding his iPad. She pulled up alongside him.

"Hi Chester," she said. "I was here yesterday? I brought the caboose?"

"I remember," Chester said.

Summer put the truck in gear, but Chester tapped on the hood.

"Hold on there, Miss," Chester said.

"Yes?"

"Where did you say you were going?"

"I thought you said you remembered me."

"I did say that. And I do remember you. But rules is rules."

"I'm here to see Bale Bar…I'm here to see *Bale's Tiny Dreams*."

Chester scrolled through his list.

"Here it is," Chester said. "Okay, you're clear."

Summer nodded and once again threaded her way through the rows of miniatures. The parking lot was full of tiny houses now, all lined up and ready for the big opening. She could see the caboose, blazing red in the late morning sun. She drove past it, watching passersby stop and admire it. She parked Big Red, proud that the showstopper was hers. She didn't see Bale as she and Shortie walked up to the caboose. She stopped and studied her home. Something seemed wrong, but she couldn't place it.

"Hi there, little lady," Bale said, startling her.

She dismissed her unease. It was great to see Bale, with his handsome, nonjudgmental smile.

"Hey," she said. "Everything all set?"

"Yep," Bale said. "Are you hungry? I just made some soup."

Summer realized she was starving. She followed Bale toward the Shiny Olive. Bale scooped up Shortie at the front steps and brought him inside.

Would Keefe do that?

Don't think about Keefe.

Summer chatted effortlessly as Bale ladled out the soup.

This is how adult relationships should be. Easy and not full of drama.

"This is the last meal I can cook in here until the show's over," Bale said. "So eat up! No more home cooking until we pack up and head home."

Summer wondered where home would be for Shortie and her.

Bale handed her a steaming mug of soup. She sipped at it. It was comforting; just what she needed. She looked out the window and took in the caboose again. She lost track of what Bale was saying. The caboose seemed to be trying to tell her something.

"What do you think?" Bale's voice interrupted her thoughts.

"I'm sorry," Summer said, embarrassed to be caught zoning out. "What did you say?"

"I said," Bale didn't look at her. He stood at the sink, looking out at the sea of tiny homes. "How are thing going in Cat's Paw?"

"Complicated," Summer answered truthfully.

"How complicated?" Bale asked.

He turned to her. Summer felt her eyes welling up again.

Please don't ruin this moment, she commanded herself.

Stalling for time, she looked back at the caboose. Her breath caught as she realized what the caboose was trying to say.

"I'm not supposed to be here," she heard the caboose say. "I belong on the hill. Your grandfather knew I was coming and he laid down that foundation just for us."

You're a house. I'm not listening to you.

Summer stood up and walked to Bale. She threw her arms around him and kissed him. Hard.

"I'm still out here," the caboose said.

Don't listen, Summer commanded herself. *This is worse than listening to Shortie.*

"You have unfinished business," the caboose said. "It's not fair to—"

She tried to focus on kissing Bale and drown out the caboose.

The caboose was cut short as Bale gently guided Summer away from him, his hands firmly on her waist.

"The time isn't right, is it?" Bale asked.

Was he hearing the caboose too? Or could he tell she just couldn't commit to that kiss?

"I...I really like you, Bale," she said.

"I like you, too," Bale said. "But sometimes that's not enough."

"It should be!"

"The world is full of should-bes," he said. "Here's the thing about these tiny houses...there's no room to hide from yourself. They make you face what's real."

"If I knew that, maybe I wouldn't have bought one," Summer said. "Sounds like the house is smarter than I am."

"I don't know what exactly it is you need to face, Summer," Bale said, pulling her close and kissing her forehead. "But I'm guessing it has something to do with Cat's Paw, and Queenie, and especially Keefe. You need to settle up."

Bale smiled at Summer. He let go of her and strode to the window, looking out at the caboose.

"I picked that spot for you," he said pointing to the caboose without turning around. "Because I had a hunch you might need to make a quick exit."

He turned to face her.

"My hunch is right, isn't it?"

Summer couldn't speak. Her hair fell over her face like a curtain as she hung her head.

"It's okay," Bale said, coming back and pushing the hair out of her eyes. "I'll probably make a boatload of money on my hunches here in the next couple days."

"I could leave the caboose here until the end of the show," Summer offered. Bale shook his head.

"I think that would just make matters worse," he said. "Come on, I'll open the back gate so you came hook her to Big Red and get out of here."

Bale's expert hands had the caboose ready to go in minutes. Summer put Shortie in his car seat and Bale ruffled the dog's head.

"You take good care of your mama," Bale said.

Bale closed the door and put his hands on her shoulders. He bent down and looked into her eyes.

"I have another hunch," he said.

"Yes?" Summer said, barely breathing.

"I think you're going to figure everything out just fine."

He kissed her quickly on the cheek and went back to the road show.

He did not look back.

Summer stopped for more tea bags on the way home. Was she out of her mind? She had a real shot at romance with Bale. He was a good man. He was strong. He was kind. He cared about her. Keefe, on the other hand, was maddening! She had no concrete idea where she even stood with him. Why would she give up the stability of a man like Bale when her relationship with Keefe was so unsteady? She turned the truck around and headed back toward Seattle.

Within a half hour, she'd convinced herself that Bale was right. She did have to come to terms with her past, and especially Keefe, if she planned on moving forward with her life. She turned on her blinker and once again swung Big Red toward Cat's Paw. She turned around two more times before heading back to Flat Top Farm.

"I hope you're happy," Summer said, looking in the rearview mirror at the caboose.

* * * *

Even with her indecision on the road, Summer was back at Flat Top Farm by midafternoon. She easily got the caboose settled on the hill. Too bad Keefe hadn't seen how adept she'd become at maneuvering it.

Summer shook her head. She really needed to stop thinking about Keefe.

She was exhausted. She knew a showdown with Keefe was inevitable, but all she really wanted to do was draw a hot bath and put everything out of her mind.

* * * *

Heading into the caboose, Summer heard a low rumble coming from somewhere on the farm. She looked around and saw what it was: Keefe was driving the farm's backhoe. He was filling in the well!

Summer watched him. Keefe was not the young man she fell in love with and she was not the young girl he once loved. They were adults now. Hearts had been broken and needed to be mended. When the well was full, it would not be the same as the earth around it. It would be strong, possibly stronger than ever, but it would be patched.

She walked toward Keefe… and her future.

Chapter 31

Bale Barrett's hunch was right. He made a name for himself at the Tiny House Road Show. He also subscribed to *The Cat's Paw Chronicle*, to keep tabs on events as they unfolded.

THREE MONTHS LATER

THE CAT'S PAW CHRONICLE

Cat's Paw welcomes its latest merchant to town: Ms. Mary Lynn "Lynnie" Laite. Lynnie has moved from Hartford, Connecticut, and is selling handmade felted purses made by local artisans in both her Main Street shop and online.

* * * *

SIX MONTHS LATER

THE CAT'S PAW CHRONICLE

The Grand Opening of DOUGH FREE DOUGH, Cat Paw's new gluten-free bakery, was a huge success, with lines around the block. Queenie Murray, her granddaughter Clarisse, known to locals as Summer, and longtime manager Keefe Devlin gave out free samples to an enthusiastic crowd. Festivities were cut short when Evie Caleb went into labor. She gave birth to a healthy baby boy. Mother and son are doing fine.

* * * *

ONE YEAR LATER

Clarisse "Summer" Murray and Keefe Devlin, co-managers of the popular Dough Z Dough gluten-free bakery in Cat's Paw, announce their engagement. Wedding plans will be announced in an upcoming issue of *The Cat's Paw Chronicle.*

* * * *

Bale smiled.
And canceled his subscription.

Nanaimo Bar Recipe

Bottom Layer
½ cup unsalted (also called "sweet') butter (European style cultured)
¼ cup sugar
5 Tbsp. cocoa
1 egg, beaten
1¼ cups graham cracker crumbs
½ cup finely chopped walnuts
1 cup coconut
Melt butter, sugar, and cocoa in the top of a double boiler. Add egg and stir to cook and thicken. Remove from heat. Stir in crumbs, coconut, and nuts. Press firmly into an ungreased 8" x 8" pan.

Second Layer
½ cup unsalted butter
3 Tbsp. almond milk or 2 tsp. cream
2 Tbsp. vanilla custard powder
2 cups icing sugar
Cream butter, cream, custard powder, and icing sugar together well. Beat until light and fluffy. Spread over bottom layer.

Third Layer
4 squares semisweet chocolate (1 oz. each)
2 Tbsp. unsalted butter
Melt chocolate and butter over low heat. Cool.
Once cool, but still liquid, pour over second layer. Chill in refrigerator until chocolate is set (ten minutes to a half hour).. Cut into squares.

Chocolate Meringues

2 ounces bittersweet chocolate, broken into pieces for melting,
2 ounces semisweet chocolate, chopped
½ teaspoon vanilla extract
Pinch salt
1 tablespoon white vinegar or lemon juice
4 large egg whites
1 cup granulated sugar
½ cup finely chopped walnuts (if desired)

Melt the 2 ounces of bittersweet chocolate pieces in a microwave-safe dish or over a gently simmering double boiler. Let cool but not harden. Add the vanilla.

Preheat oven to 325 degrees F. Line three baking sheets with parchment paper.

Use a paper towel to wipe off any possible grease or dust in bowl for a standing mixer. Then use a paper towel to wipe the blades of the whisk attachment as well. Do not rinse. This procedure will ensure that the egg whites will whip to their full potential.

Place the salt and vinegar (or lemon juice) in the clean mixer bowl.

Add egg whites to salt and vinegar in mixer bowl. Beat the egg whites/salt/vinegar mixture on medium speed until foamy, about 1 minute. Increase the speed to high. Slowly add the sugar in a steady stream and continue beating until stiff peaks form, 4 to 5 minutes. (The bowl can be turned upside down without the meringue falling out.) Add a third of the meringue to the melted chocolate and mix well until glossy peaks form. (another minute, but best to use your eye to judge). Gently but thoroughly fold the melted chocolate into the meringue, and then fold in the remaining two ounces chopped semisweet chocolate. Add chopped walnuts, if desired.

Using a pastry bag, pipe the meringue into 1½-inch rounds, 2 inches apart on the prepared baking sheets.

Immediately place in the oven and bake about 10 minutes. The cookies will develop a shiny crust but will be soft inside.

Let rest on the baking sheets for 10 minutes before removing to a rack to cool completely.

Welcome to Fat Chance, Texas

If you enjoyed Tiny House on the Hill, be sure not to miss Celia Bonaduce's
Fat Chance, Texas series, including

Welcome to Fat Chance, Texas

For champion professional knitter Dymphna Pearl, inheriting part of a
sun-blasted ghost town in the Texas hill country isn't just unexpected,
it's a little daunting. To earn a cash bequest that could change her life,
she'll have to leave California to live in tiny, run-down Fat Chance for six
months—with seven strangers. Impossible! Or is it?

Trading her sandals for cowboy boots, Dymphna dives into her new life
with equal parts anxiety and excitement. After all, she's never felt quite
at home in Santa Monica anyway. Maybe Fat Chance will be her second
chance. But making it habitable is going take more than a lasso and Wild
West spirit. With an opinionated buzzard overlooking the proceedings and
mismatched strangers learning to become friends, Dymphna wonders if
unlocking the secrets of her own heart is the way to strike real gold....

Keep reading for a special look!

A Lyrical e-book on sale now.

Chapter 1

"Please don't talk to anyone at the yoga stand," Erinn Wolf said.

"Those people are dead to us."

"That's a bit harsh," Dymphna Pearl said.

"They threw down the gauntlet," Erinn replied. "Not us."

"I just don't want there to be any hurt feelings," Dymphna said, as she loaded two of her Angora rabbits into the hatchback of the car. Erinn, who was her best friend, landlady, and business partner, filled the backseat with knitwear—hats, scarves, bags, and gloves. When Erinn was upset, it was as if she lived in some medieval melodrama—or at least with the New York Mafia.

"Yes," Dymphna said, as she buckled herself into the passenger side of the car. "But we won. We have to see those people every Sunday. Don't you think it would be nicer to offer an olive branch?"

"By 'olive branch' I take it you mean 'carrot cake'?" Erinn asked as she pulled out of the driveway.

Dymphna winced. "How did you know?" she asked, eyes downcast.

"I could smell it as soon as I woke up!" Erinn said. "I could smell it before I woke up. I dreamt the gingerbread man was chasing me— until I realized it was the cinnamon and cloves coming from the guesthouse. I knew to what you were up."

Even when Erinn was in scolding mode, her grammar was perfect.

"I just think we could take the high road," Dymphna said. "I don't want to have enemies at the farmers' market."

"As Franklin Roosevelt once said, 'I ask you to judge me by the enemies I have made,'" Erinn said.

Dymphna thought that Erinn might want to rethink that particular philosophy. Did she really want to be judged by these enemies—people offering peace and spinal alignment?

Erinn drove down a deserted Ocean Avenue toward the Santa Monica Farmers' Market on Main Street, where Dymphna had a booth called Knit and Pearl. Dymphna was a bit of a celebrity, since she was the host of a video podcast—produced by Erinn—also called Knit and Pearl. The show fueled sales at the farmers' market and the clientele at the farmers' market created new viewers. Erinn, who knew what it took to get attention, insisted that a giant Angora rabbit would trump any display of yoga pants on the aisle, so Dymphna always brought at least two of her six angora yarn–producing rabbits. It seemed like a straightforward business plan, until the owners of the Midnight at the Mirage yoga stand complained the animals were disrupting the quiet zone that was imperative to the success of their business. Dymphna could see their point—people often came to her booth just to pet the fluffy fur of the animals that looked like an explosion in a cotton factory. It was anything but calm.

But Erinn would have none of it. She told the farmers' market board that Dymphna was using the rabbits as educational tools— teaching the public about the proper care of Angora rabbits and their fur. Knit and Pearl was every bit as enlightening as a chakra massage. Erinn won, but Dymphna got a stomachache every time the owners of Midnight at the Mirage looked over at a family squealing with delight over one of her rabbits. Dymphna didn't want to stir up Erinn's wrath, which was formidable no matter what the issue, but she thought maybe she'd sneak the carrot cake over to the yoga instructors when Erinn wasn't looking.

Dymphna understood all too well that sinking feeling when you thought your business was threatened. One of her greatest regrets was that she had never made a go of her shepherding business. She had tried to raise a small herd of sheep in Malibu, but when the land she was renting got sold out from under her it just proved to be too expensive. So she traded in her sheep for six Angora rabbits and moved out of the hills. Sometimes she felt guilty about trying to raise rabbits in Santa Monica. Dymphna wasn't sure city life was healthy for rabbits.

Erinn stopped the car near their allotted space and started to unload the collapsible tables and the knitted accessories, while Dymphna tended to Snow D'Winter and Spot, the two giant Angoras chosen to represent the show at the stall.

By midmorning, the farmers' market was humming. Once the booth was set up and everything was running smoothly, Erinn usually headed off to shop for produce. She offered to go shopping for Dymphna, who was stuck at the booth all day, but Dymphna could never gather up all her various scraps of paper on which she'd written reminders of what she needed. At one point, Erinn tried to relieve Dymphna at the booth so she could do her own shopping, but the customers all wanted to talk to Dymphna Pearl, designer of the knit creations, or they wanted to ask questions about the rabbits—questions to which only Dymphna had answers. Dymphna was perfectly content buying her groceries at an actual grocery store, but she knew better than to share that with Erinn.

Erinn started to gather her shopping bags and her detailed list.

She turned to Dymphna and held out her palm. "Let me have it." "Have what?" Dymphna asked.

"The carrot cake. I don't want you to have a weak moment."

Dymphna handed over the carrot cake and watched Erinn stride purposefully into the crowd. On one hand, Erinn could be exasperating, but on the other you had to hand it to her—she had amazing instincts.

Dymphna gave Spot and Snow D'Winter some fresh water. When she turned back toward the front of the booth, a tense-looking woman was standing in front of a display of knitted scarves. She didn't appear to be all that interested in them, though. Instead she was staring intently at Dymphna.

"May I help you?" Dymphna inquired.

The woman seemed startled that Dymphna was talking to her. Nothing about this woman suggested she resided in a casual beach neighborhood. Dymphna guessed the woman to be in her midfifties, her salon-highlighted hair glinting expensively in the sun. She extended a long French-manicured talon and snatched up a creamand rust-colored scarf.

"Yes," the woman said. "I want to buy this." She thrust the scarf at Dymphna.

"Great!" Dymphna said, taking a charge card from the woman and sliding it through a contraption on her smartphone. She held her breath. She couldn't believe her phone could actually ring up sales.

Dymphna handed the card back to the shopper. The name on the credit card was C. J. Primb.

"Thank you, Ms. Primb," Dymphna said. "Would you like me to e-mail you a receipt?"

Ms. Primb looked startled. "No," she said. "Absolutely not!"

"All right," Dymphna said, handing over the knitwear. "I hope you'll enjoy the scarf."

As the woman took the scarf, Dymphna noticed a small gold band on C. J. Primb's left hand. It was sitting on the index finger, between the first and second knuckle joints. Such odd placement, Dymphna thought. She herself would never be able to get any real work done without losing a ring so precariously placed.

Perhaps that's the point.

Dymphna was happy to turn her attention to another shopper, who was scanning the hats. Ms. Primb was making her nervous. She couldn't put her finger on it, but there was just something about the woman that made her very uncomfortable.

The shopper wandered over to the booth and caressed a green and blue beret. She saluted Dymphna with her biodegradable cup of chai tea, purchased from a stall across the asphalt. "I love your TV show," she said.

"Podcast," Dymphna said in a breathy whisper. "It's just on the web. It isn't a real TV show."

The shopper held the hat up to the Southern California sky. The yarns sparkled, changing colors like a prism. She then expertly popped it on her head at a jaunty angle, studying herself in the mirror. "Video, podcast, TV show, I don't care, I just love it all," the woman said, handing the hat to Dymphna with a smile. "This beret is just fabulous."

Dymphna stared down at the beret. Did the woman want to purchase it? Or was she just handing it back? There were more compliments than sales at the Santa Monica Farmers' Market. It was times like these when she wished she were a little more like Erinn—assertive and self-assured. Erinn would just come right out and ask the customer if she wanted to buy the hat. But Dymphna could never bring herself to be so blunt. She would just wait it out, until the woman made whatever decision she was going to make.

"Excuse me, ma'am, but are you going to buy that hat or not?" Dymphna looked up. Sometimes people could get pushy and she was not one for conflict. It was Ms. Primb. Why was she still here? What did she want?

"So," Ms. Primb said again to the shopper and pointed an accusing finger at the hat in Dymphna's hand. "Are you buying that or not? We don't have all day."

We?

"Yes," said the woman, handing over her charge card to Dymphna and blinking aggressively at C. J. Primb. "I am."

Dymphna hurriedly rang up the sale and started to put the hat in a paper bag. Whatever weirdness was going on with Ms. Primb, Dymphna didn't want to distress one of her customers.

The woman took her charge card back and put her fingertips on Dymphna's arm. "That's OK, sweetie," she said. "I don't need a bag. No need to kill a forest on my behalf."

"I wouldn't," Dymphna said.

"Pardon me?" the woman said as she adjusted her new hat in the mirror. "You wouldn't what?"

"I wouldn't kill a forest on your behalf."

The woman nodded quickly, first to Dymphna and then to C. J. Primb. Dymphna watched her as she drifted down the aisle to the vintage jewelry. Dymphna suddenly realized C. J. Primb was still studying the merchandise—or was she studying Dymphna? Their eyes met. Ms. Primb made no attempt to leave.

"May I show you anything else?" Dymphna asked.

"Not really. I just wanted to get a good look at you."

Dymphna tried not to show her surprise. Many people watched the show and felt as if they knew her—and could say anything they wanted.

"Well, feel free to look around," Dymphna said cautiously while looking around herself—mostly for something to do. She wished Erinn would come back. She started arranging embellished half gloves on a smooth manzanita branch that she used as a display rack. She tried to ignore the woman, who just stood, rooted, in front of her booth.

"Let me ask you something," Ms. Primb said.

"Yes?"

"If you had all the money in the world, what would you do with yourself?"

"I . . . I really don't know," Dymphna said. "I've never thought about having all the money in the world."

"Oh, really?" Ms. Primb practically snorted in disdain.

"What about you?" Dymphna asked. She had read somewhere that people loved to talk about themselves, and you could get out of practically any uncomfortable situation by asking your tormenters to talk about themselves. "What would you do if you had all the money in the world?"

"I do have all the money in the world," Ms. Primb said as she walked away.

Slim Pickins' in Fat Chance, Texas

It's been a year since an eccentric billionaire summoned seven strangers to the dilapidated, postage stamp-sized town of Fat Chance, Texas. To win a cash bequest, each was required to spend six months in the ghost town to see if they could transform it—and themselves—into something extraordinary. But by the time pastry chef Fernando Cruz arrives, several members of the original gang have already skedaddled...

Fernando's hopes of starting a new life in Fat Chance are dashed when the town's handful of ragtag residents—and a mysterious low-flying plane—show him just how weird the place actually is. His hopes of making over the town's sole café into a BBQ restaurant for nearby ranchers threaten to turn to dust as a string of bizarre secrets are revealed. But just when the pickins' couldn't get any slimmer, the citizens of Fat Chance realize they might be able to build exactly the kind of hometown they all need—but never knew they wanted...

Livin' Large in Fat Chance, Texas

From ghost town to growing community, it's been a few years since a group of strangers inherited property in tiny, deserted Fat Chance, Texas. And besides creating businesses, they've developed friendships and romances too. But plans to pave the town may put Dymphna Pearl and her beau, Professor Johnson, on opposite sides of Main Street. In his zeal for the project, he's making great decisions for Fat Chance, but not for them as a couple. Disgruntled, Dymphna heads back to Los Angeles to collect the rabbits she's created a special place for in the hot Texas climate. But the professor is in for another surprise...

Professor Johnson didn't even know about Dympha's sister, Maggie, and when he meets her in a most unexpected way, he begins to understand why. In the meantime, Dymphna is off pursuing an exciting venture to let the world know about Fat Chance—one that will bring a talented new crew to the eclectic group. The kitschy little place they call home is clearly destined for bigger, better things—-but with so many changes a-coming will the same be true for everyone in Fat Chance, including the professor and Dymphna?

Meet the Author

Celia Bonaduce, author of The Venice Beach Romances and the Welcome to Fat Chance, Texas series, has always had a love affair with houses. Her credits as a television field producer include such house-heavy hits as Extreme Makeover: Home Edition; HGTV's House Hunters and Tiny House Hunters. She lives in Santa Monica, CA, with her husband and dreams of one day traveling with him in their own tiny house.

You can contact Celia at www.Celiabonaduce.com